HUGE DARE

A STEPBROTHER ENEMIES TO LOVERS REVERSE HAREM ROMANCE

STEPHANIE BROTHER

1

ELLIE

"Tell me you're gonna be at the party tomorrow night?" Dornan says as I emerge from my crowded lecture room into the hallway that's teaming with people. I get pushed along by the tide of my classmates, but somehow, Dornan holds his ground. I guess his size is an advantage, and his years playing football. The man is a unit, and when he grabs my arm to stop me from getting swept away, I feel the power in his grip and the shelter of his body at my back.

Dornan's been my best friend since kindergarten, and ever since Maddy-Lou pushed me over in the schoolyard and he came to my aid, I've loved him like a brother.

"A back-to-high-school party? Seriously, dude? You couldn't come up with a better idea?"

"What?" he says as I turn to face him. His face splits into a wide smile, and despite my disapproval of the theme for his birthday celebrations, I have to smile, too. "You didn't love high school?"

"Not as much as you, obviously."

"Best years of my life."

We walk towards the campus coffee shop, emerging from the frenetic building into the warm sunshine outside. I inhale a lungful of fresh air, glance up at the blue sky, dusted with cotton puff clouds that fill me with happiness, and tug my bag more securely onto my shoulder.

"Aren't these the best years of your life?" I ask. "No parents breathing down your neck all the time?"

Dornan shrugs. "My parents were mostly cool. I don't know. I guess I just liked how everything was new. Now, I feel like I've done it all before."

"Yeah, Dornan Walsh. You're a pro at life these days."

He punches my arm softly, nudging me off balance. "No need to be snarky because you'd rather be a hermit than socialize with your peers."

"I don't want to be a hermit," I say. "I'm just not into parties where everyone is downing drinks like they're going out of fashion and fooling around with the nearest warm body."

"But that's what college parties are all about. Seriously, Ellie, you need to act your age because there will come a time when you're too old to act like an idiot and you'll regret missing out."

"You want me to act like an idiot?" I ask, quirking my eyebrow.

"I want you to let your pretty hair down and relax for a change. I know your mom is always breathing down your neck about your grades, but a few nights off to party won't make any difference."

"What would my mom think of you, Dornan, if she knew the truth? Her blue-eyed, blond-haired golden boy is encouraging her daughter into acts of disrepute."

"Don't tell her," Dornan says seriously. "I couldn't take it if your mom turned those disapproving eyes on me."

I chuckle because he's being serious. Mom is nice as pie if you're on her good side, and that means molding yourself into the shape she wants you to be. My stepbrothers are experts at keeping mom happy. I swear, if she raves about their perfection over breakfast one more time, I'm going to toss my cereal at the wall. And Dornan's no better. He sucks up to mom so much it's nauseating. I forgive him for it, though, because he's been a loyal friend to me for more years than I care to count. My stepbrothers don't get the same break. They've only been around seven years, and I'm certain their simpering for approval is designed to make me look bad.

We enter the crowded coffee shop and Dornan shoulders his way into the queue, ordering my favorite caramel Frappuccino with extra whipped cream and a black coffee for himself. I scramble for the first available free table, almost faceplanting in the process.

Dornan thwarts my attempts to change the subject at every turn, and by the time I need to head to my next lecture, he has somehow achieved the unachievable. He's gotten me to agree to attend his stupid frat house for a back-to-high-school party. Well, it is his birthday. Even though the idea makes my skin crawl, I'd do anything for my friend.

Dornan ordered me to wear something black and slinky so we can take cool selfies. His words, not mine. I'm sure his teammates have no idea that he comes out with things like that. When he's around them, he amps up the butch, but with me, he's a big softie.

The only black, slinky dress I have is short on me because mom shrunk it in the dryer, but I don't want to disappoint Dornan. As I approach the front door of the frat house, I wriggle my hips and tug at the hem, lengthening it for a second before it rebounds.

The music is pumping, and the sound of laughter and people yelling conversation spills into the cool night like a tidal wave of everything that makes me uncomfortable.

I'm not a big drinker, but I'm going to need something to take the edge off. As I step over the threshold, I search the hallway for someone I know. There are familiar faces, but no one I'm on a first-name basis with.

There are ten types of guys you'll meet at a frat party. The stoners spend all their time slumped in the corner, getting high. The desperate guy will paw anything he can get his hands on and usually ends up too drunk to have any success with women. The player moves through the crowds zeroing in on potential targets, motivated by his horniness. The aloof guy exists just to let everyone know he's too good for the party. The drunk makes alcohol his focus, disappearing after the first hour so he can sleep it off. The gamer will turn anything into a competition: who can drink the most, who can pull the best-looking girl, who has the best dance moves. Then there's the DJ who's obsessed with the tunes, the creepy guy who everyone does their best to avoid, the mature guy who thinks he can order everyone around, and the smug asshole with the girlfriend.

None of those types of guys do anything for me.

Tugging the hem of my dress again, I venture through the crowd, taking a left into the sprawling den, and bump face first into an insanely broad, hard chest. It must be one of Dornan's teammates. I glance up, placing my palms on two dinner-plate-sized pecs as I ease back and find myself gazing into the mesmerizing emerald eyes of Colby Townsend, my stepbrother nemesis.

"Ellie," he says curtly. "Didn't your mom teach you to look where you're going?"

"No," I say. "She was too busy letting you lick her ass."

Colby's eyelids lower slowly, and he lets out an annoyed breath. "I don't lick anyone's ass," he says darkly.

"Anyway," I take a step to the left, trying to make my way around Colby's massive frame. "As much as I'd love to hang around sharing happy family stories, I've got to

4

find Dornan."

I don't wait for Colby's snarky reply, but I feel his eyes on me as I make my way deeper into the crowd. His brothers must be here somewhere, too. They always move as a pack. I need to keep my eyes peeled to avoid them too.

People are dancing, and my feet end up covered with splashes of warm liquid, probably beer, from jostled red plastic cups.

I spot Celine slumped onto Eddie's lap in the corner and Dornan perched on the tiny square wooden table, booming with laughter at something one of his jock buddies said. When he sees me, he's on his feet in a flash, lifting me off my already sore feet and spinning me around without a care about who's trampled in his excitement.

"Ellie-Belly," he shouts, forgetting that he promised to forget my stupid nickname when we came to college.

"Ellie-Belly," three of his friends yell, holding up their cups and downing the contents.

"Dornan!" I slap his shoulders. "You promised you wouldn't."

As I slide down his body, his smile drops, and his hand flies to his mouth. "I'm soooo dumb when I'm drunk," he slurs. "I forget everything."

"Not everything," I say, tugging him around the back of his neck so he stoops low enough that I can plant a birthday kiss on his cheek. "You remembered my stupid nickname!"

"Hey, I made up that nickname," he says. "And it's affectionate, not stupid!"

"Affectionate and embarrassing as hell."

"You need a drink," Dornan says, looking around. "Here…come on." Grabbing my arm, he pulls me over to a table in the corner, where enough alcohol to kill a small army rest precariously. "Vodka, beer, or wine?" he asks.

"Or some of this…what the hell is this?"

Holding up a bottle containing liquid with a greenish tinge, he squints at the label. "Absinthe!"

"No fucking way," I say. "That stuff is lethal…and probably illegal. And anyway, I need to keep my wits about me in this place."

"Wits need to get left at the front door," he says, pouring a large amount of vodka into a cup and topping it with warm lemonade. "This is a party, not a courtroom. And it's my birthday, so you can't say no."

"Seriously, dude! How many times are you going to bribe me with the 'it's my birthday' routine?"

"As many times as it takes," he laughs, pushing his floppy hair from his face. "Now, drink that one, and I'm going to pour you another before you make your escape."

"You know me too well," I laugh. Despite the drink being a little warmer than I'd like, it tastes okay. Dornan, in his drunken state, still manages to mix exactly the right balance of bitter alcohol to sweet soda. "You'd better get the selfie out of the way now, too," I say.

"Okay…okay." He fumbles in the pocket of his black jeans, pulling out his phone with so much haste he almost drops it. "Actually, Chris, can you take a photo of me and Ellie?"

Chris, a hulking great linebacker with black curly hair and skin that's the color of crème caramel, lumbers to his feet and holds out a hand as big as a shovel, grasping for Dornan's phone. He holds it up as Dornan throws his heavy arm around my shoulder. For a second, I glance up at my friend, catching his broad smile and happy crinkled eyes, and my heart swells. Part of me wishes I could put aside all the years of friendship and fall in love with him romantically. He tried to kiss me once towards the end of high school, but it felt so weird for both of us that we laughed it off. Dornan's so special to me, but in a way that

I can only assume to be brotherly. He's like the sibling I never had.

Instead, I was saddled with triplet douchebag stepbrothers who I've come to loathe rather than love.

As Chris hands Dornan's phone back, I'm nudged by the crowd. Dornan reaches out and steadies me. "We should head upstairs. It's not as cramped."

"Sure," I say, following as he shoulders his way through. In the hallway, I glance around, expecting to find Colby, Sebastian, or Micky, but my stepbrothers are nowhere to be found.

Dornan is right. It is less crowded upstairs. In one room, we disturb a couple who should have closed and locked the door. In another, Gabriella has her hands all over a guy I recognize from the student council. When I yell her name, she pulls back long enough to shoot me a thumbs up. "Come find me later," she says before resuming the previous face-sucking. Gross.

In the room at the end of the hallway, we find a large group sitting around in a circle. "Dornan," a blonde girl with wide-set eyes shouts. "We're playing seven minutes in heaven. Get your ass over here."

I grasp his elbow as he steps further into the room, but before I can tell him that reliving the worst high school party games isn't my idea of a good night, he presses two fingers over my lips. "It's my birthday," he says again.

"That is absolutely the last time you can use that line," I say.

He tugs me down onto the floor to join the circle.

Just as I take my place, the blonde girl spins the bottle in the middle of the floor, and by sheer bad luck, it lands on me.

"You're up," she says, jabbing her thumb toward the closet.

"No," I say. "Really. I'm just here with him."

"Are you scared?" she asks. All around me, the others make chicken noises.

"I'm not scared. I'm just…"

"Dare you," Dornan says before I can finish my excuses. I cut him a murderous glance because he's playing dirty now. Three 'it's my birthday' chants were enough. Now he's wheeling out the dare!

"Dornan," I say, my voice low.

"Dare, dare, dare," he sings.

Shaking my head, I rise, and smooth the fabric of my dress, wishing it would grow an extra three feet. I cut Dornan another murderous stare because he knows I will never back down on a dare, just like he knows the movies that make me cry and the comedians who make me almost die with laughter. The truth is, he knows me too well.

"We're timing," the girl says in a sing-song voice.

"Enjoy," Dornan says.

"Whoever is in there is getting the cold shoulder," I say. "He'd better keep his hands to himself." The people in the circle exchange looks and I catch a few smiles that are quickly hidden.

"Lame," someone shouts as I put my hand on the handle.

"Wait," the girl says, holding out a scarf. "You're forgetting the blindfold."

"It's darker than Satan's armpit in there," Dornan snorts.

"The rules are the rules," she says.

Dornan quickly fixes it around my head, and darkness swallows me whole. The door creaks open and he nudges me forward. When it closes behind me, I wait in the darkness, knowing I'm about to make a big mistake, but unable to do a thing about it.

8

2

ELLIE

Whoever owns the closet has too many stinky sneakers for their own good and enough clothes to sink a ship. My outstretched hands make contact with a rail, and I stop, not wanting to touch anything. This closet is cavernous, and I can see nothing through the blindfold. Clearing my throat, I wait for the dude who's trapped in here with me to say something.

Instead, the lightest graze of fingers against my wrists makes me jump. Before I have a chance to tell them they need to keep their hands to themselves, the fingers trail up the soft skin of the inside of my arm, and I shiver.

I actually shiver. My hair is lifted off my shoulder, and a soft kiss is pressed there. Warm breath caresses, then another kiss, and for a moment, I wonder why I have whirled away from wanting to stay on the opposite side of this closet to wanting to get closer. What about this stranger's touch makes me want to lean in and feel more rather than less?

The lightness of it. The surety.

I can't explain it.

Maybe it's the sensory deprivation and the anticipation it brings.

A soft exhale of breath leaves my parted lips as fingers trail up my bare arms. "Relax," a husky voice whispers. The vodka makes my head swim, or is it him? This man who's made me warmer between my legs in three seconds than the two poor excuses of men I've dated.

"Relax," he says against my skin, his tongue making a whisper of contact.

Even though it's pitch black, I close my eyes, needing to switch off just one sense before I overload.

A hand touches my thigh, just the flick of a cat's tail, but it's enough that the air catches in my throat. For a second, I think I feel the brush of another body, but it can't be, can it? Seven minutes in heaven is a game played by one girl and one boy. Except, I'm not a girl anymore, and whoever is touching me like a maestro playing a sonata is definitely not a boy.

Lips press against the inside of my thigh, and I jump as hands clasp the tops of my arms to steady me. "Relax," the voice behind me says, this time close to my ear.

One mouth whispering, another mouth kissing. Impossible, but not.

Two men cloaked in the darkness of the closet—two men whose touch is shudder-inducing.

Before I can say we need to stop, lips press against mine, trapping my words with teasingly gentle kisses.

Three men.

Oh god.

My pussy squeezes between my legs, aching and heavy with arousal.

I feel like I'm in a dream where my feet aren't quite touching the ground, and my brain has drifted away with the fairies.

I should stop this.

I didn't want this. Or maybe it's more accurate to say I didn't expect this. In high school, seven minutes in heaven was more like seven minutes of fumbling and embarrassment.

Not seven minutes of teasing. Seven minutes of swooning. Seven minutes of bliss.

A hot mouth presses against my pussy, warm even through the fabric of my dress and panties, and my hand instinctively reaches out to touch the head of whoever is down there. Soft curls meet my fingertips as he breathes in and out, heating my skin and maybe breathing in my scent. There's a moan, and it sounds so loud in the confines of this dark space. His pleasure seeps into my bones and reddens my cheeks, and they only flame brighter when the hem of my dress rises.

Am I really going to do this? Am I really going to let this unspeakably intimate thing happen with three strangers?

A tongue on my clit is the only convincing I need. And a mouth on my tightly puckered nipple. My hands are held too, as though there's a fear in the group that I might bolt.

That uncertainty prompts just the smallest of aches in my heart.

"Just let go," the voice behind me whispers. His hips press against the round curve of my ass, and I can feel just how much this stranger needs to let go, too. His cock is like a security guard's flashlight, and I'm surprised to find myself wishing that seven minutes could morph into at least an hour so that I could discover exactly what he'd do to me with that thing.

My dress is hitched up to my waist, and my black lace panties are shifted to one side with a roughness that makes me tremble.

It's delicious to sense their urgency. As delicious as the

first hot flick of his tongue against my soft flesh.

As one man suckles and squeezes my breasts, another teases me to the point of disaster. Fingers probe my entrance, and the slickness he elicits is enough to coat his hand and my thighs.

"Fuck," I hear him mutter, as though the discovery of my wetness is driving him to distraction.

I've never been this wet, this ready. I've never felt so close to falling over the precipice of pleasure into the blackness of ecstasy.

"Don't think," the man by my ear whispers. He shifts, bringing my right arm behind my back and pressing my palm to his cock. It's a moment of selfishness. A desire for him to feel just a flicker of the pleasure he and his friends are giving me. He doesn't realize that the fierce way he forces my fingers to close around his huge, thick length is the very thing that achieves the unachievable.

The sound that comes out of my mouth when I come is something so foreign that I don't recognize it as me. His grip on my hand increases, but I willingly squeeze his erection as though it's the only thing preventing me from falling. I feel the smile of the man whose mouth is over my nipple and a swift exhale of cool air against my sensitized clit that feels a lot like relief.

Relief he got me off.

What he doesn't know is that I'm relieved too. So relieved that hot, stupid tears spring to my eyes.

I thought I was broken. Simon, the last asshole I let between my legs, hinted as much. At first, he tried hard to get me to orgasm. After a couple of failed attempts, his attention became cursory at best. A few licks so he wouldn't feel like such an asshole for fucking me just for his pleasure.

Now I know it wasn't me. It was him.

My body is capable of the ultimate release.

I'm capable of letting every annoying, tension-inspiring part of my life drop away so that I can float on a helium balloon of pleasure, and that knowledge feels like freedom.

A tear escapes my eye and rolls down the side of my nose beneath the blindfold- a cool line of realization - and I feel so stupidly grateful that my chest hitches with a sob.

All around me in the darkness is silence. Surprised or shocked? I'm not sure.

Then, before any of us can say a word, there's a loud knock on the door.

"That's it, Ellie. Times up."

Dornan's voice is booming and amused, and within the blackness around me , three men inhale in a rush.

The man behind me drops my hand like it is scolding him. The hem of my dress is tugged down, and the top is pulled up as though they're hurriedly packing me away.

Dornan rattles the door handle. "It's not eight minutes in heaven, guys. Wrap it up. I need my girl back to party with."

Pulling away, I yank at the blindfold and stumble past the man at my feet, the one at my back, and the one looming to my right, fumbling for the door handle and shoving it open. The light in the room wasn't bright when I left, but it seems bright now. For a second, my eyes don't work, and I turn back to the closet, searching for the welcoming darkness. That's when I see just the flash of a hand in the gloom before Dornan slams the closet door shut.

A hand with a familiar tattoo of a lion with a huge shaggy mane. A tattoo that graces the skin of my stepbrother.

3

COLBY

My head pounds with a headache that most people would assume was alcohol induced, but I know differently. I don't get hangovers. I don't do weaknesses. I'm a man who handles his business and maintains control, even under the influence of mind-altering substances.

No, my headache is Ellie induced.

And Sebastian induced. And Micky doesn't get off scot-free. He's the idiot that dragged me into that fucking closet. Admittedly, he didn't know Ellie would be the one who stumbled into Sex Fest 2022. I know that for sure. I was the only one who knew Ellie had arrived at the party, and she was supposed to be in the den. Micky had his eyes on Alexandra from his business class. The same Alexandra who spent the last two months asking him a million questions about what it's like to be an identical triplet. Like any of us know any different.

My brothers have been around since before I was even conscious of myself. They are such an intrinsic part of me. I sometimes feel it when they hurt themselves.

Micky was convinced Alexandra wanted to know what it's like to get between identical triplets. It wouldn't be the first time, and it won't be the last. For some reason, it's a popular fetish, one that we've mostly been happy to indulge. I mean, who wouldn't want to get involved in that kind of kinky fuckery.

Stupid high school games should be relegated to high school, not dragged into our college years, where we should always have our wits about us when it comes to sex.

Ellie has the same length of hair as Alexandra. She's roughly the same height and build too. Who the fuck would have known the difference in the silent darkness of the closet?

I didn't recognize her whimpers. She's our stepsister, for fuck's sake. That's not the kind of thing any self-respecting stepbrother would know about the girl who lives across the hall.

I'm not a creep. I don't hang outside her door listening for that shit.

As far as I'm concerned, Ellie's sex life is her own business.

At least, that's how I felt before last night.

Before I rested my lips on her neck and felt her tremble. Before I breathed in the soft floral scent of her warm skin, forced her little hand to my cock and felt that hint of eagerness to explore.

See, Ellie was nothing like I thought she'd be. Instead of pushing us away when she found out there were three of us in the closet, she warmed to the situation. She let us discover what it took to get her off, and she came like a river.

At least, that's what Micky said. He was the one who got to taste her pretty pussy. And Seb got his lips around her tight little nipples.

And me?

I got to whisper in her ear and feel her trembling

response. I got to hear just how much she enjoyed everything we did to her.

And when Dornan yelled for her through the door, it was me who felt her flinch.

Fuck.

At that moment, my life flashed before my eyes because there are things that happen between two people that it's impossible to come back from and holding your stepsister still while your brothers make her come is one of them.

Shit.

I rub my temple, closing my eyes against the bright sunlight illuminating the yard of our family home.

Family. Even thinking about the word makes my head pound harder.

"Colby, can you take this salad to the table," Lara says. Lara, Ellie's mom, has no idea what happened last night. No idea of the real reason Ellie has been up in her room all morning.

Ellie never misses breakfast, especially on the weekends. Lara makes the world's best pancakes, but only on Saturdays, in case we learn to take them for granted.

Not that there's any chance of that.

Now it's lunch, and she still hasn't made an appearance.

"Sure," I say, reaching out to take the large wooden bowl that is almost overspilling with crisp lettuce and juicy red tomatoes. My stepmother smiles brightly at me, her deep brown eyes filled with approval. Eyes that are almost exactly the same shape and shade as her daughter's.

"And come back for the potato salad."

"I'll get that," Sebastian says, jumping up from the sun lounger he was reclining on.

"You boys are so helpful," Lara says. "Unlike my lazy daughter. Where the hell is Ellie?"

I turn to Seb and find his eyes widening. "There was a party last night," I blurt. "Maybe she ate something that didn't agree with her."

"Ate something?" Lara rolls her eyes. "Do you boys think I was born yesterday? Since when do they serve food at frat parties? In my day, bowls of chips were the only things edible at those events."

"Not much has changed," Micky says, but I don't miss the way his tongue darts over his top lip like he's imagining savoring the taste of Ellie all over again. The fucker thinks he's clever.

"There was pizza," I say quickly. "And you know what those cheap pizza places can be like…no hygiene."

"Maybe I should go up there and check on her?" Lara says, glancing up at the house, even though Ellie's window is at the front.

"You have your hands full," I say quickly. "I'll go."

Seb's eyebrows shoot up so quickly that it's comical, and I get why. I'm not exactly the man you send anywhere to offer soft concern and sympathy. I'm the man you send when you need shit done. Give me a task to complete, and I'm in my element. Finding out if someone has the shits or is just hiding away from three men she orgasmed all over would be better suited to anyone other than me.

But I can't send Micky. Lord only knows what he'd say. He'd probably apologize and then tell Ellie he was hoping Alexandra would come into the closet. And Seb's go-to style under pressure is to make a joke of everything. Not what this situation needs.

"Well, that's so kind of you," Lara says. "Especially when Ellie's probably just being her usual uncooperative self."

"It's nothing," I say, already making my way to the sliding doors. The house is my father's. He and my mom bought it when we were little. They stretched themselves financially to make sure we each had our own rooms, and there was a spare room for when our grandparents stayed over to help. Now Ellie occupies the spare room, and mom's place in the master suite has been filled by Lara. I don't blame dad for remarrying when he lost mom. He couldn't deal with the demands of three teenage boys and keep his sanity and employment. Lara stepped in to run us between school and extracurricular activities. She fed us, clothed us, and ensured we kept our grades up; for that, I'll always be grateful.

I wonder if Ellie feels the same about our dad. Not that he's played much of a role in her upbringing outside of putting a roof over her head. I get that his effort would have been a lot less visible for her.

There's always been a prickliness to Ellie within this house that doesn't fit with the person she is around friends and at college.

As I climb the stairs, I remember the person she was in that closet with strangers. A different version of Ellie that I've never seen before and never expected to feel up close and personal.

Just the thought of her soft moans has my cock hardening in my pants, and the memory of Dornan's booming voice disrupting our moment makes me seethe with anger. Fuck.

It's so wrong to view Ellie sexually. I'm her stepbrother, and that should put any kind of relationship off limits. Forget how furious my dad would be, and her mom. Lara would never look at my brothers and me the same again.

But I can't stop reflecting on the soft fragrance of her skin or the way she clutched at me as she came. It's like she opened a box of secrets and let me rummage around, and now I've seen what's in the box; closing the lid is impossible.

How can we sit opposite each other at breakfast and

not remember what happened at Dornan's party? How can we chat with our parents as though nothing happened?

At the top of the stairs, I tip my head from side to side, stretching out my neck as though I'm limbering up for a game. My hands instinctively flex into fists before loosening again. I bounce up onto my toes and then inhale a deep breath. It's not that I fear facing Ellie. Not in the slightest. But for the first time ever, I'm worried about how our interaction will go. Things between us have always been frosty. In the beginning, I tried so hard. I wanted her to feel comfortable in our home. I wanted her to like us, but she always held back, so I stopped trying. Will it be worse now we've overstepped the sibling line?

Will she hate us? Will she blame us? Does she regret what happened?

Or worse. Will she feel violated?

The thought that she might look back on last night with regret or worse causes my heart to do a fucked-up thud that feels black with dread.

Standing with my hand poised to knock on Ellie's door, I close my eyes for a second, making a vow to whoever might be listening that if this goes okay, I'll be a better man. I'll try harder. Work more. Volunteer more. Be kinder.

The thump of my fist on the wood is abrupt and loud, and I crane my ear to the door, so I can hear better. There's no noise inside, then a muffled 'go away' emanates from deep in the room.

"Ellie, you need to open this door," I say with as much conviction as possible. I've learned that a stern and confident voice can compel people to act.

"Leave me alone," she says, but it's after a pause.

"Your mom is worried about you. If you don't open the door, she will come up."

More silence, but then I hear a shuffling sound, as

though Ellie's dragging more than just her sweet ass across the wood floor.

When the lock rattles in the door, I take a step back.

It's opened just a crack, and a disheveled Ellie peers around the white-painted wood so that all I can see is a half-closed eye, messy curls, and a pair of pretty but scowling lips.

"I'm not coming down," she says. "You and your brothers know why. How about you keep my mom at bay...you always know how to twist her around your finger."

She tries to push the door closed, but I shove my foot into the gap. "We didn't know it was you," I admit.

"And you think I did?" she hisses.

"So it's nobody's fault, is it? We're all adults. We just need to get on with it. Pretend it never happened."

Her dark eyes stare into mine as though she's trying to dig past my words, deep into my thoughts and the truth of how I'm feeling. "And that's easy for you, is it?" she asks.

There's no right way to respond to her question that's been tossed into the crackling air between us like barbed wire, designed to snag and tear. Saying yes means it meant nothing to me. She meant nothing. Saying no means that I'm hung up on her in a way that's past the boundaries of acceptability.

"I'm trying," I say, treading a middle line. "That's all any of us can do."

She blinks, shocked. "Just tell mom I'm exhausted. Offer to bring me food. That should be enough to get her off our backs."

I nod once, folding in my bottom lip to moisten it. If I closed my eyes, I could conjure the taste of her skin. If I was alone in my room, I could make myself come so hard recalling the press of her rounded ass against my cock. But I can't do any of that. I just need to forget and find a way to ensure Lara doesn't come up here to bother her daughter.

"Okay."

Ellie nods and looks down at my foot. I didn't know eyes could move flesh until my leg reflexively retracts.

"It never happened," she whispers, her eyes still lowered to the ground.

"But it did," I say instinctively. Denying it doesn't seem right. Not when I can still feel the ghost memory of her body pressed against mine.

"Forget it happened then," she says.

When her eyes meet mine, they're the color of a moonless sky. "What if I can't," I say.

Her lips part as if there are words on the tip of her tongue that want to break free, but she thinks better of it and traps them again, narrowing her mouth.

As the door slowly closes, I shake my head. Ellie Franklin might want to lock herself away and deny her seven minutes in heaven, but I can't pretend it never happened.

Not to myself and definitely not to her.

4

ELLIE

Professor Anderson is my favorite lecturer. He inspires every student in an overflowing lecture hall to hang on to his every word, leaning forward as though they don't want to risk missing a single syllable. It doesn't hurt that he's nice to look at, either. Maybe that's why at least three-quarters of the class is female.

Colby is within the minority of male students, and today he does not look happy.

But that's not unusual. My stepbrother has a way of exuding a mix of anger and disdain wherever he goes. His brow is furrowed, his black hair with its annoyingly perfect wave, flopping low over his forehead as he types notes on his mac.

I shouldn't be looking at him because I don't want to get caught in the act, but I can't help myself. Since Dornan's party, I've been in denial. I've avoided seeing him other than that one time through a crack in the doorway. After our 'chat', he successfully convinced my mom that I needed rest, so I hunkered down in my room and avoided everyone.

But I couldn't avoid my thoughts. I couldn't stop

myself from going over every minute detail of what happened in the closet.

Three men.

Three stepbrothers.

Three different roles in making me come harder than I ever have before.

But who was where?

It's stupid that I care. It's ridiculous that I think I know. Colby was the one behind me, the controlling hands and whispered orders. Micky was the one who licked me so perfectly that I soaked through my panties on the way down the stairs. Seb's clever mouth tortured my nipples. They're still tipped with red and a little sore. I'd bet money I don't have that I've worked it all out correctly.

The thing is none of it should matter. I wish I could bury every memory and relegate them to the same place I pushed all thoughts of when my dad moved to another state for work and never came back.

But I can't.

Because these memories aren't bad per se. Pleasure isn't the same as pain, no matter how difficult the reality of it all is. We shouldn't have done what we did. We would never have if it hadn't been for the darkness and anonymity. But now that we have, I don't know how to feel. I don't know what to do with the tingling I feel between my legs or the yearning I have for men I try not to talk to even though we live in the same house. I can't reconcile the feelings from before with the ones from after. I feel ridiculous for letting sex thoughts cloud my mind. That's not the kind of girl I am.

Except it seems that it is because as Colby frowns again, staring at the big screen behind Professor Anderson, I get a flutter low in my belly.

Traitorous body.

"For extra credit, I'm tasking you to work in pairs to

answer this question." Professor Anderson flicks forward in his presentation. I read over the question and type it quickly into my lecture notes. "To shake things up a little, I've decided on who will work with who. I know you all have your buddies in the class, but getting to know someone new will broaden your perspectives and hopefully mean that you get more from this exercise."

A mix of chatter and groaning fills the room, and Professor Anderson raises his hands to calm everyone down. Flicking forward again, a list of names appears on the screen. I scan for my name, finding it halfway down, and my heart drops ten stories in my chest. Because, of course, who would fate pair me with but Colby?

It's a sick joke.

A doom-filled nightmare.

I don't want to look at him now. I don't want to see the disappointment and annoyance on his face.

"Gather your things and find your partners. We'll spend the rest of the time today going through what I want you to consider and options for presenting your answers."

My heart thuds so hard against my ribs that I bring my hand to cover it. Closing my eyes for a second, I inhale a long, deep breath through my nostrils. This is such a mortifying situation, but I've lived through worse. I just need to pull up my big-girl panties and get on with it. If Colby wants to be an ass, he can be. There isn't a way of controlling other people's responses, only my own.

Finally, I pluck up the courage to glance over my shoulder and find Colby still in his seat. Our eyes meet, and he raises his chin so defiantly that I want to laugh. Of course, he wouldn't come to me. Colby might as well be made of cement for all the flexibility he has in his attitude and opinions. But if he's cement, then today, I'm made of unbreakable diamond. Raising my eyebrows, I turn back to Professor Anderson, who is watching everyone trying to find their partners. I contemplate raising my hand to tell him I already know Colby far too well, and maybe we could swap partners, but that would probably get me points deducted before I've even started this task.

So, I wait.

And wait. And wait. I don't turn to Mr. Granite again. He can suck it if he expects me to go to him just because he beckoned like a neanderthal.

Just as Professor Anderson flicks to the next slide, ready to explain the task further, Colby slumps into the empty seat next to me. "Did anyone ever tell you you have an attitude problem?" he growls under his breath.

"Nope." Folding my arms, I stare straight ahead.

"Why don't I believe you?" he says, opening his laptop.

"Because you have trust issues," I mutter.

A snort is all I get in response.

For the next twenty minutes, Colby takes notes like he's going to be asked to regurgitate the lecture word for word. I swear, I've never seen a man's fingers move so fast. Especially thick, strong fingers attached to palms the size of dinner plates. My pussy squeezes, remembering how it felt to have identical fingers spreading me open. Colby and his brothers may have very different personalities, but they're so identical in their physical features, it's uncanny.

Maybe I'm wrong. Maybe it was Colby kneeling on the floor before me, serving me with hot, slick pleasure. Another glance at his fingers heats my cheeks like lava.

"Now, I want you to take the last ten minutes to discuss your ideas and potential approach with your partner. The task should take you around four hours to complete in total. Work out a schedule for when and how you're going to meet the deadline."

All around us, people chatter. It's the kind of over-enthusiastic rumble that only comes about when lots of people who don't really know each other are forced to partner up. Between Colby and I is deathly silence.

"I'm free on Thursday," he mutters eventually.

"And what if I'm not?" I say, even though I am.

"Then we find another day."

Ugh. I hate him for being so unemotional and logical. How can he be unemotional, for fucks sake? Isn't he as pent up with indescribable feelings as me? Doesn't he want to shout at me for being in the wrong place at the wrong time? Isn't he mad as hell that we overstepped a line we can never cross back over again?

What if I can't? The four small words he uttered through the crack in my door flare into my memory. He's thinking about what happened, too. He admitted it with no shame.

"Thursdays fine," I say through gritted teeth.

"Okay then. I don't mind taking the second part of the question to research. Or would you rather do that part?"

"I'll take the first," I say, relieved.

"Good. Okay." Colby types some more and then goes through his ideas for how we should approach the presentation of our results. His voice is low and even, and everything he says makes complete sense. So much so that I want to scream.

How can a man with such a handsome face and perfect biceps also be so intelligent? Like, shouldn't God have shared the good stuff a little more evenly rather than giving Colby all of it? And why am I even noticing his ridiculously thick eyelashes or the way his t-shirt is straining across his chest? They're not appropriate thoughts for an almost sibling.

If he could hear my thoughts, he'd be disgusted, wouldn't he? I'm disgusted.

And overwhelmed.

I always thought my stepbrothers were airheads who

only got into college on the back of their amazing sporting prowess. All they seem to be interested in is football and girls, and I'm not even sure which order to place those two things in.

When Colby's finished talking, I want to say yes. That all sounds perfect.

But instead, what comes out is, "How can you focus on this stupid task after what happened?"

For a flash, I see Colby flinch at my question, and his eyes lower to the computer in front of him. Then he turns his fae-green eyes to me, his jaw ticking with tension. "What do you want me to do, Ellie?" he growls. "I don't have a frigging DeLorean. There's no going back in time."

Rational again.

"I want you to apologize," I say. "At least be regretful. It's like it was no big deal to you."

"It was a kiss in a closet," he whispers. "Something we've all been doing since high school. We didn't tattoo your skin with our names, for fuck's sake. It doesn't have to be a big thing unless you make it one."

"So now it's my fault for overreacting."

"That isn't what I said," he says. "Didn't you have a good time?"

"That isn't the point."

"Well, it should be." A flicker of amusement passes across his infuriatingly perfect lips.

"If pleasure is all you care about, your life is going to be very shallow."

"I don't want to patronize you, Ellie, but you need to loosen up."

"I don't want to patronize you, Ellie, but I'll go ahead and do it anyway," I mimic.

"Listen," he growls again, leaning close enough that I can see flecks of gold in his eyes. "I felt you grinding

27

against me. I heard you come all over my brother's face. You loved every minute, so stop pretending it was something hideous and terrible."

"You might twist my mom around your little fingers, but I'm not so easily impressed," I say.

He recoils and shakes his head. "I'm not interested in twisting anyone around my little finger. Not your mom, and definitely not you."

"Good," I say, breathing deeply and quickly like I'm trapped in a flight response even though I'm coming out fighting.

"As I said before, Ellie, we're not related. We're all adults. It doesn't have to be a big deal unless you want to make it one."

"What are you insinuating?"

He meets my narrowed eyes with a quirk of his eyebrow and a twist of his lips. "You know there's that phrase from Shakespeare, 'the lady doth protest too much'."

"Fuck, Colby. You're quoting Shakespeare at me now?"

"I think you liked it. And I think you'd like to do it again, but you're so fucking uptight that you can't bear to admit it."

"I'm not uptight," I hiss.

"Oh, no." He looks down at my hands, which are balled into tight fists. His hand brushes my bunched shoulder, and then he shakes his head. "Seriously, Ellie. You need to take a chill pill. And if you can't find one of those, Micky's not the only one who's skilled with his tongue. Another orgasm like that will push the tension right out of your body."

"I knew it," I say before my brain kicks into gear and my hand flies to my traitorous lips.

Colby smiles then. A full-on megawatt smile that

doesn't seem to fit his face, even though it would look perfect on almost identical Sebastian. "You tried to work out where we all were, didn't you?" Leaning in close until his stubbly cheek almost presses against mine, he whispers in my ear. "Lucky Micky."

I jolt back at the warm gust of his breath and the way my whole body comes alive at his proximity.

"That's disgusting," I blurt, and he pulls back, staring me right in the eyes, close enough that I wonder if he'll kiss me here and now. And fuck, I want him too. I really want him to, with an urgency that I despise. I want it to be a hard, mean, closed-lipped kiss that will bruise. One I could slap him for but mess my panties over in secret. But this is Colby, and I hate Colby, I resent Colby, and I have to live with Colby.

"Keep telling yourself lies, Ellie, and one day, you won't be able to recognize the truth."

At the front of the lecture hall, Professor Anderson yells, "RIGHT THAT'S IT. YOU SHOULD BE FINISHING UP NOW," but I'm so mesmerized by Colby's close proximity that I don't move a muscle.

"Fuck off, Colby," I manage, but it comes out more like a breathy squeak than an aggressive dismissal.

"Micky was right about you," he says as he backs up in his seat, lowering the screen of his laptop.

"Oh yeah, and what did Micky say?"

Colby shrugs. "You're not ready for that now. When you are, I'll tell you."

And with that, he gets to his feet, stuffing his bag with his possessions before turning to leave.

Thursday will be torture, but when this assignment is done, there's no reason for me to have to spend any more time with my stepbrothers than I'm forced to. Micky can say what he likes about me. I don't care what his opinions are.

But as I pack away my laptop, I turn to catch Colby disappearing through the double doors and wish I knew everything.

5

SEBASTIAN

There is nothing like a shower after a game. The sweat and dirt wash down the drain, and my sore muscles loosen perfectly under the stream of steaming hot water. My brothers always complain that I take too long, but they don't understand that this is part of my ritual. Some people have pregame rituals. The things they do to hold luck on their side. I have a post-game ritual that keeps my head in the right place. I use the time to think through what went well and what I'd change if I could fix my mistakes. By the time I get into the locker room, dressed only in a small white towel, my teammates have finished busting each other's balls. I can avoid hearing the negativity tossed around when everyone is pumped with testosterone.

As I stroll out of the showers and into the locker room, I catch sight of Colby and Micky, who are dressed, and sitting next to their gym bags, their dark hair still slick with water. Colby narrows his eyes at me. He hates waiting, but he's done with complaining because he knows it won't make a damned bit of difference.

"Hey, douchebags," I say, grabbing my bag from my locker and searching out my antiperspirant. "What's the rush!" Nothing like tossing out a taunt to wind them up.

"Don't start," Micky says, holding his hands out as though they can prevent me from prodding Colby and Colby from reacting. Micky has always been the buffer between us. The middle-born child. Is that a coincidence? It must be. There are only three minutes between each of us. Three minutes doesn't make Colby the serious, mature one or me the lighthearted joker. It doesn't make Micky the triplet who empathizes with everyone so much that it burdens his soul. I guess when the universe was handing out attributes, they handed out ours in a way that is just ridiculously cliched.

"Some of us have things to do," Colby grumbles.

"Oh yeah. And what's such an emergency?"

"He's got an assignment to prepare for," Micky says with a glint in his eye.

"Don't start," Colby says. "I always have assignments to prepare for."

"Yeah, but this one's with Ellie."

I lift my brows, scanning my brother's expression for any sign of how he's feeling. As usual, he's giving absolutely nothing away. But I don't need to see his reaction to knowing what he's thinking. Since our seven minutes with Ellie in the closet, Colby's been acting like a bear with a sore head, and he's even worse than usual. None of us knew it was going to be her, but we all wanted it to be.

Colby won't admit that to me, though. He holds his cards close to his chest, but I catch the lingering looks he gives her when she's fixing breakfast in her sleep shorts and crop top with messy hair and sleepy eyes. I catch the way he seems extra riled by her over the smallest things. He believes that by maintaining his frosty, aggravated persona, no one will guess he's been lusting over his stepsister for years, but he forgets I know him and Micky better than anyone.

Micky doesn't even try to disguise his lingering looks. He stares at Ellie's ass like it's the ark of the covenant dropped from heaven in front of his very eyes.

And me. Well, I do what I always do. I use my humor to cover the fact that Ellie is my dream girl made reality.

"Is she still mad as hell?" I ask.

"Yep," Colby grits his teeth, which makes his jaw tick.

"You talking about that fine stepsister of yours?" Elias asks, looking up from packing his bag.

"Easy," Colby warns. "Ellie's family."

"Interesting family you've got." Elias grins broadly despite Colby's withering stare and Micky's slightly panicked expression.

"You going somewhere with this?" I ask.

"I heard you went somewhere with her. Into the closet."

"You never heard of minding your own fucking business." Colby lumbers to his feet, making the most of his imposing size to draw a line under the conversation, but Elias is also huge and remains unphased.

"I'm just telling you what I heard."

"Yeah. Well, maybe people need to keep their mouths shut about things that don't concern them," Colby grunts, looking around the locker room to make it clear he means everyone there.

Elias shrugs. "When it was Blake's love life getting dissected last week, you were all over it."

"Blake was all over it," Micky says quickly. "None of us were getting involved in any business that he wasn't happy sharing."

"That's the thing, though, isn't it? You guys seem very happy to share," Elias winks, and I take a step forward, knowing Colby's temper is frayed to the point of being held together by a single thread. Coach would be pissed if there were any physical altercations in the locker room, and I need shit from Coach like I need a bullet in the brain.

"Okay, Elias," I say. "You've had your fun. Time to let it go."

He shakes his head, letting out a bubble of amused laughter. "I don't know why you guys are so fucking defensive about it. She's not your real sister. Half the porn on the internet is about stepsisters hooking up with their stepbrothers.

"Ellie is family," Micky says. "Colby's just being protective."

"If you think of her as family, then what happened at Dornan's party was fucked up," he says.

A voice clears behind me, and I turn to find Dornan with his bag held high on his shoulder. I wouldn't want to be the one talking shit about his best friend right now. "You better not be talking about my friend, Elias. You know how I get when people talk shit about the people I care about."

Elias grabs his bag from the bench and shrugs one huge shoulder. "I'm not talking shit about anyone. Just trying to get to the truth behind the gossip."

"Yeah, well, you tell whoever's gossiping about Ellie that they can come to talk to me," Dornan says.

Colby steps forward. "Better still, you tell them to keep her name off their lips. And anyway, who the fuck are you? Mother-fucking-hen? Why the fuck are you interested in gossip? Don't you have more important things to think about, like football, assignments, and your own fucking sex life? Or maybe that's the problem. Maybe if you had somewhere to put your own cock, you wouldn't be worried so much about mine."

A look passes between Colby and Dornan, and Elias

shrugs. "I'll see you guys around."

He saunters off as though he doesn't give two shits about what any of us have said. Dornan drops his bag to the floor and rubs his hand through his wet blond hair. "I feel responsible," he says. "It was my stupid fucking idea to have that party. I dragged Ellie into playing the game. Now people are talking about her behind her back. This kind of gossip can stay with a person."

"If Elias has a head on his shoulders, he'll listen to the warning," Micky says.

"It's good to know that you're not adding fuel to the fire," Dornan says.

We all glance at each other, and I know my brothers are feeling aggravated at the insinuation. "That's not who we are, despite what Ellie might tell you." Colby inhales a deep breath and lets it out through his nostrils like a bull on the brink of charging. I rub my tattooed arm, feeling the air's chill but not wanting to interrupt the current flow of conversation by getting my dick out and pulling on my underwear.

"Again, good to know." Dornan glances around at the rest of our teammates, sending a warning to anyone else who might not be so protective of his friend.

I'll be honest in saying that we've talked shit about other girls in the past. Some cheerleaders put out so easily they might as well not wear panties, but Ellie's different. She didn't mean to end up the subject of speculation. She certainly didn't mean to end up with her sweet, tight nipple in my mouth.

Fuck. Just thinking about that night has my cock stirring. The sounds she made as Colby held her and Micky licked her have kept me awake at night since. I've tugged myself to orgasm more than once with just those breathy sounds buzzing around my head. The pictures I've had to conjure from my own imagination. It was too dark in the closet to see anything, and that's a fucking massive regret for me. If that's the only time I'm going to get my lips and hands on Ellie's breasts, I'd at least have liked to see them.

A few minutes later, as we're walking to my car, Colby makes a growling, angry sound in his throat. "That guy has a chip on his shoulder."

"Elias? Maybe. Or he could be fishing around for something to talk about. Not everyone has such interesting lives," I say.

"Interesting isn't a word I'd use."

"You don't think the situation with Ellie is interesting?"

"It's a powder keg ready to explode," Colby says. "She's mad as hell."

"Mad and horny," I laugh. "Maybe a little freaked out. I'll admit that when Dornan shouted her name through the door, and my mouth was in a very controversial place, my heart pounded a little harder than usual."

"Your mouth was in a controversial place?" Micky says, rolling his eyes. Yours was practically PG-13 compared to mine."

"She tasted good?" I ask, my face twisting into a devilish grin.

"Don't answer that," Colby says.

"Why? Are you telling me you don't want to know?"

"I'm telling you that the more this is talked about, the deeper the shit gets for all of us."

"I'd say we're up to our tongues in it already," I laugh. "Not sure it could get any worse."

"We could admit that we like her," Micky says, taking a big bite out of an apple and chewing it like a horse. "I mean, we're brothers. More than that. We were supposed to be one person, for fuck's sake. And we're all still pretending like denial is a fucking safe house. We're as bad as Ellie."

I gawp at Micky, trying to produce a funny retort but

finding absolutely no inspiration. Nothing. Nada. To be honest, my absence of inspiration freaks me out more than his admittance. Because there have been times when I've wondered if it was just me who was lusting over Ellie, and I've been reading more into my brothers' looks and body language than there actually is.

"Close your mouth," Micky says, winking as he takes another loud crunch of his fruit. "I know you do," he says. "Although, out of all of us, you're the least obvious about it. Colby, on the other hand…"

"What about me? You think you know what I'm feeling? You think you have an insight into my mind because we share the same DNA?"

"I have an insight into your mind because you wear your heart on your sleeve, Colby," Micky says. "You might not want to accept it with your gruff, angry-bear persona, but you do."

I stare at both my brothers with utter fascination. The vein on Colby's temple throbs through the thin skin and he clenches his jaw so tightly I worry he will fracture his molars. Micky just seems smug, as though he's relishing this new role of getting us to admit the shit we've kept private until now.

"Doesn't matter what we want, though, does it?" Colby says eventually. She's our sister, and we just have to find a way of putting everything that happened in that closet out of our minds."

"But she isn't, is she?" Micky says gently. "She's just a girl who's the daughter of someone our dad married. We're not blood. We don't share even a sprinkling of DNA. So apart from it being a little weird that all three of us have the hots for the same girl, and the fact she lives under the same roof, there's nothing really stopping us, is there?"

"You're forgetting one very important thing," Colby says. "It doesn't matter because Ellie sure as hell doesn't feel the same. And now she's at the center of a huge scandal, there is no way she'll even consider doing anything that'll add fuel to the fire."

6

ELLIE

I've been dreading working on the presentation with Colby for many reasons. I tell myself it's because he's an arrogant ass and a suck-up to my mom, but those are the easy excuses to cover a more complicated truth.

The reality is that being forced to sit near a man who whispered in my ear as I came at the hands of another man has me hot and flustered. Truly, I don't want to have these feelings. I want to hold the anger and resentment against my stepbrothers close to my heart. I want to hate them but hate and lust are strange bedfellows. How can I fantasize about them and want to avoid them simultaneously?

I know how.

It's like I've separated the closet men from the real men in my head. And that's easier to do when I don't see them. But we can't work together without sitting in the same room, and sitting in the same room will mean proximity, and proximity will mean remembering what that sweet release felt like and applying it to the real person. Or one of them.

Would it be harder to sit next to Micky now that he knows how I taste between my thighs? Or would it be more difficult to sit with Seb, whose tongue flicked against my shamelessly tight nipples?

I don't think so. Each of them played a role. Each of them is as guilty as the others.

They are as guilty as me.

A knock on my door is so loud and sudden that I practically jump out of my skin. Like the day after I stumbled into that closet, unaware of who was going to take me to heaven; when I open the door, I find Colby looming on the other side. "Are you ready to study?" he asks in a voice that sounds gruff and unused. A sexy, husky voice that trails hotly over my skin, searching out my most sensitive place.

"Sure," I say, even though the reality is NO NO NO!

No, I can't sit next to you.

No, I won't be able to process the boring topic we have to discuss with you sitting next to me.

No, I can't pretend that you don't affect me.

My whole body feels like it's vibrating, disturbing the air around us in rippling sex-waves that I'm convinced Colby can sense. He looks at me strangely, with a question in his eyes that never makes it to his lips.

I return to my room, needing to get away from his intensity and gather my thoughts. What should I take with me? Laptop, pens, paper, some frickin' common sense. Most of all, I have to banish these sex thoughts to have hope in hell of concentrating.

"Give me a minute," I call over my shoulder without turning to check he's heard me. The heavy retreating tread of his feet tells me all I need to know. Like a marathon runner at the end of a grueling race, I place my hands on the fronts of my thighs and bend at the waist. "Get it together," I whisper. "Pull your panties up and get on with it."

With a deep breath and a renewed purpose, I grab my

things and make the brief journey across the hall to Colby's room.

The door is ajar, so I cross the threshold without knocking. He's already hunched over his desk, computer open, fingers flying over the keyboard. "I've started putting something down so that we have a starting point."

"Okay." I'm relieved. Hopefully, that will mean sitting next to him for less time.

He's brought the chair that usually sits in the corner of his room next to his desk so that I can see what he's typing. I guess Colby's taking the lead, which doesn't surprise me. His bossy tone and controlling hands flash into my mind, and my knees go to jelly as I slump into the seat.

"What are your thoughts on these headlines?"

I scan through what he's written, and it's precisely the approach I would have taken.

"Looks great."

His shoulders drop a little, which is funny because I wouldn't have imagined Colby would care much about whether I agreed with him. I expected him to just take over, assuming he knows best. He's that kind of man. But the reality of how we work together over the next couple of hours is completely different. Yes, he has strong opinions, but that's okay. I'm pretty bull-headed too.

The thing is, even if I start out wanting to disagree with him, his arguments are always strong and well-thought-through. I catch him nodding when I'm talking, as though he's impressed with my way of thinking, too. In record time, we have a presentation that I'm proud of and know Professor Anderson will love, and we've achieved it without a disagreement and in record time.

We make a great team. Who could have predicted that?

It's the first time in forever that we've spent time in each other's company without getting on each other's nerves, and I don't know how to process this version of my stepbrother. Is he like this because of what happened? Is he trying to smooth things over so he can get a good grade, and get in my pants again, or is he a different person than I thought?

As Colby closes his laptop, I stand, pushing my chair back a little with my legs to make space, but it's as though Colby has the same thought and stands too. I end up with my face almost pressed to his broad chest, catching the scent of his freshly washed shirt and warm skin in the process. He looks down as I look up, and when our eyes meet, a frisson of electricity seems to pulse between us, flashing bright and blue and noisy as static. My lungs react by sucking in a noisy gulp of breath, and I quickly press my lips together so no other evidence of my arousal can squeak through. His forest-colored eyes are dark with wide pupils that feel intense as they search mine.

Seconds tick past. Seconds that feel as long as summer days.

I swallow, feeling every bodily reflex, the clenching of muscles as I brace for what may happen, the involuntary movement of my throat. I'm so small next to his huge, muscular body, so tiny and insignificant.

He'd have to bend to kiss me, I think, and then I blush because what the fuck? Why am I thinking about kissing when I should be retreating to my room, closing the door, and focusing on anything but how soft his lips look and how even though I'm looking directly at his face, I can sense his hands flexing at his sides, ready to grab me and pull me close?

God, I want that. Grabbing hands and frantic kisses. I want a man who demands things of me without asking, and who can tell when I acquiesce I do so willingly.

Colby's chest rises and falls on a long breath, as though he's trying to keep a fingernail grip on his restraint.

I'm holding my breath, waiting, waiting, either for

Colby to do something or for me to see sense. As Colby leans in, I feel like Alice, about to tumble down a rabbit hole into a world I'm wholly unprepared for.

But as unprepared as I am, I still want that kiss.

Then a loud bang on the door jolts us both from our mesmerized state. Micky's standing at the door, dressed only in a towel, and my cheeks flush hotter than lava.

Shit.

I grab my things, stacking them in my arms.

"You got some antiperspirant?" Micky asks Colby. I can't look at either of them because two Townsend men in such close confines have the potential to make me melt. As Colby reaches out to hand Micky the black and silver can, and I head for the door, footsteps pound in the hallway. Out of nowhere, Seb appears, his hand grabbing for Micky's towel.

In slow motion, it comes away from his waist. Seb makes off with it down the hall, and Micky is left naked only four feet away from me. Naked and so fucking hot that my mouth fills with saliva.

Oh god.

It takes him a couple of seconds to react with his hand over his cock, but it's a couple of seconds too late.

I've seen the size and perfection of what he has between his legs—what they all have because they're identically sized in everything else—and the image is burned into my brain. Rippling abs leading down into the v of muscle that I've never seen on a man in real life. And thighs that are powerful enough to make me salivate.

"For fuck's sake," Colby mutters, his eyes on me, watching everything. I hesitate, not able to break out of my frozen state. Micky shrugs his shoulders apologetically, even though none of this is his fault, and makes off down the hallway in pursuit of a very juvenile Sebastian. Colby clears his throat, and that's enough to jolt me towards the door, a raging blush flaming at my cheeks. "I'll send you what we did," Colby shouts after me, but I couldn't care less about the presentation.

All I can think about is Micky's clever tongue sliding over my pussy, and what it would feel like to be penetrated by a cock that long and thick. All I want to do is clamp my thighs together to relieve the ache. When I'm in my room, I slam the door and lean against it, my knees almost giving way and my heart thudding so hard, it's like a bass drum inside me. I can't believe the physical reactions I've had to something I want to feel repulsed by but can't.

Shit.

I've got a problem. Actually, it's more like three huge problems.

Placing my laptop and book on my desk, I go back to the door to press my ear to the cool wood. I don't even know if it's possible to hear anything, but I want to know what they're talking about. The distant manly rumble of voices isn't intelligible through the door, though. Damn.

Flopping onto my bed, I need a distraction to keep me from pressing my fingers to my lips in memory of a kiss that never happened or to my clit, to relieve the ache that my stepbrothers have left me with.

Instead, I bring up Dornan's number on my phone and call it, knowing my best friend will take my mind off the Townsends and make me laugh. I need to laugh.

"Hey, Ellie-Elephant," he says.

"For fuck's sack, Dornan! Can you chill the fuck out with these shitty nicknames? They are not flattering."

"Who said nicknames are supposed to be flattering? They have to be cute or annoying. Them's the rules, babes. I don't make this shit up."

"Well, maybe you need to ignore the rules, Dornan. I mean, when did you become such a rule-abiding person anyway?"

"When did you, Ellie-Belly?" I ignore yet another stupid nickname.

"What do you mean? I abide by the rules."

"Seven minutes in heaven with your stepbrothers isn't in anyone's rule book," he says with an unseen smile on his lips.

"Ugh," I say. "Really. You want to bring that up now? You know how I feel about them. They're just annoying suck-ups who I have to live with, and that was a stupid dare gone wrong."

"They're not bad guys. Not really," he says thoughtfully.

"Since when?" I gasp. Although they play on the same team, Dornan has always shared my views of the Townsend triplets. I can't be sure how much of it was because of what I think and have told him, and how much is his own view.

"Since they were defending your honor in the locker room," he says.

"They were what?"

"Defending your honor. What happened at the party got out, sweet pea. A few of the team were talking about it. Colby, Sebastian, and Micky were quick to shut it down. They didn't want anyone saying anything bad about you."

"Are you serious?" I ask, not believing it could be true. Why the hell would they be bothered if people were gossiping about me? If anything, I would have imagined them having a field-day talking about what we did. Isn't that what men do? They brag about their conquests. And what could be better to brag about but fucking around with the stepsister you don't even like that much? I mean, why would they care about defending my honor? We're not related. What I do sexually with anyone doesn't affect the family or them at all.

"Yeah, I'm serious. They tore Elias a new one, and he

wasn't even saying anything particularly bad. He was just asking them to confirm that they messed around with you in the closet."

"That was it?"

"Yeah. I stepped forward because no one talks shit about my best friend, but I didn't need to. They were already on it."

I let out a soft breath. I'm not often surprised, especially when it comes to my stepbrothers, but if what Dornan says is true, they've done the exact opposite of what I expected in the circumstances.

"So people are talking about me?" I ask.

"Don't worry about it," Dornan says. "Believe me, it's nothing. No one knows what you did in the closet, not even me. You could have all stood around trying not to touch each other. Your stepbrothers didn't confirm shit."

"Okay," I say, feeling relieved.

"But you came out of that closet with very red cheeks," Dornan says slowly. "And a damp hairline. And a ruffled hem."

Clearing my throat, I shift in my seat. "Dornan," I say in a warning tone.

"What? You don't want to confide in me? Am I not your best friend?"

"You are," I say. "But…"

"But you don't want to tell me that your three stepbrothers got you off like a rocket."

"Dornan!"

"What? Are you forgetting you're at college? These are the years you're supposed to have fun and make crazy mistakes."

"But some mistakes are better left unspoken and unrepeated."

With a long sigh, I hear Dornan shifting. "You don't

need to be so uptight, sweetie. I'd hate for you to get to your thirties and look back with regrets because you didn't let your hair down when you had the chance."

"Are you seriously suggesting I should look to repeat what happened in the closet?"

"Well, I don't know what happened in the closet, so I'm not sure I can tell you that. I'm saying that all the grumbling you do about your stepbrothers has always felt like a cover for other feelings, and if that's the case, maybe you should grow up and face what's in your heart rather than ignore it."

"I don't believe you," I huff.

"Ah, Ellie-Belly, don't be like that. You know I have your best interests at heart. Which of them are you crushing on?"

The little flutter of my heart in my chest is more ache than excitement. Dornan isn't to know that all three of my stepbrothers have wormed their way through my frosty, hard outer shell for different reasons.

"Crushing is so high school," I say, to change the subject.

"Human beings don't ever grow out of crushing." There's a smile in his voice that piques my interest.

"Oh yeah. And who are you crushing on?"

"I'll tell you mine if you tell me yours," he says in a playful tone.

"Forget it." I shake my head even though he can't see it. There's no way I'm going to get dragged into a game like that.

"I d…"

I hang up before he can say the word dare and text him with a laughing emoji and the words, NO MORE DARES! Then I slump back against my chair.

My stepbrothers defended me, and I don't know how

to process that.

7

ELLIE

"No more dares," I shout over the music pounding so loudly from the speakers that I can feel it in my throat.

I wobble and shift my feet as the last Red Devil cocktail goes straight to my head. Gabriella grins devilishly, tucking her straight blonde hair behind her ears.

"I'm not going to promise anything," she says, linking arms with me and turning us so that we're surveying the dance floor. The Red Devil bar is heaving tonight, and as the lights flash in time to the pulsating beat, I struggle to make out a single face.

"It's time to go home," I say, already worried about whether I can still carry myself to the door.

"It's time to dance," she says, tugging me straight into the throng of moving bodies, throwing her free hand in the air with abandon. I swear my friend has zero inhibitions. The only way I keep up with her is because of her overuse of my kryptonite.

Well, maybe kryptonite is the wrong way of putting it. She knows that if she wants me to push my boundaries, she needs to throw out a dare. Most of the time, she gets away with it because I enjoy the chance to do things outside my usual comfort zone. Tonight, I drank at least three more drinks than I would have.

"We need to hook up with some sexy guys," she says when she's finally stopped walking and starts dancing. Under the flashing lights, her silver sequined dress comes alive like a sparkling rainbow.

I grimace, not liking where Gabriella's train of thought is heading. "I don't want to hook up with anyone," I remind her. "I'm already the talk of the boy's locker room."

She swivels on her black chunky platform boots, scanning for potential sexy boys. There's no shortage in here, but there's no one I'm interested in. Even the sexiest man isn't a patch on just one of the Townsend triplets, let alone all three. "What about him?"

Across the dancefloor, Elias is leaning over to speak to the head cheerleader. His eyes fix on her ample cleavage. So much so that he almost topples over and lands headfirst between her breasts. "Yeah. He looks like a real catch," I say.

"Yeah. Might be hard to snog someone whose eyeballs are caught between someone else's tits."

I snort, glad that she noticed even in her drunken state.

"What about him?" This time she points to a skinny dude who's leaning against the bar, nursing what looks like a soft drink. I guess he's an art student because he has some patches of paint on his arm.

"Can we just dance?" I ask. "Or, if you want, I can dare you to snog Mr. Eyeballs Elias."

Gabriella bends over at the waist, cackling loudly. "That is the best nickname ever," she squeals.

"If Celine wasn't dating Eddie right now, she'd definitely go for the guy at the bar."

"True." Gabriella nods in agreement and carries on

looking.

"Oh," she says, her eyes widening.

"What?" I turn to follow the direction of Gabriella's gaze, finding Colby, Sebastian, and Micky standing by the entrance. I duck immediately, trying to hide behind a tall man who's gyrating with his girlfriend behind me.

"Why are you hiding from them?" she asks.

"No reason," I say. I still haven't confided in Gabriella about what happened, and the gossip must not have reached her yet. "Well, no reason other than they're annoying as shit."

The half-lie leaves a sour taste in my mouth.

Gabriella narrows her blue eyes and twists her mouth into a one-sided smile. "You know that I'm aware you lust after those gorgeous hunks of men," she says.

I open my mouth to deny it, but she claps one of her hands over my mouth.

"Don't do that, sister. Don't lie to your friend."

My shoulders drop, shame washing over me. "I can see their unbelievable manliness and 'chiseledness'–is that even a word?–but still find them annoying as shit."

"You can," Gabriella agrees. "But you know that usually means you want to have their babies, but you're hiding behind your self-constructed fear-elevated barriers."

"I think you need to drop your psych class," I say, dancing with one eye on my stepbrothers as they make their way to the bar. Their manliness is out in full force tonight. Tight shirts hug their broad backs and bulging biceps, and their jeans are snug around their asses and ridiculously muscular thighs. They move in such a similar way, their legs in synch as they walk.

"I see you watching them," Gabriella says.

"Only so I know where they are. I don't want to bump into them. They're just so dull. Always talking about football."

"I heard they've been volunteering to teach football to kids in a deprived neighborhood across town." Gabriella wiggles her eyebrows, pleased that she's found a tidbit of information that goes in the triplet's favor.

"They are?"

She nods. "It's a charity thing organized by their coach. It was on the student website."

"Mmm…"

Gabriella grabs my hands, spinning me under her arm in a ridiculous formal dance move. "Mmm is right. Not such bad guys, after all, are they?"

"Volunteering doesn't make a difference," I lie. "They're probably just doing it to make themselves feel less like douchebags.

"I don't know. Colby's been helping Kain with his classes. You know how much he struggles because of his ADHD."

"Why's he helping Kain?" I ask.

"Because he loaned Kain some notes when he saw him struggling, and then Kain said how much it helped him, and Colby offered to tutor him for a couple of hours a week."

I glance across the dancefloor at Colby, who now has a bottle of beer in his hand and is waiting for Seb to finish paying. He's always seemed so self-centered to me. He is more interested in getting his way and making other people compliment him. Out of all of them, the only one I would have thought would have been selfless in any way is Micky. A couple of years ago, he befriended a stray cat, and now it lives in his room. It's the ugliest thing I've ever seen, but he loves it.

I twist away, not liking where Gabriella's stories are taking my train of thought, because if Colby, Seb, and Micky aren't the assholes I've convinced myself they are, then I have way less reason to suppress all my pent-up sexual feelings about them.

My conversation with Dornan echoes through my mind. Which one are you crushing on? He asked me. What I didn't tell him is that I can't separate them in my mind. When we were in the closet, for those seven minutes, they were like one person. They were so focused on my pleasure that the three men became a single six-handed entity.

Now, when I get fluttery sexual feelings at the memory of that night, it's with all their almost identical faces in my mind. Colby with the permanent furrow between his dark, serious brows. Micky with the small scar that runs along his chin and the soft look in his eyes. Seb with that quirk of a grin and his devilishly sexy dimple. I imagine them standing over me, Colby with his arms folded, Micky reaching out, and Seb leaning against the wall.

I can't separate them, even in my fantasies.

"You're thinking about them, aren't you?"

"I was thinking I need to use the bathroom."

Gabriella flashes me another knowing smile and grabs my hand. "Awesome. Me too. And on the way, we can say hello to your manly chiseled stepbrothers."

"No…" I blurt, but as soon as it comes out of my mouth, I realize they're now standing directly in the path to the lady's room, and there's no way to avoid them.

"Hey, Micky, Colby, and Seb," Gabriella says smoothly. "Looking good."

They know my friend, but they're not exactly on super friendly terms, mostly because I've avoided hanging out in their vicinity whenever she's come around.

"Hey," Colby nods. I can see his brain working to remember her name.

"Hey, Gabriella," Micky says. Of course, he'd be the one to remember.

Seb nods in my direction. "Ellie."

"Hey." The greeting sounds more like a squeak, and I blush, dying inside at how awkward this all is. "Nice dress," he adds, his pretty eyes trailing down the full length of my body. I know I don't imagine him folding in his bottom lip seductively, the same lip that teased my nipple.

My dress is nice. It's emerald-green stretch cotton, almost the same color as the Townsend's eyes, and it clings to every curve. Paired with my New Balance, it's cute and comfortable. But I don't want him to notice anything about what I'm wearing because when he does, it reminds me of how urgent their hands were in pushing up my dress in the closet and how easily they accessed all my most private places.

Gabriella is staring at me with the most annoying smug look on her annoying smug face.

"This was nice," I say, stepping around Colby and dragging Gabriella with me.

"Nice," she snorts as I push open the restroom door. "You are really uptight, my friend."

"I am not uptight."

"Soooo uptight," she says. "So uptight, you're almost ready to snap."

Maybe she'd be less critical if she knew I came face to face with Micky's perfect cock last night. Probably not. If I described it in all of its glory, she'd tell me I was a fool for not dropping to my knees right then and there.

We disappear into the stalls, and as I relieve myself, I clasp my face in my hands, trying to regain my composure. Seb, Colby, and Micky don't even need to touch me, and I'm an overheated mess of a person.

"You know what?" Gabriella shouts through the partition.

"What?"

"I dare you to fuck at least one of those sexy hunks of men. In fact, I don't just dare you, I double dare you!"

"You can't dare me to fuck someone," I squeal, shoving my dress down over my hips, my eyes bugging out at the thought.

"Why not?" We open the doors simultaneously, and I stare at my friend in disbelief.

Dares are usually about fun and lighthearted stuff. More alcohol, a fumble in a closet, a kiss with someone, maybe. That's as far as anyone has ever gone. But sex is a totally different matter.

"A sex dare shouldn't be a thing," I say, already praying that Gabriella's going to see the error of her ways and take back the dare.

"A sex dare should absolutely be a thing," someone says from inside an occupied stall. "I wish someone would give me a sex dare."

Gabriella claps her hands, her silver bangles jingling like bells at Christmas. "I'll give you a sex dare," she says. "Anything to help a girl out."

"Gabriella," I say. "This is a disaster!"

"I didn't dare you to fuck them all," she says, resting her hands on her hips. "Although that would be mind-blowing fun. Think about all those gorgeous muscles rippling and working to give you pleasure, all hot and sweaty with arousal." She fans herself with her hand. "All I'm daring you to do is fuck just one of your sexy stepbrothers. Just to know what it'll be like. I mean, they're all identical. How different could they be in the sack?"

I could tell her right now what happened in the closet. I could tell her about the damage Dornan's dare has already done, but I don't because that's not how dares work. And as much as I'm objecting, now she's set the dare, there's no getting out of it.

The last words my dad said to me ring in my ears.

You're a coward.

It was a cruel, throwaway comment from a man who never understood the power of words. It's a comment that's lodged deep in my heart like a shard of glass that can never be removed for fear of bleeding out.

Because I think he's right. I am a coward. I never push myself hard enough. It's one of the reasons that Mom spends so much time gushing about my stepbrothers. They're dynamic go-getters, and I'm just happy coasting, apparently. The only time I ever let myself go is with a dare. And every time I go through with a dare, however stupid, it's like I'm sticking a big fuck-you finger up at my dad.

Dares make me brave, and I like being brave.

"You can take it back," I say hopefully, just as the girl who's one hundred percent into sex dares steps out and beams at us. She's dressed like a crazy art teacher, with brightly colored clothes and frizzy multicolored hair; an abstract painting brought to life. Gabriella and I look at each other and smile as we have the same idea.

"The guy in black," we say simultaneously.

"What?" she asks.

"Your sex dare," Gabriella clarifies. "There's a guy out there to the right by the bar, dressed all in black. He has paint on his arms."

"Paint? Sounds cool."

I want to tell her that the word cool is no longer cool, but I don't because she seems so happy. She washes her hands and then proceeds to give both Gabriella and me a hug.

"Good luck with your sex dare," she whispers in my ear, giving me a wink as she leaves.

"You see," Gabriella says, pressing her hands to my inflamed cheeks and squashing them like an overzealous Italian grandmother. "I'm like a sex genie, making everyone's wishes come true."

"You think I've been wishing to fuck one of my stepbrothers?"

"Yes. Yes. Yes, I do. In fact, I think you wish you could fuck them all. But I won't go that far with the dare. Not now. Not until you tell me it's what you want."

"Oh, that's so kind of you," I huff. "You want to make sure your sex wishes actually end in satisfaction."

Taking me by the hand, she heads for the door with me trailing behind. "Well, I can't guarantee you a good time. I just hope whichever one you choose will deliver."

I don't tell her I already know one who is guaranteed to provide satisfaction. Micky and all the special things he can do with his fingers and tongue. I guess if I'm going to go ahead with this dare-and just the thought of it has my panties wet–I should choose the one who's already proven himself. And I've already seen him naked. Somehow, that makes this whole thing less daunting.

"You're crazy, you know that?" I say as we hit the dancefloor again. The alcohol in my body is making everything way fuzzier than is ideal. If I was sober, maybe all of this would freak me out rather than make my nerve endings buzz with anticipation.

"No, my darling. You're the crazy one because you're going to go through with this dare, aren't you?"

8

MICKY

"This conversation is pointless," Colby grumbles as he drives us home from the Red Devil. It was a good night, with a great atmosphere and the chance to watch Ellie dance wearing her clingy green dress. Hell, I'd have stayed longer, but Colby's mood fucked with everyone's mojo.

"I saw how close you were to kissing her," I say. My brother is still in denial, even though he has no reason to lie to Seb or me. "You were leaning in, and she was waiting. If I hadn't stumbled in there like a fucking cock block, you would have kissed Ellie as she wanted."

"You didn't see shit," Colby says, his denial sounding hollow. He grits his teeth in that fucking stubborn way that makes me want to punch him in the face and plead with him to take a chill pill. Sibling vibes.

"Maybe that's his game," Seb says. "Maybe Colby's telling us that Ellie's not interested, and we need to keep our distance for the sake of the family so that he can stake his claim behind our backs."

"Is that your game, Colby?" I ask doubtfully.

"No, that's not my game. What kind of asshole do you

think I am?"

"Then what the fuck is going on?" I flick the radio off, wanting us all to concentrate on this conversation. "I know what I saw. Why won't you just admit it?"

"He won't admit that he likes her because he knows what will happen," Seb says.

"And what is that?" Colby growls.

"We'll fuck her. And we'll want more. And maybe everything Colby suspects will happen comes to pass. Our dad will skin our cocks, and Ellie's mom will use the skin to make a new purse," Seb laughs, but neither of those thoughts is funny. I shift uncomfortably in my seat.

"But what's the alternative?" I ask. "I'm sick of trying to find another girl I like as much, only for them to never match up to Ellie."

"Me too," Seb says. "And it's worse now we've had a taste of what it could be like. Before the closet, it was just me and my own filthy imagination. Now it's me and the actual memories of Ellie. It's a fucking miracle I'm out of my room, and my cock is tucked away right now."

"Gross," Colby snaps. "We have to forget it for Ellie's sake. Her relationship with her mom is already strained. We can't do anything to disrupt it. It's not fair."

"You forget that there are these things called secrets. They happen when people don't tell everyone what they're doing. You know, it's normal for people our age not to disclose our sex life to our parents." I smile as Colby swivels his head to take a measure of my expression quickly.

"I thought Seb would have been the one to push this," he says. "He's usually the one who cares the least about the implications of his actions."

"Thanks," Seb says from the back seat, genuinely pleased with that description.

"It wasn't a compliment," Colby growls.

"You're also forgetting that we've already fooled around with her," I say. "Maybe if we were talking right now, and we hadn't had that seven minutes of heaven, I'd think differently."

"He's had a taste," Seb says. "And now he's addicted. It's pushing all his usual restraint and empathy out the back door."

"I still have empathy and restraint, dude. But I see how Ellie looks at us now, and it's different. She feels it too."

Colby lets out a stressed-sounding breath. "She wanted to kiss me. I'm ninety-nine percent sure of that. And I probably would have done if you hadn't appeared in the doorway."

"See. I told you."

"But my moment of stupidity and seven minutes of unintended fooling around shouldn't lead us down a path we can't return on."

"How very philosophical of you, Colb," Seb laughs. He tosses a ball in his hands, forever restless.

"Nothing philosophical about me wanting to preserve some sanity in our house."

"Sanity is overrated, brother," Seb says, "but you know what isn't? Accepting how you feel about someone and doing what needs to be done to satisfy both of you."

"Satisfaction is overrated," Colby replies. "You can get your dick wet any night of the week, if that's all you're looking for."

Seb drops the ball on the floor and leans forward, wrapping his arms around both our seats so that his head is almost level with ours. "But it isn't just about getting our dicks wet, is it? That isn't what any of us really want."

"Oh yeah, and what do I want?" Colby snaps. "Tell me, little brother."

"We all want to make that girl happy."

I snap my head around, staring at my brother, who always tries to lighten every situation, but just jumped headfirst into the emotional zone.

He raises his eyebrows and grins because he knows he's hit the nail on the head, and none of us will deny the truth of his words.

We want to make Ellie happy, but what does that mean? What will it take to put a smile on her face?

I don't know, but I hope I get to find out.

9

ELLIE

I wake to a message from Gabriella.

Gabriella – Did you do it yet? I want the deets.

Me – No. I got home before them last night and went straight to sleep.

Gabriella – Not good enough, sweetie!

Me – Gimme a break. I'll do it.

If Gabriella knew how hard my pussy just clenched at the thought of fucking Micky, she wouldn't doubt my intentions one bit.

But I guess she's worried that a girl who needs a dare to act on her obvious physical urges is cowardly enough to pull out of a dare. It's something I've never done. Ever.

Throughout classes and library study time, all I can think about is how Micky looked with a surprised expression on his face and his hand cupping his cock. He wasn't embarrassed, that's for sure. In fact, I'm sure he was pleased with the chance to reveal what he has to offer.

Show off.

Maybe he and Seb planned the whole thing. I wouldn't

put it past either of them.

Maybe they hoped that one look at the most exceptional cock in the northern hemisphere would be enough to tempt me over the line again.

Without the dare, all it would have done was driven me a little closer to sex-fueled fantasy insanity . The dare is the icing on the cake, because now I know exactly what I'm going to get.

If he wants to go through with it, that is.

The later it gets in the afternoon, the more restless the butterflies in my belly become. Instead of finishing an assignment, I mentally calculate the pros and cons of approaching the dare. Do I just come out and tell him about Gabriella's challenge and hope he's happy to help me out? That feels lame. Do I act all seductive and hope he makes a move? Difficult to achieve with his brothers and our parents around. Do I message him and ask him to meet me somewhere? A hotel room, maybe? Logistically and financially risky if he doesn't turn up. And a message will leave evidence for him to show his brothers or even other people. My last idea is to slip into his bed in the middle of the night and hope that my hands on his skin is enough to pique his interest.

By the time I'm done imagining each of the scenarios, my panties are damp, and my body is shivery with lust. I'm aching to come again, hungry for the way he made me feel in the closet. Part of that is because orgasms are awesome, but it's also because when he succeeded in tipping me over the edge, he reassured me that I'm not actually frigid at all.

Having that fact underlined multiple times would be good. Spectacular, actually.

Gabriella messages me at four-thirty with a clock emoji. I respond with a gif of a puppy slowly shaking its head. She sends a laughing emoji back, and then I stick my phone in my bag, pack up my files and laptop and head out of the library.

Maybe she imagines me jumping him after a lecture and dragging him into a restroom. Not my style at all.

Outside, the sun is perfectly warm, settling a yellow glow over the paved quad and imposing buildings. I scan the crowds for anyone I know, but it's mostly freshmen, as far as I can make out. I'm almost in my car when my phone rings. By the time I fumble for it, it's close to clicking into voicemail, so I don't look at the screen before I answer.

"Hello."

"Ellie." Mom's voice is breathy and a little panicked.

"Yeah. I'm okay. Just couldn't find my phone."

"Oh, okay," she says. "Listen. I've got a flat, and I can't make it to drop the refreshments at the school downtown."

"What school?" I say, confused.

"The one where the triplets are coaching. I was supposed to take the drinks and snacks."

"That's a shame." I rest my bag on the floor, clutching the phone between my shoulder and neck as I search for my keys.

"I need you to go to the closest store, get the stuff, and drop it off. I'm going to send you all the details."

"Mom," I whine. "I've got too much to do." Too much that doesn't involve witnessing my stepbrothers doing altruistic things.

"It won't take long," she says. "It's important. It wouldn't hurt you to get more involved in some community outreach. The triplets have just as much work as you, and they have football training, too. They still have time to make the world a better place."

There she goes, highlighting all the amazingness of her golden stepsons and bringing me down in the process. Ugh. The resentment I feel towards them bubbles up all over again. Sighing loudly, I know that saying no will only make her mad and even more disappointed in me, if that's even possible. "Send me a list," I say.

"I'm on it."

Before I get in the car, and without even saying goodbye, mom has hung up the phone.

Perfect.

I wait for the list to come through and pick a store I know will have everything. It's going to cost a lot, and against all my bubbling angry feelings, I am kind of proud that my family is doing helpful stuff like this.

In the store, I fill a cart with drinks and snacks. It takes me a while to pack it into bags and set it into my trunk, and then I tap the address into my phone so that I can follow directions. The closer I get, the more my stomach feels fluttery. The neighborhood isn't great, but my nervousness doesn't come from concern for my safety. It's the anticipation of seeing Micky and his brothers with the knowledge of what's going to happen later.

The most brazen dare I've ever pulled off.

I drive slowly into the lot next to the field and scan for familiar faces. Colby is working with one group of kids, and Seb and Micky are running drills with another. I sound my horn and wave, catching Micky's attention. His expression is surprised, and then he jogs in my direction as I exit the vehicle.

"What are you doing here?" he asks when he's close.

"Bringing refreshments," I say. "My mom has car trouble."

When I open the trunk, Micky's eyes go wide. "Wow. That's some haul."

He steps closer to look into the bags, and I get a lungful of the sexiest man smell ever. Oh god. Even sweaty, Micky is lickably gorgeous, and I feel like a sex-starved loon for wanting to get closer and breathe him in.

"Yeah, it's big," I say, my mind all foggy from his pheromones and the lingering memory of his cock. Big? What am I even saying? Sweat prickles under my arms as I blush hotter than the sun.

"Yeah," Micky agrees, sounding confused. When I risk glancing in his direction, one of his dark brows is quirked, and the corners of his mouth are pulled upward.

Shit.

He's laughing at me.

"So, do you want to take this stuff or not?"

"I do. Can you help me carry it, or shall I call Colby?"

"I can help."

We each grab two bags and carry them over to a bench at the edge of the field. Colby and Sebastian look up and follow our progress. Micky walks ahead, and I keep my eyes focused on his ass because it's so goddamned perfect it's mesmerizing. That ass could crack walnuts. As the powerhouse behind his perfect dick, it could split me in two.

I shake my head, trying to jolt some sense back into my addled brain. Seriously, Ellie, what the fuck? The dare is ringing in my ears, and I only have a few hours before my lack of dare fulfillment feels uncomfortable.

"Just put them here," he says, dropping his bags onto the bench and unloading the contents. The juice boxes are all wrapped in plastic, and Micky splits them.

"Shall I help you with that?" I ask.

He pauses what he's doing and fixes me with that surprised look again. "Sure. That would be great."

Behind us, Colby is yelling instructions. I hear Seb's laughter and turn to see the kids all doubled over at something he's said. With the sun shining down on us, there is something so unbelievably wholesome about this arrangement.

"Have you guys been doing this for long?" I ask Micky.

"A few weeks," he says. "It was only supposed to be a short-term thing, but we're going to carry on. The kids are awesome, and they're making great progress."

"That's good," I say.

"Yeah. It feels good to give something back."

"I can see that."

We continue unpacking as silence settles between us. There are so many things I want to ask Micky. Even though we live in the same house, there seems to be so much that I don't know about him and his brothers. It feels weird that I've built up this image of them as selfish douchebags, when in reality, they seem different.

I swallow involuntarily at the realization that it's me who's the selfish one.

What the hell do I do to benefit the community? How am I making anyone's life any better?

Ugh.

I already have my mom making me feel like a disappointment. I don't need to be doing it to myself.

"You know, we need someone to organize the refreshments every week," Micky says softly. "Dad has agreed to pay for it. Some kind of tax write-off. But we don't get time to pick the stuff up before we come...there just isn't enough room between classes and the start of the sessions."

"Instead of mom, you mean?"

"Yeah, but obviously only if you have time."

He eyes me cautiously, his long lashes casting shadows over his chiseled cheekbones. My gaze drifts to his mouth—his perfect, orgasmic mouth—and my lips tingle to kiss him. Would his mouth move over mine the same way as Seb's did? Will he be as bossy as Colby when we're alone?

"I guess I could," I say, still not able to fully focus on what I'm saying.

"That would be awesome." The smile Micky gives me is broad and genuine, his perfectly straight white teeth a bolt of pure joy in my otherwise stress-filled day.

The sound of the kid's laughter and chatter builds, and when I turn, I find Colby and Seb leading their groups toward us. They're all sweaty and ruddy-cheeked and smiling like they've been having the best time. I grab a few drinks and hand them out. There are oat bars and fruit too, and the kids take everything gratefully, settling onto the grass to enjoy a break from training.

Colby and Seb wait until everyone else has been served before accepting a drink and a snack themselves. "I didn't expect to see you here," Colby says, nodding slowly as though my presence is something that requires change of his opinion of me.

"I asked Ellie if she'd help every week, and she said yes."

"That's great," Seb says, taking a massive bite from an oversized red apple.

"Yeah, awesome." Coming from Colby, it comes with an undercurrent of suspicion.

It's a suspicion that I understand. We've never been friendly. Not even when we were younger. I've always held them firmly at arm's length, so why are things changing now?

I once heard someone say that people are like onions. You peel off one layer and find so many other layers beneath. It's like my experience in the closet peeled off their outer shell, and now suddenly, all their other layers are visible.

I turn my attention back to them, trying to hold up the old lens against each triplet. Self-righteous Colby. Foolish Seb. Suck-up Micky. But the lens doesn't work because it's been cracked with new knowledge.

Is it better that I've begun to see them as better people?

Does it make going through with the dare tonight easier or harder?

I chew the inside of my cheek, sneaking a look at Micky, and decide that it's a bit of both. Easier because I can relate to him more, but harder because relating means being closer to him, and getting closer means having feelings.

Feelings don't have a place between us.

Feelings are messy and hurt-filled and best avoided at all times.

"So, are you going to hang around and watch?" Seb asks with a wink.

"No," I reply quickly, even though I'd enjoy seeing the kids have fun. I don't want their good Samaritan ways to seep through the cracks in my exterior any more than they have. "I'd better go."

"Shame," Seb says, and I don't miss the warning look that Colby spears in his direction.

"See you at home," Micky says as I turn to make my escape.

I don't stop, but I call over my shoulder. "Yeah, see you there."

I'll see him at home for a dare and nothing more. I'll go through with this because that's what I do and because I want his body and all the skills I know he can use to make me feel good.

But when it's done, I need to do whatever I can to fix that old lens. I need to find the strength to hold them at arm's length again.

I can't let them get under my skin.

Not now. Not ever.

10

MICKY

I know I'm dreaming when the bed shifts behind me and Ellie's voice whispers 'sssshhh' close to my ear. I know I'm dreaming because there's no way my stepsister would slip into my room and slide her hand over my abs and up my chest like she's reading braille.

"What?" I say, blinking in the darkness. Flashes of my shadowed room hit my vision as Ellie snuggles closer, her breast pressing against my back.

"We have to be quiet," she whispers. "My mom is a light sleeper."

I blink again, my mind whirring over the fact that Ellie's voice in my dream is as clear as it would be in real life. And her fingers on my skin feel as real as they would if this wasn't a crazy, vivid sex fantasy.

"What?" I say again; my voice is so husky that it hurts my dream-throat.

"Micky," she says, her lips pressing against my neck. "You made me come so hard in that closet. Now it's my turn."

Fuck. Fuck. My balls draw tight, my cock already

hardening. *I'm too old to have a wet dream*, I think, shifting against the too-warm mattress.

Blinking again, I see the time on the clock on my nightstand; one-fifty-three am. The middle of the fucking night. I suck in a long, whooshing breath as I finally come awake enough to realize that this isn't a dream. I'm not asleep. I'm just dozy as fuck and too delirious to register the amazing truth. That Ellie is really in my bed, and her hand is really trailing over places that are coming to life with shivery anticipation.

"Fuck," I mutter. "Stop." My hand grips her wrist tightly, a reflex that hits me through the confusion.

"What?" she says as I roll quickly to face her. "Don't you want me to?"

Even in the darkness, I can see the mortified expression on her face. She had the courage to slip between my sheets almost naked, but now she's worried she's gone too far. Before she has time to mentally travel further in the wrong direction, I press my lips to hers. It takes a few seconds for her to register what's happening. I release her wrist as I tease my mouth over hers, my hands exploring the soft warmth of her body.

Damn. I know I've already had my tongue between her legs, but I missed the awesomeness of the build-up. I skipped the exploration of her body, and I will not make the same mistake twice.

Fuck what Colby keeps saying about us having to deny what we want. Fuck always having to do the right thing.

This can't be wrong when it feels so right.

"Micky," she whispers as I pull back long enough to check she's into this.

"Ellie, baby," I murmur against her neck, pushing away all the questions I want to ask her. Why me? Why now? Why the change of heart? With her warm breast in my palm, I don't want to risk anything destroying this moment.

Ellie tastes too good, and as she trails her hands down my back until her palms are resting at the curve of my glutes, I can't focus anymore.

I have to hear those little whimpering sounds she made in the closet. I have to feel her trembling thighs clutched around my face, taste her arousal, and feel the pulsing of her pleasure against my tongue.

My big hands search out her slender wrists and force her arms to the bed next to her head. I loom over her, taking in her parted lips and wide eyes as I nudge her thighs apart with my knees.

"I made you come once," I say, my voice still husky with sleep. "I want to do it again."

She nods, and that's all the encouragement I need. In a flash, I'm shoving at the sheet that's covering us and sliding down her body. The negligee she's wearing isn't something I've seen before. Pink, with pretty lace at the hem. It's something a woman would wear for a boyfriend, not around the house in front of parents and stepbrothers. It's something Ellie put on specially to come and sneak into my room. It's something she's worn just for me.

When I push it up, I find she has left her underwear behind.

Shit.

Sexy nightwear and no panties. Ellie is my perfect woman, real, warm, and already shivering with anticipation.

I'm torn between rushing and taking my time because of where we are and who's asleep in rooms separated only by thin walls. I can't imagine that Ellie locked my door on her way in, either. The locks in this house are clunky and loud. The risk would have been too great.

But as I kiss over the curve of her belly, already scenting her arousal, going fast becomes impossible.

Making this woman moan is my sole focus. Building up to her pleasure is what I need. Proving that she made the right decision when she came to my bed is my mission.

Her legs are slack with anticipation as I rest my rough palms against her soft thighs. There's no resistance as I use my thumbs to spread her pussy, finding soft, wet flesh, just begging for my tongue.

A shiver of anticipation runs up my spine, and my balls tighten in readiness for what my body hopes is coming.

Ellie's body shifts under my palms impatiently.

Leaning closer, I brush her sweet clit with the tip of my nose, using my tongue to find her tight little hole. Shit. This is so much better than the closet. No need to rush. No awkward angles. Knowing it's Ellie whose body is opening and quivering at my touch.

She tastes as I remember. Sweet with a side of eagerness, as desperate to come as I am to make her. It's then that I realize why she chose me first. I'm a known entity—a guaranteed orgasm. If I could work out her body in seven minutes in the darkness of a closet, I'll have no trouble playing her like a maestro in my bed.

I smile as I run my tongue along her folds, searching out the tight bud of her clit. She whimpers as her hand grips my hair. It's like she doesn't know whether to push me closer or pull me away. More would feel so good, but more could also be too much. It's always fascinated me how pleasure and pain exist in such proximity. Even more how one can be triggered by the other.

"Don't worry," I murmur, flicking my tongue. "I'm going to make you feel so good."

"Please," she gasps, and I can't help but blink with shock in the inky darkness. Ellie isn't the kind of girl I ever imagined begging for anything. She's tough and a little frosty, always on the defensive. She's a person who never shows her feelings but would kill for her friends and family. It just shows how different a someone can be once they've surrendered to losing their tough outer shell.

"It's okay, baby," I whisper. "Just lay back and relax, and I'll take care of everything."

It's as though I've uttered the secret code, the open sesame to Ellie's metaphorical cave. Her legs drop further open, and her hand leaves the mess of my hair and flops to rest on the pillow by her head. She surrenders entirely to my ministrations, and it's the sexiest thing I've ever witnessed.

I love eating out. There's so much power in taking a woman to the point where she's clawing and incoherent, leaving her hanging at that moment between tension and release. The vulnerability that comes after when their thoughts aren't quite their own is amazing, too.

I feast on Ellie's body, using my mouth and my fingers, twisting inside her while I tease her most sensitive place, watching her body undulate and her eyelids flutter, watching her get ready to tumble over the edge into oblivion. I savor every moment because who knows if this is a one-off or if she's planning on making midnight visits to my room a regular thing? And when her thighs clamp tightly around my head and fingers almost tear my hair from its roots, I know I've given her what she came for. What I don't know is if that's it. Will she get up now and leave?

My cock is like an iron bar between my thighs. Whether she goes or stays, he's going to require some attention.

Climbing over her, I press kisses above her navel and between her breasts, feeling the heaving of her ribcage as she pants for air. I watch every second of the aftermath of a very spectacular orgasm, and I don't give a fuck if I sound like an arrogant douchebag. There are many things a man needs to know about life. How to walk into a room with presence, give a firm handshake, and open a bottle of champagne, but nothing is more important than how to make a woman's knees turn to jelly.

When Ellie's eyes open, she stares up at me as though she's seeing me for the first time.

"Oh my god," she whispers. Her hand touches my cheek and explores my features, mapping the hills and plains.

"That good, huh?"

"You have no idea." She blinks her pretty eyes, and long lashes cast dancing shadows across her cheeks.

"The pleasure was all mine," I say.

"I doubt that." As if to illustrate her point, her hand finds my rock-hard dick and squeezes it enough to make my eyes roll.

"You don't have to," I say softly as she strokes me with more purpose.

"Oh, I do. I really do."

Her words are like music to my ears.

❧❧❧❧

11

ELLIE

Oh, my god. Micky just broke my brain again.

And I'm really here, in my stepbrother's bed, holding his hot and heavy cock in my palm.

I can't believe it. I can't believe I'm really doing this with Micky.

This is what it's like with dares. My mind buzzes with the freedom to let go and have someone else take responsibility for my actions. This is Gabriella's idea, Gabriella's task.

She's given me the nudge I needed to get what I want, and what I want is more of this.

I can't believe how hung he is. I got a glimpse into Colby's room, and their sheer size should have been a clue. My stepbrothers lumber around our house like bears, so gruff and massive. And their shoes are the size of cruise ships. But that doesn't always translate to the size of other things.

In the closet, I got my hand on Colby's cock, but it was through two layers of fabric, and my mind was blown with pleasure, so it didn't really register.

For a moment, I drift out of the moment to consider that all three of them will be equally well-proportioned. The prospect of them all naked in front of me with all their perfect abs and pecs and shoulders and biceps and thick thighs and ohhhh...

Micky leans in to kiss me, and I'm immediately back in the room.

He lowers his pelvis until the rigid underside of his cock settles against my too-sensitized pussy. There's a question between us as he strokes down the line of my cheek and palms my breast.

Will we fuck?

Even though I know the answer—I knew before I tiptoed into his room and slipped between his sheets—I like the fact that Micky's not assuming anything. There's something chivalrous about the idea that he could serve me with enough pleasure to fracture the top of my skull and not expect anything in return.

But as much as I enjoy making him wait, I don't know how much time we have before everyone sleeps more lightly, and I need to make the risky journey back to my room. I push at the waistband of his boxers, hoping he'll get the hint.

His eyes meet mine, curious.

"Do you have a condom?" I ask.

His arm shoots out, practically tearing the drawer from his nightstand. In a flush of controlled rustling and searching, he pulls out a silver foil packet. I don't think I've ever been so relieved to see a rubber.

When he kneels between my thighs, I lose my breath at the sight of him. In the low light, the shadowed dips between his muscles sculpt his body like the Roman masters. I trail my finger down the v of muscle on his left side, getting closer and closer to his cock. Shit. I want to tell him to hurry, but there's no way I'm making myself look any more desperate than this dare already has.

The condom is a very snug fit, and he takes tantalizing seconds to roll it down, down, down until there's no more latex to spread. His dick looks less than half covered, but I guess the important part is protected.

His eyes flick up to mine, and a quirk of a smile pulls his perfect lips. "See something you like?"

"I wouldn't be here if I didn't," I whisper.

Resting his hand on my thigh, he considers me for a moment. "You sure about this?"

I nod because finding the words to tell him the truth, that I need this from him and hate myself for it, is too confusing for me to comprehend, let alone articulate.

"I can't say I'm not surprised." With his cock in his hand, he lowers over me, notching at my entrance and pausing to stroke my hair from my face. "Even though I had a feeling."

"You had a feeling?"

"Yeah. That I wasn't the only one wanting more."

Even though I've been naked in front of him, I still flush bright from his words.

His eyes stay fixed on mine as he pushes to enter me. Is he searching for my stunned expression because he gets it in full force? My god, the stretch is unbelievable.

I don't think my body can accommodate Micky's full girth, but he knows exactly what he's doing. Slow, shallow thrusts spread my wetness and allow my body to relax. He bites his lip in concentration, and I want to smile at his effort to make this pleasurable rather than painful. I groan as he hits deep, and his hand flies to my mouth, cupping it gently and making a ssshing sound. "You'll wake everyone," he smiles.

"But it feels so....gooooood," I say into his palm, arching my back and rocking closer, so my clit brushes his pelvis.

"It's about to feel even better," he says. "But you have to promise me to keep these pretty lips shut. Swallow the moans, baby. Keep all of it inside."

On anyone else, his claims would sound like bravado, but Micky isn't a showoff. He just knows his capabilities and owns them, and there is something so unbelievably sexy about that.

When he moves faster and deeper, I clamp my mouth shut and close my eyes, letting my body become one with his, undulating like the ocean around the stern of a boat. I dwell in the darkness behind my eyelids, concentrating on keeping quiet even as I whisper his name and tell him harder, faster. Micky doesn't need instructions, though. He holds the perfect even tempo, building and building, drawing me tighter and closer until I have to open my eyes and stare at him because he's about to achieve the impossible. He's going to make me come while he's inside me.

It's never happened before. No matter how hard I've tried to get into the right position with other boyfriends. No matter what instructions I've garbled or how I've moved to get the friction right, a penetration orgasm has always been elusive.

But not with Micky.

Because he knows what my body needs. He grips my wrists against the bed with one hand and uses the other to tip my hips, and then it's there, smooth and sparkling, like I'm slipping into a warm sea while the fourth of July fireworks light up the sky.

"That's it," he hisses, as his control seems to slip. I understand why. My pussy has clamped down so tightly it must be hard for him to withdraw. I guess he likes it like that because he closes his eyes and arches his spine, and then it happens.

I watch my stepbrother tumble into oblivion too.

Well, I say tumble into oblivion. In reality, he looks more like he's been yanked into the depths of hell. His face pulls into a grimace, and his body seizes. Everything suddenly looks painful. But that's how I know it's good. So good.

When he eventually returns to the land of the living, Micky stares down at me with his emerald eyes, blinking fast as though he's seeing me for the first time. His hair is flopping messily over his brow, and the skin on his chest is slick with sweat. He's messy and panting and perfect. A different person now we've shared this epic experience together. Like a cardboard cutout made into 3D.

"Fuck, Ellie." He shakes his head, those dark curls flopping in a way that tempts my fingers to touch. His hair is soft, and he closes his eyes as I gently pet him.

"That was…" I trail off, not knowing how to express what a life-changing moment I just experienced. How can I tell him he proved that I'm not broken? How can I tell him that every sexual experience I had before him was unsatisfying and disappointing?

We might have just done the most intimate thing possible, but somehow the emotions behind the physical act seem more sensitive, more private.

"It really fucking was," he says. There's a surprise in his tone, too. I can't imagine that I'm the first girl who's ever had that reaction, so maybe he's just shocked that I did.

Maybe he's always thought of me as frigid and uptight, and the reality is such a surprise.

Maybe he just created a new reality because, as stupid as it sounds, I don't feel like the same person I was when I snuck across the hall and slipped into Micky's bed. I feel like a ripe fruit that's been peeled and devoured. I feel like a woman who's been shown into a room that's filled with treasure and told there are more rooms and infinite treasures, and all I have to do is keep coming back.

Could I? Without a dare to push me, could I make this a regular thing?

I don't know.

Because there isn't just Micky to show me the riches of the secret treasure sex rooms, there's Sebastian and Colby too.

"Why now?" Micky asks.

I shrug, allowing my hands to trail his sweat-slicked back and take in the warmth of his crazy-fit body.

"I don't know," I admit. "The party…"

"I know," he says, and with those two small words, he shows me he gets it. He felt it too. It wasn't just me.

His brow furrows as he chews his cheek, considering me closely. "But right after, you were so angry about what happened. You looked at us like we'd violated a trust. What changed your mind?"

I could lie and tell him that my feelings have changed. I could use seeing them at the football training as the trigger for my mindset shift but doing that would be risky. It would mean admitting to feelings, and that isn't what this is about.

But you like him, a little voice whispers. You like more than just how good he makes you feel. You saw how sweet he was with the kids and that stupid cat. You've noticed the gentle way he looks at you and all the times he's changed the subject when mom was finding reasons to pick at you. You've seen the way he shields Sebastian from Harry's derogatory comments. He's a good person.

A good person with the potential to get under my skin.

My heart pounds with panic at the thought of what would happen if I admitted any of that. "Gabriella dared me," I blurt, knowing that the truth is the best defense against heartache.

"She dared you to fuck me?" Micky pulls back, resting higher over me on straight arms. The space between our bodies is suddenly cold.

"She likes to get me to act on impulses that I usually stuff in a tightly sealed box."

"So, you wanted to fuck me, but you only did it because she dared you?" He seems totally confused, and I'm suddenly hot with embarrassment. The truth might protect me from admitting how squishy my heart feels when he's near me, but it makes me sound so frickin' stupid.

"Why the dare, Ellie?"

I shrug, not wanting to admit that I'm a coward, but he doesn't let it go. He waits, and waits, and waits for me to answer the question and in the end, the silence between us is too big and too loud for me to deal with.

"I'm not good at doing things that aren't sensible," I say. "I'm not good at stepping out of my comfort zone. Not without dares."

When Micky rolls to his side, propping his head up on his hand so that he can stare down at me and touch my hair at the same time, I pull the sheet over my nakedness. He pushes it down again with a raise of his eyebrows.

"Did someone dare you to go in the closet at Dornan's birthday party?"

"Dornan did."

Micky nods, and I can almost hear the turning cogs of his brain as he works through this piece of information that has many implications.

"Why dares?" he asks.

I shrug, knowing that I've already spilled too much. Sharing makes me vulnerable, and I'm not ready to open myself up any more than I have.

We shared something amazing. And I realize, with a

sudden rush of blood to the head, that I trusted this man with more than I've ever admitted to past lovers. I trusted him to tell him about a fragile part of me.

Stupid Ellie.

I need to draw a line under this conversation and get out of here. I need him to understand that it won't happen again, but that I'm cool with that. "I'm happy she dared me, and that's all you need to know," I blurt.

Micky nods and hooks his hand around my waist, pulling me closer. He smells so good, even after sex, in a way that makes me feel a little trippy. Is this what attraction is supposed to be like? Who knew?

"Can I ask you something else?" he whispers.

"Sure." I kiss his stubbled jaw for no other reason than I want to taste the salt on his skin. That and it's a distraction.

"If I dared you to fuck Colby, would you feel the same way? Is it an impulse you haven't acted on? One that you would if I dared you. Like what you did with me."

"Why Colby? Why not Seb?" I ask, feeling the penetrating way he's watching me.

"It could be Seb. Would you prefer it if it was Seb?"

Would I?

I had considered none of this. Gabriella's dare was a one time thing, and I picked Micky. The memory of Colby's whispered words and Seb's flicking tongue set goosebumps racing over my skin. I shiver, and Micky feels it. He knows. I'm like an open book; my pages spread wide in front of him. But I'm not ready to answer his question. I'm not ready to reveal any more about my desires or feelings.

Shrugging, I kiss his mouth, and we explore each other deeply and slowly for long, liquid minutes. Long minutes we don't have.

Eventually, my sensible self returns. "I should go."

"You didn't answer my question."

As I slide out of bed, tugging my nightdress back over my body, I smile. "That's not how dares work, Micky," I say.

"I dare you to fuck Colby." His eyes never leave mine as he watches for telltale signs that would give away how I feel about his challenge. He won't see any because I keep my face impassive.

"Don't tell your brothers what we did," I say.

A frown pulls his brows together, and he cocks his head to one side.

"I'll take the dare," I say. "I always do."

The smile he gives me lights up the darkness. "You want them, too?" he asks, full of bubbling hope.

I want them, too, I think, and my heart skitters with the truth of it. But I don't tell Micky that.

"I'll take the dare," I repeat.

When I sneak back to my room feeling like a thief in the night, I curse how relieved I am that Micky gave me another dare.

Another chance to experience mind-altering sex.

Another opportunity to live out my fantasies, however annoyed I am for having them.

Colby's next.

And however fearful I am of the risks associated, the only thought that lingers in my mind is: I wonder how he'll react.

12

COLBY

"Ellie, I want you to go with the triplets to get the things we need for Harry's barbeque," Lara says, sounding stressed.

"How come?" Ellie asks.

"Harry was supposed to help me, but he's got other more important things to do." The last part is said with dripping disdain. "And let's just say the triplets have a tendency not to get everything I put on the list." Lara looks pointedly at Seb, who shrugs and grins. She's not wrong. My brother always takes the opportunity to buy things that aren't on the list and charge it to our dad's card. Maybe Lara thinks Ellie will rein Seb in.

"Sure." Ellie glances at Micky. As their eyes meet, her cheeks turn a rosy shade of pink, and I immediately narrow my gaze. There's something different about my brother this morning. I caught him humming on his way down the stairs. And now Ellie is looking at him softly rather than with her usual daggers.

I didn't see them acting particularly friendly yesterday. If anything, Ellie was her bristling self. But she's different today.

Interesting.

"I'll drive," Ellie says quickly.

"No way," I object. "There's no way your trunk will fit everything."

"Are you seriously going to get into a my-trunk-is-bigger-than-yours is competition with me?" Ellie rests her hands on her hips. I expect to hear frustration in her voice, and malice, but instead, there's a smile dancing at the edge of her pretty lips, and amusement in her tone.

Has the world slipped off its axis without me realizing it?

"My trunk is definitely bigger," I say, smirking.

"My trunk is the same size as his," Seb murmurs, just quietly enough that Ellie's mom doesn't hear. Micky shoots him a warning glare.

Also interesting

"Here's the card," Lara says, fishing around in her large designer purse and pulling out a shiny Amex to hand to her daughter. "At least Harry's going to make some kind of contribution to this get-together...and the list."

Ellie takes both, watching her mom with one eyebrow raised. It's not only the frustrated, angry way Lara is talking about dad—it's been bubbling between them for the last month—but also that Lara is trusting her daughter.

The world really has slipped into another dimension.

"Come on, huge trunk guy." Ellie nods in my direction and sashays out of the kitchen and towards the front door, flicking her hair over one shoulder.

Seb snickers. "I've never heard it called a trunk before."

"Get your mind out of the gutter," I grunt as I follow Ellie, my eyes fixed on her ass and the way it jiggles in her cream sweatpants. The sliver of bare skin between the gathered waist of her pants and the cropped black tee she's wearing is so tantalizing, I lick my lips. I imagine pressing kisses along that inch of skin, making her shiver. Then I shake my head.

Off limits, I remind myself and then decide that they are my two least favorite words.

I'd like to test Ellie's limits. I could take her to the edge again and again and hold off giving her a release until she's begging. I could push her into doing things that make her cheeks flame, knowing that she'd love every minute of giving over her control to me.

She's sassy as fuck, but I felt how much she reacted to my dominance in the closet. She was like putty in my hands.

Ellie forces her feet into her sneakers, grabbing her purse from the hooks by the front door. I take a little longer to get ready as I search for my Nikes amongst my brothers' mountain of huge shoes and then sit to tie the laces.

"I thought it's supposed to be girls who take the longest to get ready," Ellie snorts, her hand already on the front door.

"These divas don't count," Micky says. When I turn, he's stuffed his big feet into sliders.

"You're seriously going to the store in socks and sliders?" I ask.

"I'm on trend," he says. "Ask Ellie."

"It's true," she says. "Not saying I love the trend or anything, but all the celebrities are going out like that these days."

I make a disapproving sound. "Next, you'll tell me that mullets are coming back into fashion."

"Yep," she says, grinning. "Check on Insta. All the fashion influencers are rocking mullets."

"No way," I say, my mouth hanging open. "You're lying."

"Nope," Ellie tucks a curl behind her ear, and her eyes drift to Micky again. The slight blush I spotted in the kitchen paints her cheeks. What the fuck is going on?

I lumber to my feet and follow as Ellie trots down the front steps, light on her feet as though she's about to head into a jog. She's by my SUV in a flash, but I slow, turning to my brother. "What the fuck is between you and Ellie today?" I mutter.

His eyes shoot to her immediately and then to me. He has a rabbit-in-headlights look about him I recognize immediately. It's the same look he had when I caught him eating my Halloween candy. The same as when he wore my new sneakers that I was saving for best and got them covered in mud. His guilty look.

"Nothing," he says quickly, but I don't believe him at all.

"It better be nothing."

"Why? You jealous?" he asks.

"There's nothing to be jealous of, is there?" I say, glaring.

Seb comes up behind us, clapping his hands against both our shoulders. "Come on, brothers. Our stepsister is waiting. And I'm sure she doesn't want to hear us bickering like a bunch of toddlers."

When I unlock the car, Ellie climbs into the front passenger seat and slams the door. Micky and Seb glance at each other, but rather than being pissed that she's taken the shotgun position, they grin.

Nothing is quite as it should be.

"I don't know what the fuck is going on today," I say. "But I don't like it."

Ellie grabs a cart at the supermarket and leads us inside like a mom with three errant kids in tow. She gives each of us a few items to find, and we separate to search them out. I grab three cases of beer and carry them back to where I last saw Ellie. On the way, I bump into Micky holding a stack of bags of chips. "I know you, Micky," I say. "You better tell me what's going on."

I can't," he says. "I promised. But you'll find out tonight."

"What do you mean, I'll find out?"

"You'll find out," Micky says. "That's all I can tell you without breaking a confidence."

"You know what dad always says. The most important people in our lives are our brothers. No one else matters," I remind him.

"Yeah. But you not knowing for a few more hours won't kill you," Micky says. "You just have to be patient."

"Patience is not a virtue I possess," I admit, not for the first time.

"Then it's one you're going to need to cultivate," Micky says.

"What does Colby need to cultivate?" Seb asks, appearing behind us like the ghost of Christmas past.

"A sense of humor." Ellie's voice carries from the next aisle. We can hear her but not see her. I swear she has the hearing of a hawk.

"She's got you there," Seb laughs. "I can't believe I didn't think of that one."

"Let's just get this shopping and get out of here," I grunt, hating the feeling that I'm out of the loop when it comes to my brothers and Ellie—hating that she's managed to get between us, even if it's just for a few hours. "I don't like this," I grumble over my shoulder as Micky heads off in the other direction. I watch him leave, noting the slight swagger to his step. The swagger that comes with getting laid.

That can't be it.

There is no way Ellie and Micky have hooked up.

I sound big-headed in my mind when I decide that if she wanted to hook up with any of us, it would be me first.

We might have a fractious relationship, but I'm the one who's had the most contact with Ellie. Surely that would count for something.

But as I watch Micky and Ellie for the rest of the shopping trip, I'm not so sure.

There is a weird chemistry between them, like they have shared a secret. And I'm not talking about a PG-13 secret.

When we return to the house, Ellie wanders up to the front door and disappears inside, leaving us to unload the shopping. That's fine by me. What the hell is the point of being a big, strong man if you can't work your muscles in order to assist the fairer sex? All afternoon, Ellie helps her mom prepare amazing-looking salads and appetizers, leaving only thirty minutes to get ready before the guests arrive. After my shower, I descend the stairs expecting Ellie to be still holed up in her room, but she's welcoming the first guests—some of my dad's workmates.

And she's a knockout.

Tight black denim shorts with shredded hems and an emerald green top that only has fabric at the front and ties in tantalizing crisscrosses at the back. Her hair hangs in waves that my hands itch to grab hold of.

I imagine her on her knees, mouth open for my thick cock, my hand twisted into her long, soft curls. It would make directing the depth and speed so easy, and in my fantasy, Ellie takes it all so well.

A voice clears behind me, and I whip around to find Seb's eyes on Ellie's ass, too.

"I can practically hear the filth dripping from your mind," he whispers.

"You think you know it all."

"If there were no consequences, you'd be all over that

like a deadly contagious rash."

Ignoring my triplet, I stride into the kitchen, trying to leave my stupid fantasy behind.

Consequences. What the hell does Seb know about those? He lives his life with a foot over the line, and whenever trouble bites him in the ass, he laughs it off or laces his excuses with a joke or two. He gets away with so much more than I ever could. I don't like the bitter taste of resentment that I find sticking my tongue to the roof of my mouth, but he's right that I wish I could throw all consideration of consequences out of the window and take life a little less seriously.

"Colby, grab this platter and take it out to your dad," Lara says, thrusting a huge tray of raw meat into my hands. "He should have started grilling an hour ago." Grateful for the distraction, I stride into the yard, finding my dad and assorted friends hanging out and drinking beer like they don't have care between them.

"There he is," my dad says proudly.

"Colby, you're bigger every time I see you," Mr. Conolly, our old neighbor, says.

"All my boys are training hard," Dad says.

"I bet they eat you out of house and home." Mr. Conolly raises his beer as if to say cheers. Behind me, someone laughs in a light and tinkling way. When I turn, Ellie is out in the yard. Our eyes meet, and she brushes her hair over her shoulder, looking straight at me as though she read my mind in the hall and is now taunting me with the very curls I want to grip.

"I'll check if Lara needs me for anything else," I say, wanting to get away from Ellie's temptation. Before the closet, I could keep my urges under control. Now, it's as though everything has been unleashed. I'm a rabid dog, circling my prey, desperate to draw on my previous instincts and failing.

And that's how it is for the rest of the night. Ellie enters my orbit, shining as bright as the sun, and I skulk off like a dark planet or frigging wormhole, desperate not to obliterate her. At one point, when we're wedged together by the crowd and making my excuses would be too awkward and obvious, I find myself offering for Ellie to present the work we did for Professor Anderson's class.

"Are you sure?" she says. "Shouldn't we do it together?"

"You came up with more of the ideas," I tell her. "You should have a chance to earn extra credit." So she doesn't think I'm turning soft, I add, "plus, I'm already acing that class."

"Of course you are." She shakes her head, her mouth tugging at the side as though she's trying to work me out. It's not possible to do. I live inside my fucking head, and I don't know whether I'm coming or going half the time.

"Colby," dad yells across the yard, and I finally have an excuse to move on.

I work hard to stay away from everyone messing with my head for the rest of the evening.

I don't even talk to my brothers when the party is over. I stomp up the stairs to my room and close the door. I throw off my smart clothes and slump onto my bed, resting my head on my hands while I stare at the ceiling, breathing as fast as if I just ran the last nine yards.

Slowly, the house quiets while I contemplate the next few years of living with a perpetual boner and fighting to stay clear of Ellie whenever I can. There will be a whole lot of cleaning up to do in the morning, but for once, we're all too spent.

For once, too, I don't slide into sleep immediately. My mind churns over those minutes in the darkness of the closet. I recall every moan and movement, every twitch of pleasure and moment of resistance. It's like the sweetest torture because I want to jerk off and relieve the buildup of tension in my balls, but it feels wrong. Those images are too laced with reality. An image of Ellie laughing tonight, her face bright with amusement, tangles its way in, and nothing feels right.

This is not who I am.

I don't give in to temptation. I have the self-restraint of a monk and the self-control of the best athletes in the world. I know what's good for me, and I stick to the straight path. Deviation is for the weak.

Except, when the handle turns, and Ellie appears in my doorway dressed in nothing but a lacy nightdress, her beautiful hair hanging in soft waves, I know that all of that self-restraint and self-control is about to be obliterated.

Because there is no way I could resist this girl, ever.

She is my kryptonite. My sweetest temptation.

I was right about there being something between her and Micky. And now there's going to be something between us, too.

13

ELLIE

I don't plan to find Colby awake. He's always been such a heavy and immediate sleeper. , On movie nights, he usually only makes it ten minutes into the film before he's off into the land of nod.

But as I open Colby's door, the light on his nightstand is still on, and he's lying on top of his comforter. As our eyes meet across the room, he shifts, shocked. His gaze rakes over my barely clad body, but I don't see rejection there. I see heat and hunger. I see the moment his resistance seems to slide away like snow down the side of a mountain.

I feel the same way.

Too much time has passed. Too much longing has built up, and the fight to resist all these feelings – focusing on the bad in my stepbrothers and never the good - has gone on too long.

Micky dared me, and so I'm here.

"Ellie." Colby's voice is deeper than usual, with a huskiness that tickles the skin on the inside of my thighs.

I don't say anything because I know the power of

words. They can drive action, but they can also halt it. If I let him talk, I know Colby could destroy this precious moment with his seriousness and desperate need to be responsible.

The tent in his boxers tells me all that I need to know. He wants me. I've felt that buried need in him for so long. I've felt his fight to stay an appropriate distance from me, as though our parents' marrying has made us real siblings, not just unrelated people who live under the same roof.

He's tried his best to be a big brother, stifling me at every turn, building resentment as well as lust. But I understand him now. And I understand myself.

It's time for me to take what I need. It's time for Colby to face up to the fact that he wants me too.

Dornan's words slide into my mind. These years of our lives are supposed to be about fun. They're supposed to be about us taking risks. They are years I don't want to waste on relationships with men who do nothing for me, experiencing sex that makes me want to write shopping lists in my head rather than cry out with ecstasy.

What we have together is too good to suppress.

And I know I'm being greedy. I know that wanting all three of my stepbrothers is fucked up. But choosing between them would be worse. Driving a wedge between them would be the most selfish thing I could do. At least this way, we're all invested in the same secret. And at least this way, I don't have to compartmentalize my heart.

In silence, I close the door and walk towards Colby. He shifts on the bed, pushing to sit straighter against the headboard. His fists are balled, and his shoulders are bunched tight as though he's braced to escape, but he doesn't move as I straddle his lap. He doesn't push me away as I cup his stubbly cheeks with my palms.

His eyelids droop as I use my thumbs to stroke the soft skin beneath his eyes, and the breath he releases feels like he's been holding it in for an eon. "What are you doing?" he groans, his tone tortured and gruff.

"What we should have done a long time ago," I whisper.

I expect to lead Colby forward step by step, to chip at his resistance. But what happens is very different. In a flash, his hands grip my wrists, and before I take a breath, I'm on my back, restrained against the mattress with Colby's huge form looming over me.

"Is this what you did to Micky last night?" he asks.

When I nod, Colby looks away, focusing on the corner of his room as his glistening chest rises and falls. His hands are tight around my wrists, and I still can't tell if it's because he doesn't want me to touch him because he sees this as wrong or because it's what he gets off on.

"You picked him first because he's a soft touch, didn't you? You knew he wouldn't have the heart to say no."

For a second, I'm stunned, and then I smile. "You want there to be a reason that I didn't come to you first, don't you? You're jealous." Colby makes a low growl in his throat, and I know I'm right. For all the walls he erects and the masks he wears, he is so easy to read. "I went to Micky first because he's the one who went the furthest with me in the closet. It seemed easiest to take the first step with him."

The way Colby looks down at me with his assessing green eyes tells me the truth was a good answer. "And now you're ready to take a step with me?" His hips lower against mine, and the thick ridge of his cock rubs against my clit. It's like punctuation to his question.

"Can you just kiss me, Colby? For fuck's sake!"

"Maybe I can," he says, with a twinkle in his eyes that sends heat rushing between my thighs. I raise my hips, searching for more pressure, but he pulls back just enough that I'm left wanting.

"Kiss me, or get the fuck off me," I huff.

Dipping lower, he grazes the tip of my nose with his and hovers his lips so close to mine that I can feel his warmth without us touching. The buzz of electricity between us is crazy. I want to bite him, scratch him, and slap him for being so stubborn and in control. I want to lash out because he makes me feel crazy, and I don't want to vibrate with need for someone who is so pigheaded. But I hold myself in check, suspecting that he needs this messed up mental foreplay before he gives in to what we both know he wants.

He needs to flip the narrative. I came to him, but he's now the one in control. He'll make me bend to his will. He'll make this hard for me and easy, too.

Because as much as I rebel against Colby, I want to melt in his arms. I want him to coax me into doing new and terribly amazing things. I want him to push my boundaries while I lay back and pretend not to like any of it.

I want to submit to him, but only in bed.

His tongue flicks the underside of my top lip, and I jump at the incredible feeling.

"You're not ready to be in my bed," he says. "You're not ready to give every ounce of your will over to me, are you?"

If he could read my mind, he'd know the truth, but that would take the fun out of this for Colby. He wants me to be resistant so he can be dominant. I've never been with a man like him before; so complex and challenging.

"Nothing worth having comes easy," I say, raising my eyebrows.

Colby folds his lips like he's trying to suppress his amusement. "No one could ever describe you as easy, Ellie."

I struggle against his grip, and the flash of his eyes tells me exactly what I want to know. He likes the resistance. He wants to tame me and claim me. I'm ashamed to admit that the thought makes me hot and soaked between my thighs.

I remember what he said in Professor Anderson's lecture about Micky not being the only one who's skilled with his tongue. Will I get to find out what Colby can do?

"Have you ever been tied up?" Colby whispers, his eyes already flitting around the room for an available restraint.

"No." I struggle again, and this time, Colby lets me go.

"Would you like to be?"

The way he looks in the low light sends a shiver of anticipation up my spine and over my scalp. There's so much power coiled in his body. His massive bicep is tight under his weight, pecs rounded and smooth, and abs rippled like a ladder to the promised land. I can't stop my eyes from drifting over everything, lower and lower. When I glance up, half dazed, he's smirking. "If I say yes, doesn't that make this less fun for you?" I ask.

"I want to know that you're okay and not just playing along because it's something I want." As a second thought, his hand drifts between my legs, and his fingers probe. When he discovers the aroused mess down there, a whoosh of breath passes through his lips. "Oh yeah. You want it."

"Do you have to be such an ass about everything?" I say indignantly.

"Just bouncing off your energy, baby."

Colby slides from the bed and disappears into his closet, returning with a black tie that he wore at his great uncle's funeral and a foil packet.

Before I can object, he snags my wrists together, binds them, and secures them to the headboard. I tug against the restraint, testing, while Colby bites his bottom lip at the sight of me. The loss of control is even better than I imagined it would be. Colby drops his head to one side, clicking his neck, and fuck if it doesn't get me hot. What more could a girl want than a sexy, athletic man limbering up to give her a good time?

He doesn't rush to get on the bed, though, and I'm eager for him to get started. "Now you've got me all tied up; what are you going to do with me?" I whisper meekly, slipping into a submissiveness that I didn't know lurked in the shadows of my psyche.

"Whatever the fuck I like," he growls.

As if to illustrate the point, he flips me over until I'm on my front, the tie twisting on my wrists, and tugs me until I'm on my hands and knees. Behind me, his hands trail my back and my thighs, fingers grazing the skin of my ass in rhythmic passes, over and over, closer and closer until they touch my taint.

"Now, if our parents weren't in the next room, I'd be slapping this ass."

"Why?" I whisper, pulling my knees closer as though that will make a difference to Colby's access to my body right now.

"Because you're a bad girl, aren't you, Ellie? A bad girl who wanders the hallways and creeps into her stepbrother's room in the middle of the night looking for sex. And it's not only me, is it? You want Micky and Sebastian too. You want all of us to make you come, don't you?"

"Yes," I gasp shamelessly as his thumb brushes my entrance.

"You liked it when all three of us were playing with this body, didn't you?"

"Yes," I say again, this time weakly, the admission pulsing heat through me.

"You want all of us to fuck you at the same time, don't you?"

I don't answer his question because admitting it is too shameful. And I don't need to admit it because he knows. They all know. They knew from the moment I shuddered and came in that closet without even realizing it was them surrounding me.

"Don't you?" he says, this time more firmly. Thick fingers push inside me, and I grunt my agreement. As he pulls them out and pushes back in, slick noises fill the air.

"You're so ready for me," he says, knocking my knees open with his so that he can move behind me. A foil wrapper is torn, and a condom is rolled on. There's no finesse with Colby, just brute force as he notches his big cock at my entrance and pushes forward.

Oh god, the stretching feels so good. Balancing on my tied wrists, I close my eyes and breathe deeply, willing my body to relax and accommodate every huge inch he has to give. And he has many, many inches.

Part of me is grateful that Micky went first, letting me get used to just how big the Townsend triplets are. Colby impatiently grips my hips and rocks forward, deeper and deeper, until he bottoms out. "Fuck, you're so tight," he hisses, digging his fingers into the flesh of my ass, holding still as he gets used to the clasp of my pussy. Here I was, thinking that this is a challenge for me, but it's as much of a challenge for him. Maybe more. Colby has to restrain himself enough to make this good for me. The man is a perfectionist at life. There is no way he will be anything less than a perfectionist in bed. All I have to do is stay in this position unless, of course, he wants to flip me back over or bend me into some other contortionist state. I'm at his mercy, after all.

"You're so big," I moan because I know how men love to hear it, even if they know.

"Yeah? Do you like it big? Do you like me stretching out this sweet pink pussy? You like me buried up to your navel, Ellie? Not such a sweet little stepsister, after all."

"Oh, I'm sweet," I say. "Micky will tell you just how sweet I am."

"Oh, don't worry, I'll get a taste," Colby says, starting to move. He rocks his hips maddeningly slowly, and if I could watch him, I bet I'd see his eyes fixed on where our bodies join. I bet he loves the sight of me stretched around him. I'd put good money on the fact that he relishes the idea of splitting me open, of forcing my body to accommodate him. Of bending me to his will.

I love it too.

"Fuck, Colby," I gasp as his finger finds my clit and taps. I'm so sensitive there, but there's no way I can stop him from doing anything. I'm totally in his control.

"Yes, Ellie. You want more?" He rubs my clit this time, incredibly slowly, and I try to shift my legs, but he pins me in place, working me into a mindless puddle of goo.

"More." I shudder, already feeling as though I'm approaching the precipice, already anticipating the tumble into oblivion. For someone who's only had three previous orgasms, all at the hands of Micky, I'm getting remarkably good at achieving them.

Or, I should say, the Townsend brothers are remarkably good at giving them.

"Did you come with Micky's cock in your pussy?" Colby asks me.

"Yes," I gasp.

"Shame," Colby soothes, running his hand down the length of my spine and pushing so that I arch my back and raise my ass. "I would've liked to be the first to feel this pussy clamp down on my cock."

"Mmmmm," I moan as he thrusts faster, still stroking, stroking, stroking.

I close my eyes, remembering the urgency of his cock in the closet, the way he held me tightly, the way he forced me to hold his dick and squeeze. I recall his powerful body, the golden rings in his green eyes, and the fierce way he approaches everything in his life. I think about how much he lit up when we worked together, and he saw my abilities.

Colby might be a bossy, moody asshole, but he's a good man. A hard-working man.

A sexy, controlling brute of a man.

And when it happens, when I start to come, I have to flop forward onto the bed. There's no strength left to support me. All of it has pulsed through me in a rush. Like a fire igniting too much fuel, I blaze hot and burn in wave after wave of pleasure.

I'm expecting Colby to carry on until he comes too, but he pulls out and flips me back over, settling between my legs to lick up my arousal like a ravenous dog at a bowl. My legs are jello, my heart a wild drum pounding out a fierce beat. Sweat beads on my top lip, but I have to lick it away because my hands are still fixed tightly over my head. He winds me up like an automaton with his tongue, matching his brother's skill, but he doesn't let me come again. He teases me to the brink of insanity and smiles against my trembling flesh when he stops just before.

When Colby's had his fun and eaten his fill, he spreads my pussy lips wide with his thumbs and pushes his thick cock back inside me. This time, I watch the undulations of his hips and the rippling of his abs as he works and works. I salivate at the sweat tricking between his rounded pecs and wish I could move so I could lick the salt from his skin. Our eyes meet, and Colby smirks, so damned pleased with himself and me. I can see the happiness in his expression, the relief, as though months of holding himself in a certain posture are now over, and he's free to relax.

This is the Colby that I saw glimpses of but was never sure really existed.

This is the Colby who can break me open, physically and emotionally.

He licks his thumb so lasciviously that I blush and slicks it over my clit. It's too much but, at the same time, not enough. But Colby knows. He seems to know what to do, stroking around but not making direct contact. Working me until I'm so close again that lights flicker behind my eyelids, and my body arches hungrily toward him.

Twice?

Is it really going to happen twice?

Of course, it is. I don't know how I ever doubted. Colby is competitive to a fault.

This time we come together, me with my neck arched and eyes so tightly closed that my eyelids hurt, Colby gripping my thighs so viciously it's as though he's fearful of floating away and never returning.

He flops forward, bracing over me on one arm, his body heaving with each breath, sweat dripping and cooling between my breasts. Our eyes meet, and in his, I see the same expression as when old friends bump into each other unexpectedly after many years. It's like I'm familiar but also a surprise.

"Oh god. I've wanted to do that for too fucking long," he says.

"And you pretended all this time to hate my guts."

He shakes his head. "It's you who hates our guts. Well, mine mostly."

I shrug because explaining our fractious relationship over the past few years would open wounds I'd rather leave bandaged. Getting into my resentment and jealousy of their interactions with my mom would make me sound pathetic and destroy the moment. And admitting I'm jealous of them for having a father who sticks to them like glue would be even worse.

"I think the fact that I'm half naked and tied to your bed speaks a different story."

His hands reach out to loosen the tie, and I bring my arms down, grateful to have some movement in them again. When he sees the red marks that cuff each of my wrists, he brings one to his lips and kisses it softly. It's the gentlest gesture I've ever seen Colby make.

"You know you haven't kissed me yet."

"I haven't?" He cocks his head to one side.

"You almost did the night we were working on our presentation."

"I wanted to." The admission comes with a shoulder shrug. "I could have killed Micky and Seb…but maybe it was for the best."

"How come?"

"Kissing is different from fucking?" He shrugs again. "I know how to make you come using my body. I'm good at that part, but I don't know what you want from this, Ellie. Sex is one thing, and I can't believe I'm saying this, but kissing is relationship territory. Kissing is about connection. Is that what you want from me? From my brothers?"

Now there's a question I never thought I'd hear from Colby.

The man I thought was made of steel is holding back because he doesn't want to misunderstand my intentions. Inadvertently, he's shown me a chink in his armor, a vulnerability I would never have expected.

"I don't know," I admit, remembering last night and how sweetly Micky teased my lips with his. It was so easy for him to slip into affection as well as pleasure, but nothing's easy with Colby.

"Well, when you do know, we can talk. Until then…"

He rolls onto his back and rests his head on his open palms. I turn to look at him and let my fingers trail his tan skin stretched tightly over muscle. Now that I'm free to touch him, I'm not going to waste the opportunity, especially because this is going to be the only time.

"I wasn't going to come to your room," I say.

His eyes dart to mine, surprised at my admission. "So, why did you?"

"Because Micky dared me."

"Dared you?"

"It sounds stupid."

Colby grabs my wrist and holds it against the center of his chest, where his heart beats with a determined thud. "Explain."

When I shake my head, embarrassed, he stares at me with narrowed eyes.

"You can't drop that and not explain what you mean, Ellie."

"I'm not good at being impetuous," I admit in a rush. "I'm not good at taking risks. Before my dad left, he'd dare me to do things I was too scared to do, you know, like climb to the top of the climbing frame or dive into the swimming pool. When I wouldn't take the dare, he'd call me a coward or a chicken. He'd make clucking noises."

"That doesn't sound kind," Colby says seriously. He looks away, lacing our fingers together. It's a sweet enough gesture to inspire me to continue.

"It wasn't." I sigh as the sad knot tied tightly inside me loosens just a little. "When he left, doing anything I was dared to became a way of me saying 'fuck you' to my dad. It's stupid because he doesn't know and won't ever know, and probably more stupid because I'm still too much of a coward to do crazy things without a dare."

"You're not a coward, Ellie," he tells me, squeezing my hand. I know he's trying to be kind, but it doesn't help. If anything, his kindness makes me feel worse about myself and what I'm doing.

"I'm a coward through and through," I say. When

Colby tries to tell me again, I put up my hand, and he blinks slowly in defeat.

"So Micky knew this?" he says after a beat.

I told him that Gabriella dared me to take a chance with one of you guys. "

"So you picked Micky first because he'd already made you come…you thought he'd be a sure thing."

"Yeah." I blush hard, realizing how ridiculous all of this is, but needing to be honest. "And when he asked me why I went to him, and I told him, he dared me to come to you."

"Shit." Colby shakes his head. "So now what? You want me to dare you to go to Sebastian's room tomorrow night?"

I shrug. "Dares aren't about what I want," I say. "That's not how this works. It's about what you want me to do. I know it sounds fucked up. I don't get myself half the time."

He shifts, using his elbow to prop his head in his hand. There's a gentleness in his expression as he gazes down at me. It makes me feel fragile and a whole lot broken. His fingers are tentative when they play with my hair, so unlike Colby's usual way of being. "We're all a bundle of complexities, Ellie. You're not alone."

"I wish I had more guts. I wish I didn't always need external motivation to take the big steps in life."

"At least you're willing to take risks and stretch yourself. External motivation aside, it's still brave as fuck to do what you did."

"You mean, in case you said no?"

"Rejection is always a possibility."

"You've been looking at me like you want to swallow me whole for years," I say. "The risk was negligible."

"Cocky, much!" Colby smiles and pinches my cheek.

"Realistic, more like."

"I dare you to go fuck my brother tomorrow," Colby whispers. "If you leave Sebastian out, his ego will never recover."

"Ah. Such a nice brother," I laugh. "Looking out for your triplet's mental health."

"Looking out for my mental health, Ellie. I'd never hear the end of Sebastian's wailing."

I raise my head so that I'm close to Colby's ear. "You think you can just pass me around?"

Colby licks his lips and closes his eyes. If we were all together, I could just imagine him sitting in the corner and watching the scene he'd be directing. He likes that thought too. Being in control of who I fuck and when.

"I know you'd never do anything you didn't really want to, sweet Ellie, with a bitter bite." Leaning in, Colby nuzzles my cheek with his nose like a lazy cat showing its owner affection. Then he does something that steels the breath from my lungs. He presses a soft kiss to the corner of my mouth, lingering as though it feels too good to withdraw from.

It does. It really does.

I wrap my arm around his big chest and tug, wanting to feel his weight on me. Needing him to kiss me longer and deeper, but Colby doesn't budge.

When he pulls back, he folds in his lips, sneaking a taste of me, and then he's up and off the bed, pinching the condom to discard it in his wastepaper basket. I get a glorious view of his muscular back tapering into his perfectly rounded ass. Oh god. That ass is enough to make me want to go again, even though I'm shattered and sore.

I guess it means tonight is over. And it's fine because I got what I came for and more.

Two delicious orgasms, an insight into my dominant, control-freak stepbrother, and another dare that can free me from my self-imposed restrictions so that I can do what I really want.

Live and fuck the consequences.

Be another Ellie. A brave girl who isn't shackled by expectations. Ellie Franklin, who isn't a timid little girl anymore. Ellie Franklin, who's never a coward.

14

SEBASTIAN

When I hear Colby whistling while the coffee machine percolates, I know something is going on. This dude is never cheerful in the morning unless he's gotten laid. It's like when he comes, he exorcises his grumpy demon for as long as it takes for it for his internal tension to build up again.

I glance at Micky, and he's watching Colby too, but instead of wearing a frown to match mine, the small smile on his face makes him look fucking ridiculous.

Now I'm feeling paranoid. Have they teamed up about something I don't know about? I roll my lips between my teeth and spread butter thickly over my toast. Colby stirs sugar into his coffee and hums.

What the fuck?

I guess I could sit here for the next five minutes and pretend I'm not noticing all the weirdness going around this house, or I can just demand answers. The latter seems like more fun. "Is anyone going to tell me what's going on? It's like I walked into a room after someone told the punch line of a joke, and no one wants to fill me in!"

Colby glances at Micky and then focuses on his coffee again. I swear he'll wear a hole in the bottom of that cup if he doesn't stop stirring soon.

"I've got to head in early today," Colby says, ignoring my demand for answers. "I'll see you guys at training."

"Errr…" I wave the knife in the air as my brother heads for the door, his travel coffee mug in hand, but Colby doesn't respond. As he disappears through the door, Micky stands quickly, his chair scraping the tiled floor. "And where are you going?"

"Early start," he mumbles, folding his toast into an awkward sandwich before quickly leaving his plate on the counter.

"Of course," I say, narrowing my eyes. "I've never seen you two so keen to leave in the morning."

Unlike Colby, Micky has the decency to glance at me with an apologetic grimace before following the route our older triplet took seconds earlier.

And then I'm left alone in the kitchen to chew on my toast and my paranoia.

When, minutes later, Ellie walks into the room with a bounce in her step and starts humming, too, I'm pretty sure I know what's going on. What I don't know is why I'm the only one who's left out.

"Morning." I nod in Ellie's direction, and she beams a smile at me, her eyes seeming to linger on my bare chest. Usually, she'd say something about the inappropriateness of me walking around only half-dressed when I share a house with her, but today, her tongue darts out to moisten her lower lip and blush pinks her cheeks.

Interesting.

"Morning, Sebastian." She heads to the coffee machine and searches for her preferred pod before loading it up. She used my full name. Curious. "Where is everybody?" she asks.

"Early starts all around today," I say. "It's like my brothers were desperate to escape my company!"

"I'm sure that's not true," Ellie says brightly.

"But you don't seem to be so eager to get away from me." I cock an eyebrow and watch her blush deepen. Not for the first time, I wonder if she had that same flush to her cheeks in the closet.

"Keep talking like that, and maybe I'll leave early, too," she says.

"Ah… there's my Ellie," I say, smiling at her usual sass.

"My Ellie?" She rests her hand on her cocked hip, and my dick kicks beneath my sleep shorts. I love a perfectly manicured girl as much as the rest of them, but I prefer a woman who's mussed from sleep and scrubbed free of makeup.

"You could be, you know," I say, pushing a little to see if my suspicions might be correct. "I can keep a secret. Our parents wouldn't have to know."

"Sebastian!" she gasps, but the flush that started on her cheeks has crept over her chest. Her chocolate eyes are sparkling with mischief rather than anger.

"It's not like we haven't already done things we're not supposed to, is it? I know it was dark in the closet, but my mind conjured up many images. Maybe it's time I got to see if the images are anything close to reality."

Before Ellie has a chance to reply, my dad lumbers into the kitchen like a grumpy, middle-aged cock block. It's unusual for him to be around at this time. I guess the party and the copious amount of alcohol he consumed have made it harder for him to get out of bed. "Morning, son," he says. His bleary eyes search the room for Colby and Micky. "Your brothers left already?"

"Yep. It's like I have cooties or something," I say.

"Or maybe they have more motivation," dad replies, and for the millionth time in my life, he makes me feel like the lesser triplet.

"Sebastian has a whole lot of motivation," Ellie says. "He's acing his classes." Glancing up in surprise, I wonder how the fuck she knows how I'm doing at school.

"Is that right?" dad says. Even with his ridiculous bed hair and his striped shorts tucked under his belly, he still manages to appear condescending.

"It is right."

"Well, that's good to hear." Dad frowns at Ellie as she passes with her coffee in hand and gives me a sly smile. She sits on the opposite end of the table. Our eyes meet, and a jolt of electricity crackles between us. Reaching out, she grabs the corner of the piece of toast on my plate and snatches it, taking a big bite.

"Mmmm...." She rolls her eyes at the deliciousness of the thickly spread peanut butter. "How do you eat this and not put on any weight?"

"You should run drills with Coach," I say. "I reckon I could eat a horse, and he'd still find a way to make me burn off the calories."

"Colby has bulked up," Dad says. "He's focusing on eating clean and lean."

"I don't see any difference between them," Ellie says, taking another bite. A little peanut butter lingers at the corner of her lips, and when her tongue darts out to lick it away, I follow the movement with a fascination that borders on the obscene. "Anyway, peanut butter is loaded with protein."

Dad grunts, opening the door to the refrigerator and staring into its depths. I want to point out that he's developed quite a gut over the past few years and could do with going clean and lean himself, but I don't have that kind of relationship with him. He's the kind of man that likes to deal out advice and criticism as thickly as I spread peanut butter but would hate to receive it in return.

Ellie reaches out to hand back my toast, and I take it, purposefully eating where she bit first, remembering the sweet taste of her mouth and the warmth of her skin against my tongue. Her eyebrows raise as I lick my lips with relish.

"Will you make it to our next game?" I ask my dad.

"Nope," he says, closing the refrigerator. "Busy putting peanut butter on the table." His eyes focus on the empty jar in front of me. He turns away to stare at the open door. "Lara. Will you come and make me some eggs?"

Out of sight, Ellie rolls her eyes. Her mom appears with her makeup and hair done to perfection, dressed in a bright purple yoga outfit. I don't miss her pinched expression. "Of course, honey," she says.

I guess I don't really understand their relationship at all.

In two huge bites, I finish my toast and rise from the table. Watching Lara cook eggs while my father waits for them is too much for me to deal with so early in the morning. Plus, having dirty thoughts about Ellie with our parents around feels completely wrong.

All day, I contemplate my brother's avoidance and Ellie's cheerfulness. At training, I focus on my dad's dismissiveness, which motivates me to push harder. In the locker room, my brothers are strangely quiet, and for the first time in a long time, we all drive home separately. Colby and Micky choose to eat dinner in their rooms, blaming assignments and late-night online study groups.

Ellie chats with her mom over the pot roast in a way that feels surprisingly bright and without the usual undercurrent of tension that is often detectable between them. In a way, Ellie's relationship with her mom reminds me of my relationship with my dad. There is friction in place of affection, disappointment, and disapproval in place of pride. Ellie usually bristles in response, but she's happy today, and her mom seems to go along with the mood.

I head to bed with a swirling washer of different emotions. Questions linger at the edge of my mind as I drift into sleep, curled around the spare pillow that is a poor substitute for the warm body of a willing woman.

When an arm slides around my waist from behind, I stir in the darkness. "Ellie?" my sleep-addled self murmurs, and she chuckles lightly behind me.

"You were waiting for me?" she whispers.

I twist in her arms, coming into wakefulness. Her eyes are sparkling, even in the darkness, as my gaze rakes over her mussed hair and delicious state of undress.

My asshole brothers.

Is this what's been going on behind my back? Nighttime bed swapping with our sexy stepsister. And I'm the last to experience the fun. It's not fucking fair!

"What can I say? I'm the eternal optimist," I smile, using my fingers to push Ellie's curls back from her pretty face.

"That and your brothers are terrible at keeping a secret," she says.

"They didn't tell me, but Colby's humming and Micky's shifty expressions were revealing."

"Colby was humming?" The brightness of Ellie's smile makes me laugh.

"Yes. I was as surprised as you."

"I must have done something right."

"I'm sure you did everything right."

"So confident in my sexual abilities," she laughs, swatting my arm, and God, I love how she looks with her pretty curls spread over my pillow and her peachy skin fresh and dewy.

"Have you not learned yet? Men are simple creatures. If

you're willing and make the right noises, we are as happy as can be."

She brings her lips close to my ear. "We can't make any noise, Sebastian, unless you want your dad in here giving you pointers on what Colby could do better."

"Fuck," I mutter, shaking my head before I snort. This girl is not only pretty as a picture, but she sees it all clearly too.

"We might be triplets, but our similarities are only skin deep. You must have worked that out by now."

"I have," she says, stroking my face. "Micky wears his heart on his sleeve. Colby puts everything in neat boxes and keeps them tightly shut, and you use laughter as a defense mechanism."

"Defense, or maybe just a tool to diffuse. You know I don't like it when a conversation gets heavy."

Ellie shrugs, and I feel she likes her original idea better. Who the fuck knows why I always turn to humor? Maybe it's just my character. Maybe it's because I had two serious brothers, and the family needed someone to be the fun one. We're all shaped by the other people in our lives and chiseled by our experiences.

"You don't always need to be the fun one," she says, reading my mind. "Like now. You don't need to make me laugh. This doesn't have to be anything other than the two of us making each other feel good."

It's not until she says those words that I realize how braced I am to prove something. My shoulders are tense, and my mind is whirring over everything she's saying and doing. I am waiting to pick up tiny expressions and adjust how I respond. I guess I've never been aware of how much I need to mold myself around other people.

"You don't want to laugh?" I ask, still attempting to take the seriousness out of the moment, trying to divert her eyes away from who I really am, but it doesn't work.

"I don't want to feel like we're here to prove anything to each other. I just want to play. Just kiss me, Seb," she says. "Just use that smart, funny mouth of yours like you did in the closet when you didn't know it was me and I didn't know it was you."

So, that's what I do.

I kiss my stepsister, in my bed, in the dappled moonlight that bleeds through my drapes. I use my mouth to search out her secrets, find the place Micky got to explore during our seven minutes of heaven, taste Ellie's sweetness, and listen to her soft moans. I feel her come against my lips and I smile against her damp flesh, knowing that I made her feel as good as it's possible to feel.

When I climb over her spent body, I expect to find her eyes closed, but she gazes at me with a wide, bright smile.

"Now it's your turn," she says.

My turn.

"Sit on the edge of the bed," she instructs, her tone bossy as she slides off my mattress and kneels on the floor.

"You don't have to…" I start to say, but she puts up her hand.

"Just do as you're told, Sebastian."

God, the way she says my name makes my cock kick between my thighs. When I do as she's ordered, Ellie shuffles forward until she's kneeling between my legs. I've been given head before, but never like this. No girl has ever looked at my cock so hungrily before from such a subservient position.

I don't know why, but my cheeks feel hot, and I run my hand through my sleep-mussed hair as she wraps her cool fingers around my length.

"Either my cock is huge, or your hands are weirdly child-sized," I say.

"No jokes," she says before she dips her head and takes me between her slick lips, and damn, I just about lose my fucking mind. Even if I wanted to tell a joke, I wouldn't be able to formulate one. Not with her cheeks sucked in and her lips wrapped tightly around her teeth. Not with the moans she makes, swallowing me into her throat like my dick is the most delicious dessert she's ever eaten.

I rest back on my hands and close my eyes to regain control, but I can't keep them shut for long. I want to watch Ellie swallow me deeply. I want to commit the image of her on her knees to my dark and filthy memory.

I let her suck me until my thighs are trembling and my hips won't keep still, and my hands are itching to grab her hair and ram her mouth deep onto my cock. I let her suck me until I explode in her throat, holding my mouth tightly closed so I can't groan or curse or tell her that she's the most beautiful, perfect woman I've ever had the privilege of having in my bed.

She swallows me down, staring up at me with puffy lips and bright eyes, and I can't believe my luck. "Fuck, Ellie," I mutter when I've eventually regained control of my brain.

She climbs onto the bed next to me and I throw my arm around her shoulders, pulling her close and planting a kiss on the top of her head. "We might have to leave that part for tonight." She pats my thigh.

"I don't think so," I say, taking hold of my cock, which is already semi-hard. With a few more tugs, he's ready to go.

Ellie stares at it, then up at me with wide, bright eyes. "Are you serious?"

"What do you think?"

Before she can object, I roll onto my back, taking Ellie with me until she's straddling my lap. Her pussy is hot against my cock, and I know how perfect she will feel wrapped around me. I reach for my nightstand drawer and find a condom. I tear it open with my teeth and hand it to Ellie. "It's time to wrap your present, sweetie."

I put my hands behind my head and watch her get to grips with stretching the thin latex over my hard, thick cock. Biting her lip, she struggles, and I just want to laugh with the sheer joy I feel in the moment. " People aren't supposed to wrap their own presents, Sebastian," she says eventually. "Do you want to give me a hand?"

"I want to give you my cock," I say. "Is that not enough for you?" Taking over, I use my tightly closed fist to roll the condom down, and then I grab Ellie, manhandling her into the right position. All the while, she's smiling down at me, her hair hanging over her soft breasts, nipples peeking through, teasing me to the point of delirium.

"Give it to me then," she whispers, shifting her hips until I slide in just an inch. Clenching my glutes, I shove upwards against the grip of my hands on her hips, and I'm buried deep in an instant. Ellie's pretty midnight eyes roll back at the sensation. She's so fucking tiny, and I'm so big, but somehow, we're totally made for each other.

When she rolls her hips, leaning forward to brace her arms on the bed, I lean up to kiss her mouth. "That's it, baby. Fuck me. Fuck me good."

"Do you kiss my mom with that filthy mouth?" she snorts as her eyes roll back with pleasure.

I kiss her pretty lips, teasingly soft and slow, until her mouth parts, and she allows me deep and deeper. Her tongue slicks across mine with the same rhythm as her hips move, and we become like one.

In the darkness behind my eyelids, my mind recalls flashes of Ellie over the years; the first time we met her over burgers when she was a shy teen dressed in chunky black boots and an oversized sweater; the day she moved into our house with uncertain eyes scanning everything in sight; the first time she fell asleep on the couch with her hair spread in a tangle over the pillows like sleeping beauty. She's grown and changed before all our eyes, becoming a beautiful, confident woman who's capable of unraveling me like a cat with a ball of wool.

The closer she brings me, the stronger the need to feel her against me. Pushing up from the bed, I sit with her in my lap, face to face, chest to chest, helping her grind closer, deeper, pushing from beneath until our bodies are slick and we're panting loudly in the dark.

"Fuck, Seb," she gasps, throwing her head back as her pussy tightens around my dick. I watch everything hoping that I'll get to experience this again, even as I suspect I won't.

Because Ellie hasn't come to us to build a loving relationship. She hasn't changed the way she looks at us. We're still her stepbrothers.

Loving relationships don't start with furtive fucks in the dark while our parents sleep in the next room.

She's come to scratch an itch we created in the dark closet at a frat party when none of us knew what we were doing.

And once she's scratched that itch, she'll want to return to how things were.

But I don't think I can.

Pleasure tightens my belly and my chest, but I won't come without Ellie's orgasm first. "Shit," she gasps, digging her nails into my back. "Shit, don't stop."

As if I could.

The temptation is there to pound into her harder and faster, but that isn't what she needs. More of this tempo will take her over the edge, and then it'll be my turn.

When she comes, she draws blood on my shoulders, but I don't give a fuck. The surge of my orgasm strips me of any kind of care. I cling to her, holding my cock as deep as she can take me, unable to even gasp her name.

We flop against the bed, a sweaty heap of ecstasy, and I bring her into the crook of my arm, kissing the top of her head with a fierceness that shocks me.

I've never felt a primal urge to own a woman before. Girls come and go, and that's always been fine with me. As long as it's lighthearted and fun, I'm in my element. But with Ellie tucked against my chest, I suddenly face the knowledge that I want her to be mine. The idea that another man will get to feel this way with her makes me sick to the pit of my stomach. Well, another man who isn't my brother. I'd share anything with Colby and Micky. I'd give my life for them, and I feel the same about Ellie.

Mine.

The word surges through me, and my arm grips her more tightly.

"Why now?" I ask her.

She tips her face, and her eyes dance from left to right, searching for the motivation behind my question.

"You really want to know?" she asks softly.

"Of course."

She blinks and moves to put distance between us, but I don't let her. If we're sharing truths, we're doing it closely.

"Gabriella dared me to fuck Micky."

"Why? That seems like a fucked-up thing to do."

"Because she thought it was something I wanted," Ellie says softly.

"I sure hope it was." I frown as thoughts scramble inside my skull.

She nods.

"And Colby?"

Her mouth twitches. "Micky dared me, and then Colby dared me to come to you."

I turn my head away from her, staring into the corner. Suddenly, everything we've done seems enveloped by shadow. A person's intentions change a physical act and knowing that Ellie came to me because of something Colby instructed is like a stab to the heart.

Ellie must sense my disquiet, because she rests her hand against my face and turns me until I'm forced to look into her dark eyes. "This was good, Seb. Really good. Better than I could have ever hoped for."

"But you came because you were coerced," I say.

"I came because you're an amazing lover," she grins. It's an attempt to lighten the mood, a page out of my very own playbook.

"I don't get it," I say. "If that was the reason, why do you need the dares? Why leave it until after Micky and Colby?"

She turns in my arms until she's staring at the ceiling. "It's hard to explain."

I guess she doesn't want to say more, but I leave the silence between us in case it encourages her to open up. When she doesn't, I stroke her arm.

"Do the dares make you happy or sad?" I ask.

"Happy," she says quickly. "Can't you tell?" I shrug and bring the sheet around her so that she doesn't get cold.

"So, should I give you another dare? Is that what you want from me?"

"That's not the way dares work, Sebastian," she says seriously.

Staring at the ceiling, I count all the things that I love about this moment with Ellie. The warmth of her skin against mine. The comfortable way we relate to each other. How easy it's felt to move from stepsiblings to lovers. What we've done should feel complicated, but it doesn't. Being with Ellie feels familiar, and that isn't something I've ever had with a girl.

I don't like the idea of daring Ellie to do anything, but if that's what it's going to take to show Ellie just how good it could be to have a relationship with me and my brothers, then I'll do it.

It's too important an opportunity to pass up.

"After class tomorrow, I dare you to meet me, Colby, and Micky at Molly's Motel. I'll message you the room number."

Ellie inhales long and deep. "You serious?"

"As a heartbeat."

"Why?" she asks, still staring at the ceiling. I wonder if she's noticed that there's a crack in the plaster that's shaped like an eagle's head.

"Because I think you want it, and I definitely want it. After what happened in the closet, I want to show you how good it can be with all of us."

She turns in my arms and looks deep into my eyes, and for a moment, I wonder if I've done the right thing. "Molly's?" she asks.

Fuck. I thought she was going to say no.

I rest my hand against her heart, feeling the soft thud beneath my palm. "Tell me you want it? Make me believe it's true, or the dare is off."

She clasps her hand over mine and presses it harder against her warm skin. "I want it, Seb."

Ellie waits to see if she's done enough to convince me. I lean forward and kiss her, invading her mouth, needing to be inside her again. She groans and tugs at me, and I feel the truth in her touch. I believe her.

Drawing back, I smooth the hair from her face, resting my hands on both her cheeks. "Molly's," I whisper. "And don't wear any panties."

A small nod and a wide smile are her responses, and it's enough.

It won't be the first time I've shared a girl with my brothers. That aspect won't be a big deal for us, but it will be for Ellie. Three against one. It's a huge dare to give her. And we're not small guys. Three massive guys and one small woman. She's gonna need courage to take on those odds.

15

ELLIE

When the alarm goes off, it feels like some kind of sick joke. Three nights spent having amazing sex have caught up with me.

I wouldn't say that it's too much of a good thing as such. It's more that my college schedule is getting in the way of me having a good time.

And boy, have I been having a good time!

The inside of my thighs feels bruised. My pussy is heavy and sore, and the tips of my nipples are practically raw. My lips won't stop tingling or smiling.

So this is what awesome sex is like. It doesn't just make you buzz when it's happening. It fills you with butterflies and sparkles like tiny fairy lights. I'm practically vibrating with satisfaction. Is that even a thing?

Today is going to be different. There are no secrets between us now. They all know. We've all done the deed.

The stupid dare at Dornan's party and Gabriella's determination that I break the drought in my love life have resulted in three spectacular nights of ultimate satisfaction. Dornan would probably burst a blood vessel if he knew, and Gabriella and Celine would shatter glass with their squeals.

Me? Well, I'm feeling brave and proud for going through with the dares, and tingly at the prospect of the next one.

Dornan was right. This is the time of my life to live outside my comfort zone. I should do crazy things that I can smile about one day when I'm gray and old and past lusting after men.

In fact, as I outline my eyes with smoky brown shadow and lengthen my lashes with mascara, I realize I haven't confided in my best friend about any of it. He's usually the first person I call to discuss my car-crash of a love life. He's commiserated with me over every terrible sexual experience I've ever had, promising that better will come. And now better has come multiple times, and I've been keeping it all to myself.

I'm about to dial Dornan's number when there's a knock at my bedroom door. "Come in," I call, waiting to see who it is.

When the door opens, Colby, Micky, and Sebastian gather in the doorway. It's like a wall of perfect men, a veritable buffet of prime meat. There isn't an inch of the men currently smiling at me I wouldn't lick like the most delicious popsicle.

"We're leaving now," Colby announces.

"Oh, okay."

"See you later?" Sebastian is the one to ask, and I wonder if he's told his brothers about the next dare. Do they all know everything now, or are they still keeping secrets?

"Yeah. Later. Message me." Stupidly, I blush at the implication of that sentence. I'm asking my stepbrother for a booty-SMS. I'm instructing him to tell me where to meet three men for an afternoon of sex. My panties are already stupidly damp, and I squeeze my thighs together, trying to squash the ache that I know is going to linger, hot and heavy between my legs, all day.

"I will," Seb says. "Have a great day."

I don't imagine the slight flush to his cheeks before he turns to leave. Micky follows, and Colby lingers just long enough to look me over. I get the feeling there is something resting on the tip of his tongue, but for whatever reason, he decides not to say it.

As I'm stuffing the last of my things into my bag, I hear their vehicle leave. I grab my phone, thinking about Dornan again, but I don't have time to call him and get to class on time. When I arrive at college, I'll send him a message to meet me for coffee around eleven when I have a free hour, if he can.

Then I start to flap about what I need to take with me later. Maybe some freshening wipes because I won't want to turn up at the motel after a whole day of running around without cleaning up. And some deodorant and perfume, and some powder so I can touch up my makeup.

My underwear doesn't really matter because I'll remove my panties before I arrive, as instructed. My black lace bra is pretty enough, but they're not going to care about what I'm wearing, and I won't be wearing anything for long.

I dare you to meet me, Colby, and Micky at Molly's Motel.

Without a doubt, it's the most thrilling and heart-pounding dare I've ever received.

In the car, my phone rings, making me jump. It's Celine, who's in my morning class. "Ellie, please tell me Professor Dorkerson isn't expecting our assignment today," she says in a rush before I even say hello.

Professor Derkson, as he's actually named, is notorious for setting the most convoluted assignments known to man and hitting us with unachievable deadlines.

"It needs to be in tomorrow," I say, and snicker at Celine's theatrical sigh of relief.

"I'm so behind," she moans. "Eddie's been so horny recently. I swear, since I put on a few extra pounds, he hasn't been able to get enough of me, and usually, I wouldn't mind, but I can't keep up with my work while he's flipping me through the Karma Sutra."

"TMI, sweetie," I laugh, signaling to turn into the parking lot.

"Even a visit from the red fairy last week didn't put him off. My god, the man's insatiable."

"You're just that gorgeous," I tell her because it's the truth. Celine is a goddess with cascading red curls that touch her butt and freckles as pretty as the stars in the night sky. She's been dating Eddie on and off since she met him as a freshman. Every time she breaks up with him, I believe it's over forever. She'll mess around with other guys, and I'll be convinced she's moved on, and then suddenly, they're back together again. It's the weirdest relationship ever.

"If he doesn't leave me alone, I'm going to rub my armpits with onions and stuff cheddar into my socks."

"Don't forget sardines in your panties," I laugh, slightly gagging at the thought.

"Men are disgusting," she scoffs. "He'd probably like that. He's down there like a shot, even after I've done a ninety-minute workout."

"Oh god," I gasp, remembering about the wipes I have in my purse and my concerns about freshness.

"Exactly. I don't know what else to do."

"Have you tried talking to him, sweetie? Wild idea, but communication seems to be the basis of every successful relationship."

"I've tried talking, but as soon as I mention sex, he's all over me again. Just the word is like a flame to a tanker of gasoline." She laughs, but there is a genuine exasperated edge to it, and I start to feel sorry for her.

Would there ever be a time when I didn't want to have sex? Absolutely. Especially in all the circumstances she's mentioned. Poor Celine is struggling with just one man, and here I am, considering having sex with three. It's on the tip of my tongue to tell my friend what's going on in my life, especially after she's filled me in on hers in such graphic detail.

If anyone is going to hear the juicy details of my sex life and egg me on, it's Celine. She might only have a body count of one man, but she's not prudish in any way. And, like Dornan, she's moaned about my lack of interest in standard college pursuits. If anything, she told me she wants to live vicariously through me. If she can't sow her wild oats in college, then I should damn well be sowing mine.

"Anyway," she says. "I'm going to stop talking about Eddie now. He's in my mouth enough! What's been going on with you? I heard some wild shit on the grapevine, but I don't believe it because if it was true, I know you would have called me to dish, wouldn't you?"

"I've been busy," I say. "And so have you."

"I would have interrupted sex to talk to you about a closet foursome. What kind of friend do you think I am?"

"The best kind."

"So, dish. Or I'm going to question you in front of our entire class."

"Let's have coffee after class."

"No, you're being the worst kind of friend," Celine moans. "The kind who delays sharing gratification. I've always told you how hot your stepbrothers are, and now you have some dirt on them, you're leaving me in the cold, dark wasteland of not-knowingsville."

"Don't you think you're being a little dramatic?" I

laugh, sticking the car into park. "I'm not going to walk through campus spilling my guts."

"It's the talk of the campus already, my friend. How do you think I found out?"

I slam my car door with too much force. "Seriously, do people have nothing better to do than gossip about me? I'm so boring."

"It's not you. It's those Townsend boys. Anything they do is the subject of whispering and speculation."

"I'm glad to hear I'm so popular," I scoff.

"Popular, now you're in with the Townsend triplets. Don't tell Eddie, but I'd pay good money to be the ham in that club sandwich…in another dimension, obs."

I'm striding toward our lecture hall when I see Celine waving frantically. We both hang up our phones and she tugs me into a fierce hug. "Let's get in there," I say before Prof. Dork has an aneurysm."

Throughout the class, I can't focus. Should I tell Celine what's happening later? She's not judgy at all, but I know she won't keep quiet if she thinks I'm making a mistake.

Once a dare has been given, I don't want to debate the pros and cons anymore. That's the beauty of the dare.

"Miss Franklin. Are you with us?" Professor Derkson yells, and I jump from my trancelike state back to reality.

"Yes, Sir," I say, my hands poised over my laptop. "Sorry."

He scrunches his face so that his gray caterpillar eyebrows almost obliterate his eyes, but he carries on with whatever he was droning on about before. Celine scribbles 'Lost in a sex dream' on the corner of her notepad.

Ugh. This is what I was worried about. Already, real life is creeping in to disturb my dare-inspired fantasy life.

After class, when I've packed up my things, Celine links arms with me. "Right. I'm not taking no for an answer.

You will tell me what's gotten you losing concentration in Dorksons class."

She practically frog-marches me to the cute coffee shop on this side of campus. It has a giant brown coffee bean character outside, grinning with his thumbs up, and inside, it's all distressed wood and black metal. Industrial chic combined with animation. What's not to love?

"Two caramel Frappuccino and don't be stingy with the cream," Celine says to the guy behind the counter. Max is used to her demanding ways and rolls his eyes theatrically. She pays before I pull out my phone and strides over to our favorite table in the corner, which has been strangely available the last few times we've met up.

"While Max is slowly whipping our drinks to perfection, spill." She rests her head on her hands expectantly.

"It sounds like you already know what happened." I shrug and pick up a packet of sugar, letting the grains fall back and forth inside the paper envelope.

"What I know is that you had seven minutes in the closet with your stepbrothers and came out looking flushed. Speculation is that you all fucked in there, but I call that bullshit because there's no way one of those men could finish in seven minutes, let alone three of them."

"You're assuming they would have gone one after another," I say before I realize what I'm insinuating.

"Fuck, yeah. Is that what happened? There are three of them. You have three holes. Was it a centipede situation?"

"Centipede! That doesn't sound sexy at all."

"You know what I mean. One joined being with many legs."

"That is gross and also strangely clever," I laugh.

"FRAPPUCCINO WITH EXTRA CREAM," Max yells from the counter. Celine stands and struts to grab our drinks.

"Thank you, Maxy-Waxy," she croons.

"Please don't call me that," he pleads as the customers waiting in the queue snigger.

She places my drink in front of me but doesn't let go of it. "The Frappuccino isn't a free coffee, my darling. The one who drinks it must tell all or suffer a curse akin to sleeping beauty." Her voice lowers at the end like an old-world storyteller foretelling doom.

"I'll tell you," I huff, grabbing the drink.

I swear Celine's eyebrows hit her hairline. She almost misses her chair when she sits; her eyes are so concentrated on me.

"Dornan dared me to play the stupid game."

"I knew it had to be a dare," she gasps. "There was no way that sensible Miss Ellie was going to join in something ridiculous like that without being nudged into it."

"And when I went into the closet, it was so dark I couldn't see anything through the blindfold."

"So you didn't know there were three of them in there?" she whispers conspiratorially.

"Of course, I didn't know. I mean, who would assume there would be more than one guy in the closet? It never happened in high school."

"None of us were that kinky in high school," she says.

"I guess. Anyway, I was going to tell them to keep their hands to themselves, but…" I trail off, not knowing how to articulate what happened. I'd sound ridiculous if I told her they bewitched me with their touch, and even though I realized there were three of them, I let it happen.

"But you let them rub their hands all over you, right? Please tell me you had some freaky fun with those gods you live with."

"Believe me. They aren't gods. They're just normal guys."

"Now I know they did something to your brain because you have never referred to them as normal guys before. It's always 'spawn of Satan' or 'those assholes.'"

She's not wrong. Funny how things can change so quickly. "Yes, I had seven minutes of mind-blowing fun with my stepbrothers," I whisper. "Is that what you want to hear?"

"YES!" she yells, like the mere thought of it is enough to send her into a sex-frenzy. "You go, girl."

"We didn't do the sex thing," I say. "I mean, they did stuff to me."

"Stuff…what kind of stuff? Are we talking a finger bang or mouth stuff?" Celine's voice has gone up a few decibels, and I turn to make sure no one is listening to discover that at least three tables of our peers are staring right at us. It must have been the words finger bang. There's no pretending that means anything other than it means!

"Can we reduce the volume?"

"Sorry," she says, whispering and bringing her finger to her lips.

"Mouth stuff," I whisper.

Leaning back in her chair, Celine fans herself. "Who? Which one did it?"

"Does it matter? They were all there."

"Watching…that is so hot."

"There was no watching anything," I say. "It was as dark as a serial killer's heart."

"Oh yeah. But still hot. So who? I bet it was Colby. That man has always looked at you like you're O-neg, and he's a vampire."

"Lovely analogy," I snort. "No, it was Micky."

"Really. The dark horse. Was he good? Tell me he was good."

"Good is an understatement."

"YES!" Celine fist pumps the air, completely forgetting her promise to be quiet. "Please tell me you've been inviting him into your room for repeat sessions ever since. You're my friend, and I love you, but I've considered an intervention over your sex life, honey. It's been Sahara for too long."

"Sahara?"

"Yeah, dry as the fucking desert!"

Celine will combust if I tell her what has happened since the closet warm-up. And I want to see that happen. "Listen, you cannot tell a soul," I say, leaning in until I'm half bent over the rustic wood table, holding my drink so I don't spill it.

Celine does the same, her wide green eyes frantically searching my face for clues. "Tell me now or we aren't friends anymore!"

"There's been three more dares since," I whisper. "And three nights that were the total opposite of Sahara dry."

"Monsoon wet?" she whispers, her face deadly serious.

"Monsoon wet," I nod in agreement.

"Fuck…"

For the first time since Celine and I became friends during our first Professor Dorkson lecture, I see her lost for words. "You really did it?" she asks eventually.

"I did."

"With all of them."

"Yep."

She shakes her head and sighs. "If I was wearing a hat, I'd take it off to you."

"It's not me," I say. "It's the dares."

Celine takes a long drink of her sweet coffee concoction and nods. "Your dares are way more fun than the ones I've been challenged with in the past."

"Fun," I nod.

"And a little dangerous."

"Dangerous?"

"The danger of discovery," she says. "You better hope your parents are sound sleepers."

"They are."

"The danger to your heart, too."

I look up from my coffee to find Celine gazing at me more seriously than she ever has before. Hearts are not things we talk about much. We're fun friends, and that's cool. I don't expect every friend I have to be all things. Celine is awesome to have a good time with. She's encouraging and cool, and I love her a lot. But serious issues haven't been a part of our relationship until now.

"They're just dares," I say. "The triplets know that. They're not expecting anything else from me, and I'm not expecting anything else from them."

"If you say so." Celine glances at her watch. "Ugh. I've got another class to get to."

"Me too," I say.

As she stands, she smooths her purple dress and hooks her bag onto her shoulder. "Expectations can be funny things, sweetie. We think we know what we want and what we expect until we realize maybe we were lying to ourselves all along."

I snag my coffee from the table as her words settle inside me awkwardly. "I'm not lying to myself. Dares are cool, but I'm not looking for anything from them."

"Other than monsoon-wet sex."

"Exactly."

"Mmmm…" Celine doesn't sound convinced in the slightest. "And what about them?"

"I'm sure more monsoon-wet sex is awesome for them, too."

"You don't believe that any of them have deeper feelings for you? I mean, ya'll live together. That's a whole extra level of connection."

"Exactly. They see me in the morning with no makeup and my resting bitch face out in full force. Why would they want more of that?"

"Except they do, don't they? They've seen you at your best and worst and still want more than a weird housemate-faux-sibling relationship."

"I guess."

The cool air hits me in the face as Celine opens the door. It's like a wake-up of sorts. A warning. Dare number five is taking us into entirely new territory, and I'm just striding forward without weighing the implications.

That's what dares are about for me.

Freedom.

No consequences.

But Celine has sowed a seed of worry. What if my stepbrothers do feel more for me? What if all of Colby's searing looks, Micky's soft smiles, and Seb's humorous jabs are more than just resentment or politeness? What if beneath the sex, there are actual feelings?

I don't want to hurt them almost as much as I don't want to hurt myself, but they have to realize that this can't be anything more than five stupid dares and scratching an itch that's been driving us all crazy.

They have to.

But do they?

16

COLBY

"Molly's Motel. Why the fuck did you pick this place?" I ask Seb as we pull into the parking lot. It's half-empty, which doesn't say much about the quality or desirability of the establishment.

Seb shrugs. "What do you want? The Ritz?"

"I don't know." Glancing around, I wonder how Ellie will react when she turns up and finds this shabby building is her destination. Not exactly Paris, roses, and romance. My brothers reach for the door handles, and we all exit the vehicle in synch. I stare at Seb and Micky, still damp from their after-practice showers, dressed in comfortable sweats, soft cotton shirts, and sneakers, then I glance at my ruined Nikes.

Is this seriously what we're doing? Daring a girl to meet us in a dingy motel room dressed like this?

I feel bad.

I know that life isn't about the places you go but the company you have on the journey, but this feels fucking ridiculous.

"What are you thinking?" Micky asks.

"That Ellie deserves more."

"This was Seb's dare." Micky nods at Seb, who slams the door shut and smiles like he doesn't have a care in the world.

"What's so different about this than Ellie coming to find us in the dead of night in our bedrooms?" he asks.

"A whole lot," I say. "I don't know why, but while it was happening at home, it was more relaxed…unexpected. This feels like a date."

"Colby's right," Micky agrees. "We should have bought chocolates or flowers or something."

"And freak Ellie the fuck out," Seb says, strolling towards the main door to the motel reception, not waiting for us to catch up.

"What do you mean, 'freak Ellie the fuck out?' I ask.

"Ellie doesn't want hearts and flowers from us," Seb says, turning and shrugging. "She wants dares and orgasms. She wants guilt-free sex with three men she knows won't hurt her because the consequences are too high."

"All girls want hearts and flowers," Micky says.

"Nah." Seb rests his hand on the handle and pauses. "Some girls want the chance to be bad, to put all expectations aside, but they know there's risk to that. We're safe. Like a male best friend. Or the boy next door."

"I don't want to be safe," I say.

"Safe doesn't have to mean boring," Micky pipes up. "Safe is good. It means she feels free to do what she wants…let her hair down."

I frown as this entire conversation makes my head hurt. "That sounds okay, I guess."

Seb shoots me an exasperated look. "How long have you wanted to fuck this girl? How many times have you told me we can't, and here we are, doing the very thing you've been denying is possible? Don't you want to enjoy the opportunity? Yes, I'd like it if Ellie wanted more from us. If she expected to be treated like a girlfriend rather than a hook-up. But I'll take the hook-up if that's all she's comfortable with. Just appreciate the ride, bro. As long as she's happy and we're happy, what's the problem?"

After Ellie and I were together in my bedroom, all I've been able to think about is her. After a second time at Molly's Motel, how am I going to feel? How many times will I need to fuck Ellie to get her out of my system?

More than twice, that's for sure.

You won't ever get her out of your system, my inner voice whispers. She'll get under your skin even more than she has already, and then what? You'll scratch and scratch, but you'll never be able to forget what it was like to move inside her, to watch her come and witness the indescribable bliss.

And what about when she moves on? I'll have to witness her with other guys; douchebags who don't deserve to touch a single hair on her head. Douchebags who are nothing compared to my brothers and me.

There isn't a man out there that would be better for Ellie than we are.

"I'll take the hook-up," I say, nodding. "But mark my words, this won't end well for any of us."

Seb shrugs as though he agrees, but he still swings the doors open and disappears inside, holding the door for me and Micky to follow.

The bald man at reception eyes us suspiciously when we ask for a family room. "You in town for something in particular?"

To screw our stepsister, I think, but Seb goes into a long lie about a family reunion across town, and it's so convincing the guy processes our booking and wishes us an enjoyable get-together.

The room we've rented is in a separate block on the other side of the parking lot. "You go check out the room," Seb says. "I'll message the details to Ellie and find out where she is?"

"She'd better be close," Micky says, sounding unusually impatient.

"Why?" I ask

"Because my balls are fucking aching. Aren't yours?"

"No." I run my hands through my hair, feeling the usual frustration that builds any time I'm attempting to collaborate on something with my brothers. Shit. Has Micky not heard of jerking off, for fuck's sake?

"I guess I should go first then," Micky says with a wink, and straight away, I see the game he's playing.

"Ellie goes first," I remind him.

The door to room one-zero-three-three is green and covered with chipped paint. Someone has carved two sets of initials with a heart in the middle, which somehow makes this destination even less romantic. I turn the key in the stiff lock and throw the door open. There are three large beds inside and a carpet that matches the door. To say the faded bedcovers look like they have seen better days is a gross understatement, but at least it's clean.

"Should we push these two beds together?" Micky asks from behind me.

"Yeah. And drape that top sheet across the two mattresses so that Ellie doesn't fall in the middle."

"That's assuming she's underneath." As Micky shoves the bed forward with his knees, he wriggles his eyebrows.

"True." I smooth the sheet over the bed, pulling the edges as tight as they will go.

"How do you reckon Ellie is feeling right now?" Micky stuffs his hands into his pockets and gazes around the room. If he's wondering what her impression will be when she sees it for the first time, I'd guess at disappointed.

"Nervous," I say. "If I was in her shoes, I'd be nervous."

"There are many jokes I could make out of that sentence, but I'm not going to."

"Good."

"If you went last, would you have given her this dare?" he asks.

"Seb has always been the most impetuous. I'm not sure I would have."

Micky nods and worry lines form across his brow. "As much as I loved being with her, if I'd gone last, I would have waited to see what she did next."

"Without a dare?"

"Yeah. I mean, dares are fun, but at some point, you have to be prepared to go with your own motivation."

"I guess Seb didn't want to leave it to fate or to Ellie's dare-less decision-making."

"He thinks if we can show her how good it is with all of us together, she'll be convinced to make this official."

"Seb is the most impetuous and also the most idealistic."

"You don't think it'll work."

"Do you? There's a big chance this will scare her off for good."

Micky slumps into an old wooden chair that's resting alone in the room's corner. "If it does then it wasn't meant to be."

"You getting all philosophical?"

"Not philosophical. It's more that I'm trying hard not to analyze everything in my life. Sometimes, just going with the flow feels better, like the universe has a direction that is just for me, and I can choose to wade against it, or I can just let it carry me."

As I sit on the edge of the mattress, my eyes fix on the door, impatient for Ellie to arrive before Micky moves on to the meaning of life. "So how do Ellie's dares fit with the direction of the universe."

Micky purses his lips thoughtfully. "You could say the dares are the universe flow, and she's allowing herself to go in that direction. Or maybe our dares are interrupting Ellie's correct direction and forcing her to wade upstream."

"You're confusing the fuck out of me now!" I say, shaking my head.

"I'm confusing the fuck out of myself," he laughs.

As if my body can sense Ellie's arrival, my heart beats a little faster. It's warm in the room, and I wish I wore shorts rather than my thick grey joggers. I inhale deeply and slowly, trying to calm myself and hating the nervous sensation in my belly. This isn't like me. I'm the one who keeps his head in a crisis. The one who always has a plan.

Except this isn't my plan. It's Sebastian's. Maybe that's why the footsteps outside the door, and Ellie's gentle laugh, set me on edge.

When she walks through the door, the atmosphere in the room changes. Our eyes meet, and the electricity that pulses between us is so powerful, I brace my arms behind me. She scans for Micky and smiles when she finds him waiting for her, too. Seb closes the door behind them, and then there is a long moment of silence.

Static-filled silence.

This is a mistake.

Even as the thought registers, I hate myself.

Ellie bounces on her toes like she's readying herself for a race, and I guess she is, in a way. What happens next won't be easy on her, physically or emotionally.

I get to my feet, rising to a foot over her.

"You sure about this, Ellie?" I want her to say yes with absolute certainty. I want her to tell me that this isn't just about sex. I want her to confirm that the urge I have to possess this woman, mind, body, and soul is reciprocated.

Her dark eyes fix on me and gazing into them feels like being drawn into a vortex. "I'm here, aren't I?"

"Not without a dare."

Sebastian clears his throat and wraps his arm around Ellie's waist. "Well, I am thrilled you are. In fact, you can feel just how happy I am right now." He takes her hand and presses it to his cock, and as Ellie grips his length and moves her hand, her eyes find mine again, this time narrowed with defiance.

Despite the unanswered question hanging in the air, seeing Sebastian's hand roaming under Ellie's white tank while he mouths her neck makes my cock swell. I didn't really believe that this was going to happen until now.

Micky rushes to take place in front of Ellie. When he kisses her, she hooks her free hand around his neck and stands on tiptoes so that he doesn't have to bend too far.

Watching my brothers make a sandwich of the girl who's dominated my dreams for years is fire-hot, but I'm also the only one standing around like a spare part. In the closet, I had Seb's position, and I enjoyed being behind. I enjoyed being the one to whisper in Ellie's ears and hold her wrists. I relished having that place of control.

When Micky drops to his knees and lifts Ellie's skirt, revealing her bare pussy, I almost fall to my knees too.

"No panties," Micky practically gasps.

"Good girl," Seb says, pinching Ellie's nipple.

And what does Ellie say?

"Colby, are you going to stand around watching, or are you going to get involved?" She bites her lip and cocks an eyebrow. Everything about her posture and expression is a challenge.

A challenge to possess her physically but not touch her heart. A dare to go further than we should go with our stepsister, but not as far as I want.

Can I do it? Can I follow the path that Seb has set us on? Can I let Ellie get away with taking what she wants and holding the rest at arm's length?

Now those are some excellent questions.

🚩🚩🚩🚩

17

MICKY

If Colby fucks this up, I swear I'll kill him.

I'm inches away from the prettiest, sweetest pussy I've ever tasted, and my triplet picks this moment to have a conscience implanted in his dick.

For a moment, I acknowledge it would usually be me who's the most bothered about people's feelings.

Why has Colby had a triplet personality transplant suddenly?

Because he has deep feelings for Ellie? It's the only reason I can come up with.

Whatever the reason, I can't let him ruin this for the rest of us. Seb's right. We must believe that this dare can take us in the right direction. Closer to Ellie.

Leaning forward, I let my tongue slide between Ellie's legs, feeling the nub of her clit on the very tip, flicking with just enough pressure to make her moan.

Colby mutters an expletive under his breath, and I look up to find Ellie in a staring contest with my him. I have no idea how she's keeping her eyes open while I'm doing this, but her challenge to my bossy older brother makes me smile.

"You're not the boss of me," Colby says, his voice low and dark. "Just because my brothers are on a mission to serve you doesn't mean I am too." There's a pause, and I expect him to walk out the door. That's how seriously disapproving he sounds. But as I lick Ellie's clit again, Colby clears his throat.

"On your knees, Ellie," he growls.

Before I can step back, Ellie responds, dropping to the carpet so that we're face to face, and Seb is left standing alone.

"Turn and face Seb. Take out his cock. Show him how hungry you are for him."

Like a dream, Ellie does exactly what she's told, easing down Seb's joggers and underwear and wrapping her lips around his length.

Shit, that looks so hot. Colby doesn't tell her how to suck Seb. He just watches as Ellie takes him deep, leaving our brother's cock slick with her saliva. Seb's cheeks flush with arousal, and he bites his lip, trying to smother his desire to moan. Shit, I want to moan, and it's not even my cock getting sucked.

"That looks good, Ellie," Colby says smoothly. "Now, Micky's going to take your hand and wrap it around his cock. You can jerk him off while you suck Seb, okay."

The okay at the end isn't a question. It's said with a determination that she will listen to instructions and obey, and she does.

Oh, she does. Her hands might be small, but she has a firm grip that makes my thighs tremble with every pass. I watch Ellie's throat work around Sebastian. I take in the wateriness of her eyes as she uses all her skill and breath control to take him deeper than should be humanly possible, and I know why she's trying so hard. It's because she wants to please Colby just as much as she wants to please us."

When he tells her she's a 'Good Girl' her eyelids droop with pleasure.

"What about you, Colby?" I ask. "Don't you want Ellie to play with your dick, too?"

"Oh, she'll play with my dick, but right now, I'm enjoying watching her fuck with you two."

Ellie draws back and casts Colby a narrow-eyed look over her shoulder, and I'm fascinated at the dynamic between them. I would never have thought of her as a natural submissive. She doesn't seem to like the fact that Colby is exerting power over her, but she's so willing to comply. This isn't about dares. He hasn't used the word once. This is about something inside Ellie that enjoys being compelled. She needs to be told what to do, and Colby loves being in charge.

It's the perfect combination.

Colby edges closer; his eyes fixed on Ellie. "Suck Seb's cock, sweet girl. Let him push that thick meat into your throat. You make me so hard, watching you take it so well."

Ellie looks at Colby's crotch, her eyes drifting over the bar of his erection, and then does as he's asked. I shift closer, sliding my hand over the curve of Ellie's stomach, relishing the warmth and softness of her body. My fingers find the point of her hardened nipples and play at twisting just enough to make her moan.

Colby finally reaches out to touch our stepsister, letting his fingers tangle in her dark waves. "That's it, baby," he says, and I feel Ellie's body shiver at his words. "Touch her pussy, Micky."

I don't need to be asked twice.

Access isn't a challenge because she helpfully arrived with no panties. I find her slick and warm. Running my fingers back and forth through her wetness is easy.

"Oh, she likes that," Seb says. "I felt her mouth go really tight when you did that."

"Her pussy is fluttering around my fingers," I tell my brothers, enjoying the back and forth between us all. In the closet, we were mostly silent, but there is something arousing about speaking during group sex. Ellie likes it too. The more we talk, the wetter she gets.

"Are you hungry for Colby's cock?" I ask her.

She moans her agreement, never losing rhythm.

"Do you want him to fuck you?"

A slight nod of her head affirms.

Colby squeezes his cock roughly but takes a step back. "I think you should fuck her, Micky. Show her what you're made of."

Ellie's pussy clasps my fingers, and I pull away from her hand, kneeling behind her and lifting her pretty skirt over her nicely rounded ass. "So pretty," I say, and Colby moves to get a better view of her slick pussy. I roll a condom tightly over my cock, appreciating the time to get myself under control.

I know what it feels like to be buried deep in Ellie. I haven't been able to think about much else since she snuck into my room. The chance to feel it again makes my balls draw tight, and when I feel the clasp of her around my length, I can't hold myself back. I'm balls deep in one thrust, and the stretch is enough to force her mouth from Seb's cock when she cries out.

"That feel good?" Colby asks, stroking her cheek.

"Yes," she gasps. "Yes."

"You like getting fucked by my brother's big cock?"

"Yes," she pants, this time resting her hands on the floor and pushing back against me with every thrust.

"Shit," Seb says, watching as I rest my body over her back, using one arm to support myself and the other to grip the back of Ellie's neck.

"That's it," I murmur, pressing a kiss between her shoulder blades. "That's it, Ellie. Fuck me back."

"Oh god," she cries out as Seb drops to the floor and finds her clit with his fingers.

"Make her come," Colby orders, like the idea is his, and we're not already close to achieving it. "You see this," he says, pulling out his cock. Ellie looks up and nods. "This is what you're getting last when your pussy is swollen, and your clit is sensitive. When my brothers have made a mess of you, and you can't take any more, this is what you're going to get."

As I thrust harder, feeling Ellie's back arching, she comes around my cock, milking and milking me until I release too. Seb shoots me a lopsided grin, allowing me only a few seconds before he shoves my shoulder. "Come on, man. You're hogging the good stuff."

"Let's get her on the bed," Colby instructs coolly.

"Give her a minute." I touch the small of Ellie's back, wanting her to feel my reassurance, not sure whether she's okay or feeling vulnerable.

"It's okay." Ellie rises until she's kneeling and then uses the edge of the mattress to help her stand. She's still almost fully clothed, which doesn't escape Colby's notice.

"Take off your clothes."

"Everything?"

"Everything," he nods.

"Maybe you should do it for me," she whispers.

"Maybe you should do as you're told."

There's another standoff between them before Seb steps forward, unfastening the button at the back of Ellie's skirt and encouraging it to drop over her hips and onto the floor. Ellie steps out of the pool of fabric as Seb lifts the hem of her shirt, tugging it past her breasts and over her arms and head, leaving her wearing just a pretty black bralette.

"Everything," Colby says.

Ellie touches the strap of her bra and gently rolls it over the ball of her shoulder, allowing it to drop, then does the same on the other side. Seb takes over, hooking his fingers into the straps and gently pulling until all that is holding the fabric in place is Ellie's hardened nipples. Colby's eyes practically singe the fabric away, giving away his impatience and tenuous grip on his control.

"Want to see?" Ellie asks.

Seb's fingers run along the lace at the top of the bralette until they're poised close to her nipples. "I want to touch," he says, brushing the very tips, causing Ellie's arms to break into goosebumps.

I want to touch, too. My mouth practically salivates for a taste of Ellie's nipples. I might have come, but that doesn't mean I'm done.

When Seb finally pushes the bralette down, I find the strength to stand.

"Lie down," Colby orders, and Ellie quickly obeys. When she's on her back with her dark wavy hair spread across the pillows and her knees pressed together, my heart skitters in my chest. The way she stares up at us is intoxicating. I want to fuck her again and see her face when she comes, but more than that, I want to take this girl into my arms and hold her. I want to tell her she's special and beautiful and capable of so much. She doesn't need stupid dares to do the things she wants to do. I want her to understand that she's enough. More than enough.

The perfect girl for my brothers and me.

Before Colby barks any more orders, I lay beside Ellie and turn her face to mine. I kiss her lips gently, stroking her cheek with the pad of my thumb, trying to convey everything that I'm feeling. She turns into me more, hooking her arm around my waist and pulling me closer. Even though my brothers are watching us, it still feels so intimate.

Colby and Seb stand back, giving us time to connect on a deeper level. When Ellie pulls back, her eyes search mine, and I sense confusion. I suspect she wasn't expecting me to be tender with her. She came expecting sex, but not affection. "You're so beautiful," I tell her softly, kissing her forehead. Ellie blinks, looking away as though my words have hurt her, and it's then that Seb climbs onto the bed.

"You ready for me?" he asks Ellie, and the smile she gives him is warm and encouraging. The sex she can deal with. The emotion and affection, not so much.

Seb climbs over Ellie, and she almost disappears beneath his huge body. Her legs spread around the width of his hips, and her arms don't reach around his back. He nuzzles her nose with his, smiling down like she's the best present he's ever received, and I'm glad it's him going next. Seb is fun and warm. He knows what Ellie needs and doesn't want to push her boundaries too fast. It's a skill I would never have expected from him.

"Are you sore?" he asks, and Ellie shakes her head. He kisses down her neck, between and over her breasts, taking each of her nipples into his mouth over and over until her back arches and her hips search for contact. Moving lower, he licks over her stomach, trailing until his tongue finds her clit.

Ellie rises onto her elbows, staring down as he licks her pussy, his eyes always open and focused on hers.

"That's it," Colby says. "Make that pussy ready."

I stroke my cock, enjoying the way it swells in response to the sight of my brother making Ellie feel good. She bites her lip as Seb's tongue probes her entrance, lapping up her arousal like it's a sweet pudding.

Colby rounds the bed, his hand on his cock, searching

for a different perspective. When he kneels on the mattress, I realize he's looking for more.

"Time to put those pretty puffy lips to good use," he says, using his big hand to push her hair over her shoulder and lining up his cock with her mouth.

Ellie stares up at him, making him wait. I don't know what she's searching for in his eyes, but she must find it because, as Seb flicks her clit over and over, she leans forward and takes Colby into her mouth.

The hiss he makes sounds almost painful. Even though the angle is awkward, Ellie makes good work of sucking him off. The deeper she takes him, the angrier he looks, as though nothing she does will ever be enough.

While Ellie's busy with my moody brother, Seb rolls a condom over his cock.

"You ready for me?" he asks, touching Ellie's hip. She pulls away from Colby and shifts closer to Seb, focusing all her attention on him.

"I'm ready."

The past group sex we've had has been fun, sexy, and once it was even rough. But somehow, this feels different. There's a closeness between us, which is inevitable considering our connection. There's emotion behind everything, even the bossy way Colby is acting.

I wish my brother didn't have such an issue with admitting and expressing his feelings. He still lashes out like he did when we were kids, trying not to let anything hurt him.

When Seb wraps his arms around Ellie and settles into the cradle of her thighs, I see Colby look away. It's as though he wishes this could be a more distant experience, only so he can keep his feelings under a rock where he likes them best.

Seb rocks into Ellie, gently at first, smiling down at her and kissing her in a way that seems searching. In his own way, Seb is trying to get Ellie to face the way she feels about us. She responds to everything, but from an outsider's perspective, there is still a fracture. Just an inch of emotional space that Ellie isn't willing to cross.

"Fuck, you feel good," Seb says, and Ellie moans, closing her eyes and gripping his ass, trying to pull him deeper and closer, searching for her release. Seb doesn't disappoint.

I watch Ellie come, getting so close again that I drop my cock like it's on fire. Seb isn't far behind, falling over Ellie's body like a dead weight. I know how he's feeling. When a man puts everything into sex, all that's left is an empty shell in the aftermath.

My eyes meet Colby's, and his jaw ticks. It's like he's annoyed that Seb is whispering sweet things in Ellie's ear and still stroking her sweat-slicked body. I know Colby must be hungry for his turn, but it's more than that.

Colby doesn't do affection. He doesn't do tenderness. The line he draws between sex and love is thick and carved out in permanent marker.

This isn't love. At least Ellie has made it clear how she feels.

She wants sex, and we're happy to give her that, but at what cost?

Colby doesn't want to cross his line unless Ellie is in a place to reciprocate, so his only option is to keep on his cold and bossy armor.

As Seb rolls onto his back, his chest still heaving, Colby stalks to the end of the bed, rolling a condom down his angry-looking cock with darkness clouding his eyes.

18

ELLIE

Truth or dare?

If you asked me that question, I'd reply dare every time. Where does truth get you? Talking about the past. Baring your soul. Revealing things you might otherwise have wanted to keep close to your chest.

But dares? Dares get you on your back with your spread legs held by two of the sexiest men on this earth while another huge, gorgeous man rolls a condom down his immense cock, staring at your pussy like it's the gateway to heaven.

Dares are perfection.

"Your pussy looks sore," Colby says, matter of fact.

"It's not," I reply, although I'm not sure what he's expecting. His two equally hung brothers have already spread me open. I'm hardly honeymoon-fresh right now.

"You sure you can take it?"

There's an undercurrent in his voice, a slight smugness that feels like a dare. Big bad Colby daring me to fuck him even though it might hurt.

I'm willing to take a little pain when I know it's going

to be iced with a whole mixing bowl of pleasure.

"I took your brothers, didn't I? How much proof do you need?"

"No proof," he says, smiling darkly. "In fact, maybe your mouth needs a little more cock. I could fuck the sass right off your tongue."

"Go on then," I say, sticking my tongue out defiantly. Colby smirks, running his hands up the inside of my thighs, pressing them wider. "I could, but then again, I've been waiting for this pussy for way too long." He bends, breathing in my scent, using the point of his nose to brush my clit, all the while looking directly into my eyes. Wetness trickles out of me, running over my taint, shameful evidence of just how horny his nastiness gets me.

Truth.

I never knew I could be like this with a man, let alone three. I never imagined myself being so brazen. How could I know I had this sexy, demanding part buried deep because neither of my other boyfriends ever pushed my boundaries?

Nice missionary sex was about as stimulating as rubbing lotion into my forearm. It felt okay, but never got me off.

Now I know what it takes, and I feel enlightened but also a little scared. Colby and his brothers know what I need. They don't require instruction. I've found the perfect men who can deliver perfect sex. The only problem is they're my stepbrothers.

My throat tightens at the thought of walking away after Colby's turn and never looking back.

Finding someone else to fill their shoes is going to be impossible.

How could I ever ask for the things I've discovered I need? How could I tell another man to press his thumb against my asshole as he pushed his cock into my pussy?

And how could I find two other men to grip me tightly and stroke me softly, whispering how beautiful I am and how perfect I feel under their palms? How could I ever find the courage to explain what I want and what I need? I didn't even find the courage to get me here. Dares got me to this place of absolute physical bliss. Dares brought me the first signs of heartache.

Is it possible to find perfection once and then match it later? I don't think so.

"Concentrate," Colby barks, noticing that my mind is whirring away from what he's doing.

His hand moves to my throat and grips it with just enough pressure to get my full attention. "Watch while I fuck you. Watch while I turn this slick pussy inside out. I want to see your face when I make you come."

"Yes," I whisper because I want that too. I want everything he's saying and everything he's doing; Sebastian's hand on my breast and Micky's clever fingers pinching my nipples. I want the thickness of Colby's cock to rub the bundle of nerves inside me that only my stepbrothers have been able to find.

"Tell me how it feels," Colby says.

"Good," I hiss as he squeezes just a little tighter. My head swims, and he speeds his thrusts.

"Your pussy feels so tight and slick. Perfect for my cock."

"Mmmmm...." I moan as his pelvic bone slides over my clit.

"That's it, Ellie. You're such a good girl taking my cock. You love this, don't you? Getting fucked while my brothers watch. Letting three men play with your body and ravish and ruin you for any other man."

All-knowing-Colby keeps moving, keeps grinding his hips, and I get lost in the push and pull, my head spinning and my body climbing until I'm almost there, almost free.

"Oh god," I call out.

"That's it, baby. That's it. Come around my cock," he growls.

Sebastian moves to suck on my nipple, tugging it into his mouth in the same rhythm as Colby's thrust, and Micky presses his thumb between my lips, completing the ring of dominance that I need to trip my switch.

And that's it.

That's everything I need to find my bliss.

Throwing my head back and arching my spine, I come again, but this time it goes on and on, my pussy clamping down around Colby's working cock, clit fluttering like the wings of a hummingbird. I see stars behind my eyelids, flashing like the lights on the Red Devil dancefloor. Blood pounds at my temples, and my entire face feels hot. And all the while, Colby thrusts and thrusts, never breaking his flow, somehow keeping control through the most intense orgasm the world has ever seen.

Colby's hand releases my throat, and Seb and Micky drop my feet to the bed. I'm still breathing fast, my heart racing when I feel Colby's weight on me and then his lips pressing to my cheek. He kisses my jaw softly, grinding closer, hitching one of my legs over his arm so he can move deeper. My insides ache at the penetration, but I don't complain because when I open my eyes and look at him, he kisses my lips, and everything slips away.

A bomb could explode in the next room, and I wouldn't notice or care because as his mouth moves over mine, I swear I hear birds singing, or maybe it's angels. I don't know.

It's not so much that he's a better kisser than his brothers. Each of them has style that feels good. It's more that I know this means something more to Colby. He's giving up a boundary that he set, willingly or unwillingly. His fingers are rough, pressing bruises into the skin of my flesh. Tender and rough at the same time.

He nibbles my lower lips and tugs on it as he rises. There's something lost about his expression. Something that feels tormented.

Truth.

This isn't just about sex. Celine was right. An invisible thread tugs at my heart and tears burn my throat.

I don't dare breath for fear they'll see.

"I'm getting close, Ellie. You gonna take everything I have to give?"

"Yes," I gasp, watching his cheeks flush, and noticing the sweat at his temples and hairline, the first sign of him losing control.

"Fuck." He jerks inside me once, twice, then pulls out as though my body has scalded his.

"What is it?" I ask. Seb and Micky look down, worried.

"The condom. It fucking broke," Colby says, his hand wrapped around his dick.

"Did you come?" Micky asks, his eyes lingering between my legs.

"Yeah, but I think I pulled out in time." His breath leaves his mouth in a relieved whoosh. Or maybe he's just panting and out of breath. I can't really tell.

"That's good," Seb says. He rests his hand on Colby's shoulder and turns to me. "Ellie, you should go clean up, just in case."

I don't know what that means, but I don't ask. My heart is racing, my body is aching, and I just need a moment alone to process everything that has happened. Some cold water to shock me.

Shuffling quickly off the bed, I make for the bathroom before anyone can say or do anything else.

Shit.

I close the door and open my legs wide, running my index finger over my opening, finding more wetness there than usual. I bring it to my nose, and my heart drops because that isn't the smell of my arousal. That's clearly Colby's cum leaking from inside me.

I close my eyes and draw in a deep breath, trying to calm the pounding in my chest. I know condoms aren't one hundred percent effective, but this has never happened to me before. It's not something I ever really considered, and now I feel stupid. I'm not on the pill, and a rough mental calculation of my cycle tells me I'm somewhere in the middle. The highest risk time.

What do I do?

My eyes flick to the shower. I need to wash out as much as I can. If I stay standing, that should reduce the amount that travels. The water is still cold when I sluice between my legs. There's a lot to wash away. Despite all my efforts, I know I can't get everything.

"Are you okay?" Micky asks through the door. I know it's him from the gentle concern in his voice. He has a calming tone that's different from his brothers. Seb always has a smile present when he speaks, and Colby has that dominant edge I can tell from a mile away.

"I'm just getting cleaned up," I say. "I'll be out in a minute."

I grab a worn but clean towel from the stainless-steel rack and dry myself quickly. I'm wrapping it around myself and tucking in the end when someone's phone rings in the bedroom.

A quick look in the mirror shows a flushed and wide-eyed Ellie gazing back. Flushed from the most amazing orgasms and wide-eyed at the realization that despite all my efforts, tonight wasn't risk free.

It'll be okay, I tell myself. I've done what I needed to do. The chance that anything will happen is really tiny.

Despite every teen movie ever filmed showing the opposite, it's not that easy to get pregnant. I remember the stats from Sex Ed.

And Colby pulled out as soon as he realized. At least, that's what he said.

It'll be fine.

We can walk out of this motel room tonight, knowing we've all scratched the itch that's been building between us for years. This was the biggest dare I could have acted on. The hugest, in fact. There's nothing bigger for them to challenge me with.

As I open the door, I paint a smile on my face and scan the room. I expect to find my stepbrothers all lounging around in a post-sex state of ultimate relaxation, but what I find is Colby hunched over as he listens to someone on the other end of the phone and his brothers sitting close, listening in.

Seb glances at me, and for the first time, I see clouds over his usually cheerful expression.

What the hell's going on?

"What were you thinking?" Colby says, and I know he's speaking into the phone, but I can't help but apply those words to our situation. What was I thinking, coming to this motel room for group sex with the Townsend triplets? What was I thinking, risking getting pregnant?

I was focused on the awesome sex and living without self-constraint. I wasn't considering the future or the risks.

"But what about us? What about our family?" Colby says.

There's a moment of pause as he listens to a response. "You're seriously telling us we don't have anywhere to go?"

Another pause.

"We have assignments. We can't just roam around like

nomads."

I take a step closer, trying to hear who Colby's speaking to, but it's too muffled to make out anything than it's a man's voice.

"Fuck." Colby lowers the phone until his hand is resting in his lap, but he doesn't stop looking at it. It's as though he's expecting something more to be revealed, even though the other person has already disconnected.

"What's happened?" I ask. "Who was that?"

When Colby raises his eyes to mine, I see the same dark clouds as Seb. "It was dad. Your mom has changed the locks on the house. She found out he cheated."

"What?"

"He cheated when he was away for business. Fucking stupid, selfish fuck."

I take a step back, trying to process the implications of Colby's statement. Mom changed the locks. Harry is telling his sons they can't go back to the house tonight.

What about me?

Can I go back? It's not like I have anyplace else to go. And what will I find? Mom raging. Her anger spewing out with full force. I don't know if I can bear it by myself. I've gotten used to facing mom with the triplets in the background. Somehow, their presence has moderated her outbursts until they have become something easier to deal with.

"She can't keep you out of your home," I say, a whisper of hope sneaking into my voice.

"Dad has told us not to go back. He's worried it will antagonize Lara even more."

"Why would you antagonize her? It isn't you who cheated. You're just innocent bystanders. And her favorites."

"We're not her sons," Micky says softly. "We look just

like dad. I get it."

"You should go home," Seb says, moving to rest his hand on my arm. I stare at his fingers. The same fingers that brought me so much pleasure only minutes ago now feel like those of a stranger.

"What's going to happen?" I ask.

Colby shrugs. "Looks like dad has messed up everything for all of us."

"Does he want to break up with mom?"

Colby shakes his head. "He knows he's been an idiot. Apparently, it was with someone he works with. He says she went after him and then tried to blackmail him."

"Of course, it's a woman's fault. Of course, he wouldn't take responsibility for where he stuck his dick."

Colby's jaw ticks, and he stands, dropping the phone on the mattress. At his full height, I'm forced to crane my neck to look up at him. Even though he's still naked, there's no self-consciousness in his stance. "He was asking if we knew where you are and wanted to find out if we could get in touch with you to warn you about what's happening. He asked if we thought you'd pack some things for us. Enough for a couple of days."

"Are you asking me to pack you a bag?"

"I'm telling you about the conversation. I'm not asking you anything." His nostrils flare as he stares at me in the way he used to before we fucked. The old Colby is back. It didn't take long for him to revert to type.

"I'm asking you if you could pack us some things," Micky says softly. "We'll write you a list. We'll keep it simple. We can park on the street so your mom doesn't see the car, and you can walk the stuff to the end of the drive. We don't want to cause any additional trouble, but we need our stuff for tomorrow."

"Of course." I take a step back and fold my lips between my teeth, unsure of what to say next or even how to be around these men. After what we've done, I shouldn't feel awkward around them, but I do.

I spot my skirt on the floor and my shirt and bra nearer the bed, and I bend quickly to scoop them up. Then, before anyone can say anything else, I rush back to the bathroom to dress.

The deep murmur of voices rumbles through the door, but I can't make out anything being said. They're keeping their conversation to themselves, and the secrecy layers anger on top of my previous panic. I'm not a blood relative, but we've been part of the same blended family for a long time. What affects them affects me too. I'm not an island here, especially after what we've done. Why won't they include me in their discussion?

Even when I'm fully dressed, I still feel naked. My lack of panties isn't ideal under the circumstances. What felt exciting and risqué before now feels seedy and stupid.

Emerging from the bathroom again, I find Sebastian, Colby, and Micky, all fully clothed and standing close. Their matching eyes follow me, but their expressions are different. Micky's gaze seeks connection and reassurance. Sebastian's mouth quirks at one side as though he's fighting against the urge to make light of the situation. Colby is blank faced.

And me? I'm devastated.

I don't know what to do or how to be.

For the first time in forever, I truly appreciate the patchwork family we've had together, realizing that my situation could be so much worse. It could just be my mom and me. It could go back to how it was when dad first left, and I had to be whatever mom needed to stay happy and balanced. I might never live with the Townsend triplets again.

And that is something I just don't know how I'd deal with.

19

SEBASTIAN

I walk Ellie to her car, signaling my brothers to stay in the motel room. This was my dare, so I feel responsible for ensuring it ends well. My dad has managed to wipe out the chance for us to say what we want to say to Ellie. We don't want this to be a one-off. We want her to be our girl.

But how can I tell her that now when she looks like she wants to cry, and our lives have just been tossed in the garbage?

"We'll leave here in thirty minutes," I say softly as she opens the car.

"Maybe an hour," she stares across the parking lot, her eyes unfocused. "I don't know how mom is going to be. It might take me more time to get up to your rooms and gather what you need."

"Colby's going to send that list while you're driving, okay?"

"Sure." Her eyes drift back to the open door of the motel room, and her lips part. I wait for her to say something, but then her breath comes out trembly, her bottom lip wobbles, and she slides into the driver's seat without another word.

"It'll be okay," I say softly, leaning in to be closer to her. Staring straight ahead, she nods, but she doesn't believe me.

"You don't regret the dare, do you?" I ask.

A quick shake of Ellie's head is all I get in response. What I want is a kiss. A soft, melting kiss that tells me she feels the same. Instead, she reaches for the door handle.

"I'll bring your things to the sidewalk."

"Thanks," I say, taking a step back so she can close the door. And she puts her foot on the accelerator and speeds from the parking lot in a flash.

Back in the room, Colby is pacing like a caged wildcat, and Micky has taken up a position in the old wooden chair that is barely strong enough to hold his weight.

"She's gone," I say.

"Yeah. We got that," Colby snorts.

"Is she okay?" Micky asks.

"I don't think so." Shoving my hands in my pockets, I lean against the scuffed wall. "But how much of it is the situation she's going to walk into at home, and how much is about what we just did, I don't know." I huff a sigh and chew on my bottom lip. "Actually, strike that. I know it wasn't anything I did. I mean, sex like that only leaves a smile on a girl's face. Now Colby and his black mood and disintegrating prophylactics... that's another matter."

"You actually believe I wanted to come inside her?" My brother pauses, staring at me like I'm an imbecile.

The comment was a way to make a joke in a tense situation, but now I come to think of it, maybe my brother isn't so blameless for ending the evening on a downer. "You always want to be the best at everything. You had to fuck your way through the condom to prove a point."

"Sebastian," Micky warns.

"What? You don't think it's true. Not even a little. He only went last, so he'd know what Ellie would have to compare him against."

"I went last because I enjoy watching and because I was trying to work out how the fuck I was going to handle being inside her again, knowing it's probably the last fucking time," Colby says, and I'm surprised to see him shake his head, defeated.

Maybe I've been too harsh, but it's difficult not to suspect your triplet of something when it fits with the way they've always been. He's the oldest and the most competitive. I blame my dad for that.

"Whatever," I shrug. "It doesn't really matter."

"It fucking does." Colby's eyes widen. "You're saying I wanted to upstage you. This was about us sharing, about us showing Ellie how we can all be something better together than we are apart. And you're suggesting I wanted to create some kind of hierarchy already?"

"We all know our place, don't we?"

Colby lowers his head, and Micky clears his throat in the corner.

"This isn't the best time to be having this conversation," he says softly. "There's a lot of change happening right now. We need to be unified, or we won't get through this."

"We are unified," I say. "You know I love you both more than I love myself. I'm just pointing out something that's important. Because if any of our fucked-up ways of being together as triplets rub off on how we interact with Ellie, then we need to deal with it separately. She doesn't deserve to get in the middle of our issues."

"That wasn't what it was about," Colby says solemnly. "And I love you too, bro. I guess I just got carried away. She gets me in the sack in a way that no other girl has ever gotten me before, and I wanted to revel in it in case it was the last time I get to feel that way with her."

Outside, a car pulls noisily into the lot, breaks screeching, and wheels spinning. Laughter bursts from inside it. A bottle smashes against the asphalt, and my attention is drawn to the open door. When I look back, Colby is watching me.

"You can always be yourself, Colby. Especially around us. I hope Ellie will want to take another step with us. It was on the tip of my tongue to dare her to go on a proper date with us, but she's on her way to deal with the fallout of our parents' failing relationship. It wasn't the time."

"So, we wait," Colby says, glancing into the corner of the room to check if he has Micky's agreement. He nods, and Colby turns back to me.

"We wait," I say softly. "Looks like we might do a lot of waiting today."

An hour later, we all jump into the car and make the quick journey back to our family home. On the way, I message Ellie asking if everything is okay. All I get in response is a sad-face emoji, and my heart sinks. After our confrontation, I have little to say to my brothers, so the journey is quiet. As we're pulling up outside the house, dad calls to check up on us.

"We're going to stay at Molly's Motel," Colby tells him. I guess it makes sense. We paid for the room so might as well use it.

"We can do better than that," dad says, but Colby ignores him. "If you want to join us, we're in room one-zero-three-three."

Dad pauses for a second and thinks better of pushing an alternative plan. "Okay. I'll be there in an hour."

"We're getting stuff from Ellie right now," Colby adds. "But you need to resolve this, Dad. We'll talk more later."

Dad clears his throat, and for the first time, he seems chagrined.

Ellie must have been looking out for our car because she appears in the doorway, carrying a large bag. Wearing sliders, with her hair scraped back, I can tell from her red eyes that she's been crying. As I jump out of the passenger door, all I want to do is run up the driveway, pull her into my arms and tell her everything's going to be okay. I want to hold her head against my chest so that she feels safe and shelter her from anything negative that the world wants to throw at her.

I just want her to know that I'll always be there for her if she wants me to be.

But I can't do any of that. For all I know, Lara's in the window, watching everything.

Ellie's in the firing line enough. She doesn't need me to make it worse.

"Here," she says, reaching the sidewalk where I'm standing. "I think I got everything." She hands me the bag and takes a step back, clutching her arms around her body, her hands half hidden in her sleeves. The additional distance she feels she needs to put between us stings.

"How's your mom?"

"Not good," she says. "I've never seen her like this before. Well, not for a while."

"Are you okay?"

"No." Her voice is flat, and her dark eyes are shadowed. I reach out to rest a hand on her arm. It's the most I feel I can do to communicate what I need her to know, but she steps away.

"I should go back in," she says blankly.

"We're going to do our best to make things right," I tell her. "I know it seems hopeless right now, but we're going to make it better."

"What would make it better, Seb?" Tugging the sleeves of her sweatshirt over her hands, she twists the fabric. There's something wounded and childlike about her I've never seen before.

"My dad admitting he's the king of the douches and begging for forgiveness."

She shrugs. "My mom's not a forgiving person. I'm surprised that you haven't worked that out yet."

"Our family is worth fighting for," I say, but as soon as the words are out in the cool evening air, I realize that they're a mistake.

"Family?" Ellie doesn't speak the word as an accusation. She's not blaming me for what we've done together. I know she takes equal responsibility for it, despite it being my dare. But the question is there. What would any of us be fighting for? Fix our parent's marriage, and we're only heading to destroy it again if we allow ourselves to continue being more than fake siblings. I know for a fact that our dad would be against a relationship. Forget Lara. If one Townsend man can't be trusted, how would she ever consider her daughter shacking up with three?

It's all too much to ask.

"We'll get there," I say. "It'll get better."

"You're always such an optimist," Ellie says, taking another step back. Her eyes are glassy with unshed tears. "But sometimes life is just shit, and nothing can change it."

Then she turns and strides back up the driveway.

I watch until she's disappeared into the house and closed the door to our home behind her.

In the car, no one says anything on the drive back.

There's nothing left to say.

When we get back to Molly's, Dad's car is in the lot,

and he's sitting in the driver's seat with his head resting against the seat and his eyes closed. In the darkness, with the hollows of his cheeks and eyes shadowed, he looks much older than his years.

The noise of our car pulling in front of him draws his attention, and he climbs slowly out of his vehicle with shoulders hunched.

Looking around, I guess at his train of thought: his car is worth more than all the other cars in the lot put together.

Colby bringing him here was a good move. I'm certain that if we stayed in a luxury hotel that the direness of the situation we're facing wouldn't be conveyed half as well. This dive motel in this part of town just magnifies what he's lost, what we've all lost.

"Why the hell did you choose this place?" he asks.

"It's cheap," Colby says. He locks the car and starts walking, and dad follows, keeping in step with Micky and me.

The bed is still rumpled from earlier, and Colby tugs the sheet that we spread over the gap in the mattresses. Probably wise, seeing as Ellie might have leaked his come all over it.

He tosses it in the corner with no care for our dad noticing, but dad's too distracted to notice a soiled sheet.

He slumps into the rickety wooden chair and rests his head in his hands. "I fucked up."

It's the first time I've ever heard my dad drop the f-bomb, and I stifle my shock.

"Yeah, you did," Colby says. "And it's not just your life you fucked up."

Dad looks up, his eyes red and face gaunt, regret plastered all over him. "I know. I don't know what I was thinking."

"I don't think you were," Micky says, slumping down onto the edge of the mattress.

"I made a big mistake." Dad rubs his face and straightens, dropping his hands by his sides. "I don't know what to tell you."

"Have you told Lara it was a mistake? Have you begged her for forgiveness?"

"I don't beg anyone for anything."

I look over to Colby, whose shoulders are bunched with tension. I can see so many similarities between my dad and him. The mask they both wear to cover weakness isn't healthy for either of them.

"But you still want her? You still want our family?" Micky asks.

There's that word again. Family as a descriptor doesn't sit right with me anymore, not after what has happened.

"I do," Dad says softly.

"Then maybe you need to look at it from Lara's point of view. It's not her who's betrayed the relationship. It's not her who's broken the trust. She deserves you to crawl on your hands and knees and say a million sorrys. Whether you like it or not, that's what you're going to need to do."

"But what if she doesn't accept my apology? What if she can't ever trust me again?"

"That might be the case, but you have to take the risk. There isn't an alternative."

He exhales and shakes his head. "Women. They're nothing but trouble."

Colby snorts and rolls his eyes. "You had a perfectly good relationship, and you messed it up. Don't blame women for your selfishness. Lara waits on you hand and foot. She's cared for us like we're her own. There's not a thing that woman wouldn't do for her family. She didn't deserve this."

There's a long moment of pause, and then dad stands and paces back and forth. In his dark suit trousers and white dress shirt, rolled at the sleeves, he looks like a businessman who bet on the wrong horse. There's a stoop to his normally iron-straight posture, and it's weird because this is the first time I've ever really noticed my dad's humanity. He's always been larger than life, a mountain whose summit is too high to view. He's aloof and always in control and never shows weakness. Never lets down his guard.

And here he is, brought to the bottom rung of the ladder, in a sleazy motel room with his sons, all because of his stupidity and selfishness.

None of us is infallible. We might like to believe we are. We might want to project that to the world, but in the end, our vulnerability lingers behind the mask.

"It'll be okay," Micky says, and I wonder if he's seen the same thing as me.

"Just do what needs to be done," Colby adds coldly.

Dad stops and looks at each of us and something in his expression makes me wonder if he's truly seeing us for the first time, too. "It'll only be for one night." He stares at the three beds that we'll have to share. "I'll try my hardest to get things back. I promise. And if Lara can't forgive my stupidity, then I'll sort us out something else. Something better."

"Okay, Dad," Micky says.

Colby nods, folding his arms as if to say, 'you better'.

I look around at all the men in my family, missing Ellie and hating how somber everything has become. This isn't what I imagined things would be like after the dare. I had so much hope bubbling beneath the surface that she would find happiness in this room with us. Nothing is as I expected it to be.

I don't do serious, and I don't do negative. I just want

everything to be back to how it was, but I can't say that without sounding needy and pathetic. So instead, I do what I always do and make a joke.

"You assholes better not snore," I say, then I toe off my shoes and head to the bathroom. There won't be a sexy girl in my bed tonight, just an old dude or one of my asshole triplet-brothers.

All I can do is hope that tomorrow will be better. Maybe if I imagine hard enough that Ellie is back in my bed, I'll manifest it to come true.

20

ELLIE

I'm late for my first lecture. So late that I pause outside the door, too mortified to go inside. I know I don't look good and walking in is going to draw so much attention.

I'm a statue of grief and panic, putting off what needs to be done as I always do.

There's no one to dare me out of this funk. I'm on my own.

At least, I am until Dornan finds me.

"What are you doing out here?" he asks. "Aren't you supposed to be inside?" When he sees my red-rimmed eyes and blotchy skin, he pauses. "Hey… what's happened? What's wrong?"

Like an idiot, I burst into tears.

It's what comes from having too little sleep, frayed nerves, and forgetting to set my alarm. My mom smashing pictures of Harry and the triplets as I left the house hasn't helped either.

But mostly, I'm wobbly from knowing that Micky, Seb, and Colby didn't sleep under the same roof last night. I have no idea where or how they are right now, and not knowing makes my heart ache.

Dornan hooks his arm around my neck and tugs me towards his chest, turning so that I'm concealed between his body and the wall behind me.

"Fuck," he mutters as my sobs wrack my body. His big hand stroking over my back is so comforting that I cry harder, burrowing closer into his soft shirt that smells of the ocean. "God, Ellie. What's going on?"

"Mom and Harry are splitting up," I mumble. "He cheated."

Dornan makes a low rumbling sound in his throat. "Shit, Ellie. That's harsh. When did you find out?"

"Yesterday. She's chucked them all out of the house."

"The triplets too?"

"Yeah. All of them." My voice breaks as I speak the last word because I can't imagine what it would have been like for them to wake up with so much uncertainty. Would their dad have gone to be with them? All the questions are just overwhelming.

"Do you know for a fact they're splitting up?"

I shake my head and look up into Dornan's concerned eyes. He uses his big rough thumb to swipe away one of my tears and clears his throat. His eyes dart around the hallway like he's checking we're alone. "I haven't ever told anyone this before, and you can't repeat it, okay? You have to promise."

I nod, frowning at the serious whispered tone my friend is using. "I'm only telling you this because I want you to understand that although it seems bad right now, things might get better when they've run their course. My dad cheated on my mom when I was nine. For a few days, all hell broke loose, but dad didn't want to leave. He said he made a stupid mistake, and mom forgave him. It was touch and go for a while. It was shitty to be in the house with all that fighting, but they got through it."

"Was that the summer you used to hang out in our yard?" I ask, remembering Dornan leaving it to the absolute last minute to leave and then running home so he didn't miss his curfew.

"Yeah. Do you remember? It might not be as bad as you think." I nod, hoping he's right, and his brows draw tight as I take a step back and rub my hands over my upper arms. "I didn't know you were so invested in the blended family thing. You've always moaned so much about the triplets and your mom and stepdad."

"Better the devil you know," I mutter as heat spreads over my blotchy cheeks.

"Did something else happen?" he asks, cocking his head to one side and studying me with his best friend magnifying lens on high alert.

The wall is cold against my back, and I roll my lips between my teeth, tasting strawberry Chapstick. It's not that I want to keep secrets from Dornan. He's my best friend, and I usually share everything with him. It's just that, under the circumstances, revealing my sexual escapades feels like laughing at a funeral.

"Can we save that chat for another day?" I ask eventually.

"I'm not sure. Let me buy you one of those ridiculous frozen coffee things you love, and I'll even throw in an exploding chocolate muffin. Then we'll see how you feel." He takes my hand, and I push off the wall, pretending to be reluctant but relieved that I don't have to motivate myself to go to my class anymore.

It doesn't take us long to get to the coffee shop, and Dornan fills the journey with stories about his frat buddies and their ridiculous antics. It feels weird to laugh when my heart is so heavy, but I do. I guess that's the power of a good friend in a time of crisis.

Dornan grabs our drinks while I sit in the window, staring at the other students rushing to class or hanging out with friends. Weirdly, I carry a strange feeling of 'outsiderness' with me, as though the unsettling home environment has crept into every aspect of my life. I catch sight of Colby's back, but he disappears inside a building before I can be sure it's him. Then Dornan places an extra-large iced frap in front of me with as much excitement as would accompany a diamond ring.

I suck a long, sweet drink through the straw, and as the coffee and caramel rest in my stomach, I instantly feel better.

"Good?" he asks, slumping into the small wooden chair in front of me that doesn't look like it can hold a man as big as Dornan.

"The best."

"So, are you now in the mood to tell me everything?"

Just as I open my mouth, there's a dull thud of a fist against the glass. I almost jump out of my skin. When I turn, I find Celine and Gabriella pressing their lips against the glass the way toddlers do, making grossly hilarious expressions. When they've succeeded in making me laugh, they aim for the open door of the coffee shop and burst inside, chattering noisily.

Celine plonks herself onto the adjacent chair, and Gabriella grabs a spare from the next table, turning it so she can sit with her legs wrapped around the back.

"I hope our girl here is about to spill some good shit," Celine says. She reaches out and grabs my coffee, taking a long drink and rolling her eyes.

"Ellie's having a tough day," Dornan says.

"Why? The triplets decided not to give you the good cock?" Celine whispers.

Dornan, who was sipping his hot cappuccino, snorts some back into the cup.

"Celine, you have to chill out with talking like that in front of boys," Gabriella says, resting her hand reassuringly on Celine's shoulder. "You know that's just for women's talks. Men don't know how we speak when it's just us. They can't handle it!"

"Do they seriously believe they're the only ones who talk about cock?" Celine asks, aiming her question in Dornan's direction.

"Don't ask me," he says, wiping his lip on the back of his hand. "I'm not the voice of all men,"

"Shame," I say. "At least they'd make more sense if they were all like you."

"Trouble in triple dick paradise?" Celine asks, but Dornan is sensible enough not to comment.

"I'll give you the lowdown," he says, telling them my family's sorry tale of woe.

"Shit. He dared to cheat on your mom?" Celine says. "He's one brave man."

"He didn't expect to get caught," I snort, pealing the wrapper from the chocolate muffin and breaking off a chunk. Gabriella swoops in for a piece, too, as expected! Food is always communal.

"Yeah, but any realistic person knows secrets don't stay private forever."

"True," I nod, the secrets I'm keeping from mom making me nauseous. "Maybe he got sick of her," I say. "But I don't know why he would. She's always been like the perfect Stepford wife. And they have fun together. I always hear them laughing in their bedroom."

"That's called sex," Gabriella says, pushing her hair behind her ear.

I wrinkle my nose. "Can we not talk about parents fucking right now?"

"No, let's talk about you fucking," Celine says. Her

parents got divorced three years ago, and I know my situation is sending her back into a sad place.

"Let's just say I'm five dares in and have done about everything there is to do."

"Five dares?" Dornan says.

"Yeah. You, Gabriella, Micky, Colby, and Seb. Five dares."

"I don't want to know," Dornan says. "I didn't think seven minutes in heaven was going to be the catalyst for a sex frenzy."

"I did," Gabriella says. "I knew you liked those boys. You always denied it a little too hard."

I shrug because she's right. Behind all of my resentment and dismissiveness was an attraction that seared my core. "You seriously worked your way through them all?" Celine asks. She brings her hand to her forehead in a clipped salute. "I take my hat off to you, Ellie Franklin. You are way more woman than me!"

"Hardly," I say. "If we're counting numbers, Eddie has definitely set you up as the sex-fest front-runner."

"Yeah, but my situation seems positively vanilla compared to yours."

"I prefer chocolate," Gabriella muses, glancing over at a woman devouring a tall glass of hot chocolate with a whipped cream top.

"I didn't realize there was a competition running," Dornan says. "I must be trailing. Coach has me too busy focusing on football to find time for women."

"All work and no play make Dornan a boring boy," Gabriella says in a sing-song voice.

"Tell me they were good," Celine says. "Tell me they rocked your world."

Flashes of the multiple orgasms the Townsend triplets gave me over the past few days light up my mind and my body. But this isn't what I should be focused on right now. Mom is going through something awful, and everything about my life that has been stable will probably end up twisted in turmoil.

"They were good," I say. "They were great, but it's done. I'm not going back there again." I stare at my friends with wide, determined eyes. "And no more dares in that direction. My life is complicated enough."

Dornan nods. Gabriella turns to give Celine a knowing look. Whatever. They think I'm talking shit, but they weren't there this morning when mom almost trashed the house in a fury. Even if I wanted to let Colby, Sebastian, and Micky into my life, it's an even remoter possibility than it was twenty-four hours ago.

Behind my ribs, an ache that I've never experienced before builds. I rest my hand against it and swallow around the lump in my throat. For my good and the good of everyone else in my splintering family, I have to push away all thoughts of the tenderness my stepbrothers showed me at Molly's. I have to forget the way they made me feel.

For all of our sakes.

21

COLBY

All Micky's message says is, 'Saw Ellie crying,' but it's enough to make me want to tear bricks from the wall with my bare hands. Or maybe overturn a few bookshelves.

The library is so quiet that when a growl emanates from my throat and echoes in the space between the bookshelves, the one other dude in this section turns and gives me a weird look.

Instead of lashing out, I stuff my books into my bag, flip my laptop shut, and storm out of the building. The fresh air smacks me in the face, and I glance up into the clear sky and inhale a long breath. My hand flexes at my side, tension radiating through me.

Ellie doesn't deserve this. I don't want a single tear to run down her cheek. Ever.

And even though I'm not personally responsible, I feel guilty by association. It's my dad's fault. He's the one who's done this, and he's the one who needs to make it right.

I pull my phone from the pocket in my jeans and find dad in my contact list. When he picks up, I'm initially stumped over what to say. I know what he's like. He's as stubborn as me at knowing his mind and never wants to take advice from anyone else, but it's time for him to listen. It's time for me to stand up and let him know how important this is.

"Colby. Is everything okay?" he says.

"No," I say. "Nothing is okay." I take a deep breath and grit my teeth. "We all need you to sort this situation out. We want our family back. Whatever it takes, you need to do it."

I wait, expecting him to explode with a diatribe about it being his life and his decision, but all I get from the other end of the line is a long sigh.

"You know what, Son? For the first time in my life, I'm at a loss. I know I'm in the wrong, and I hate myself for what I did. Lara doesn't deserve this. None of you do. But I'm not good at apologizing, and Lara isn't good at accepting apologies. I don't even know if expecting her to listen to me is fair. I'd be broken if the situation were reversed."

"You just said all the things you need to say to Lara to me. You need to show her your regret. You need to let her see your humble side." I blow out a hiss of breath, finding this kind of deep and meaningful conversation with my reserved father so uncomfortable. "I know it won't be easy for you. If I was in this position and I had to tell E…" I pause, realizing the mistake I almost made. "…my wife," I continue, "I know I'd be feeling like it was impossible. But only you can make this right, Dad. Only you can take us back to where we should be."

"I know, son," he says softly. "You know, when you were a little boy, you were so determined about absolutely everything. It used to drive me mad you wouldn't listen to my directions. But I recognized myself in you. I'm so proud of the man you're becoming."

The lump in my throat is the size of a grapefruit

because dad never talks like this. He's an old-school father who puts the food on the table and demands a level of reverential respect that sets him apart within the family. He's never allowed us to see even one chink in his armor. And now, I feel as though he's set all his defenses aside.

"You can do this, Dad," I say. "I know you can. If you show Lara the same man you just showed me, I know it'll work out."

"How are your brothers?" he asks. "And Ellie?"

"The boys are okay," I say. "But Ellie's taking it badly."

The sigh that rustles the microphone on the other end of the phone is even longer and more helpless. "I'm so sorry about that. Can you tell her when you see her?"

He says it, and I believe it. And for the first time since he called me with the news that broke everything, I wonder whether he might be able to make this right.

"Sure, Pop."

When we hang up, I finally raise my eyes from the ground in front of me and find Ellie watching me from twenty feet away. I raise my hand in a surprised wave, and she does the same. Then, as quickly as she was there, she disappears through the open door behind her.

I'm hungry as a bear. Missing out on my usual breakfast made by Lara is taking its toll. In the cafeteria, I grab a tray and attempt to find something to eat that doesn't look gross. The choices are limited. As I'm staring at the burgers, a large figure looms next to me.

"Colby." The voice is deep and gravelly, and when I look to the side, I find Dornan dressed in a black hoodie that seems to magnify his size to monolithic.

"Dornan."

He clears his throat as I point to the burger, and the server behind the counter shovels fries onto my plate. "Can we grab a table? I want to talk to you about something."

When I cut him a glance and find his face impassive, I can tell from his tone and stance that this isn't to discuss football. "Sure," I say.

I lumber to the register and pay while Dornan's plate is filled, then I make my way over to a small table in the corner. Whatever we're going to discuss isn't something that should be overheard.

Eventually, Dornan places his tray on the small round table and takes a seat in front of me.

"Is this about Ellie?" I ask. "Micky said she was upset."

"Yeah, it's about Ellie," he says.

"Look, I don't know how much you know," I say, grabbing my knife and fork and clutching them in my fists, resting on the table. "But I've told my dad he needs to sort things out. There isn't anything else I can do. I can't fix our parent's marriage."

Dornan takes a bite, his bright blue eyes boring into me. He chews slowly, as though he's in no rush to tear me a new one, but he intends to. At least, that's how it feels. I've never had a run-in with Ellie's best friend. As far as I know, he's a good guy. On the field, he plays without the usual bubbling undercurrent of rage. I've never seen him fight, but he knows how to handle himself. I already feel as though I should tread carefully.

"It's good you're supporting your dad," he says eventually. "Just because they're older and parents, it doesn't mean that they always know what they're doing." Resting his half-demolished burger on the plate, he leans back in his chair, legs spread wide. It's a power pose, but I'm not sure it's intentional. Dornan is just big and used to filling a lot of space in the world. "That isn't what I wanted to talk to you about, though."

I stare at him for the first time, wondering exactly how much Ellie discloses to her best friend.

"You need to treat Ellie right," he says, arching a

warning eyebrow.

"What do you mean?" I ask, but as the words slip out of my mouth, I immediately feel like a douchebag. Dornan knows. He probably knows everything and doesn't deserve to have me treat him like a fool. I hold my hand up before he can reply. "We want to treat her right," I say. "She deserves nothing less."

Dornan flares his nostrils and grabs a napkin to dab grease from his lips. It's the same expression he gets on the field as a play is set in motion; part anticipation and part steadying himself for what's coming next. "You need to know that it won't an easy road," he says. "She's had feelings for you all for years. She just never wanted to admit it. But I've known that girl since she had pigtails and freckles. She can't hide anything from me." He closes his eyes for a moment, and I scan the twitch in his jaw and the slight downturn of his mouth. "I love her like a sister, Colby. And sometimes, when you love someone, you have to help them see who they are and what they truly want, even if it might hurt them. Do you understand what I'm saying?"

I nod and purse my lips. He's encouraged her to face her feelings for us, even though he's worried about her getting hurt in the long term. It's brave and maybe a little stupid, but I get it. He just wants her to be happy, the same as us. And right now, I need to show him we're a safe bet. Or at least safer than he currently believes. "Ellie doesn't know how to face her feelings or take steps forward when there's resistance. That's why she relies on dares so much."

"So you understand her?" Dornan nods. "The key thing is not to just become the person who's pushing her. You have to be the person who helps her take her own steps."

"Have you met Ellie? She's as stubborn as fuck."

Dornan snorts, picking up his burger again. "She's

stubborn, but she's ride-or-die. Once you're in her life and she trusts you, there's no better friend in the world."

I look across the cafeteria at all the other students eating lunch. There are big noisy groups, couples, and people by themselves, scribbling notes to catch up with late work or cramming up on knowledge from books. Every person is going through their own set of circumstances. I just wonder how many of them have a life as complicated as mine is right now.

"Our parent's relationship is about as fucked up as it could be," I say. "They can't take hearing about our feelings for Ellie or her feelings for us."

"That might be the case," Dornan says. "But as long as Ellie knows you have her back, and as long as she feels secure, she'll be okay to keep things between the four of you."

I stare at him, trying to work out how he's okay with the three of us being with his best friend. I mean, I've always suspected there is more to Dornan and Ellie's relationship than they make out. He's a good-looking guy, and she's as gorgeous as they come. Why the hell aren't they dating?

"What's the score with you and Ellie?" I ask. "Like, you must see how hot she is."

"She's fire, my friend." Dornan shoots me a lopsided grin. "You're wondering why I'm not angry with you?"

"Yeah. I'm wondering why you're so cool about all this."

He grimaces, revealing an undercurrent of his less-than-positive feelings, and I brace myself for the can of worms I've just opened. "I've been watching you guys for a while," he says, biting a fry and nodding slowly. "From the point that I suspected she was developing crushes on you, I started keeping track. I wanted to make sure that she wasn't crushing on a load of douchebags. If I thought you were assholes, I would have told her she was crazy a long time ago. I didn't notice any behavior from you or your brothers that concerned me. I was impressed that you defended Ellie when people were talking about her. And I like that you're always straight down the line with girls. I haven't heard any nasty gossip about any of you. Yeah, you might fuck around, but what guy our age doesn't? But you've always hooked up with girls who are on the same page and not played around with feelings. And you work hard. It might not be your everyday setup, but if you guys make her happy, then why the fuck not? We're living in different times, Colby. The concept of what makes a relationship isn't what it used to be."

"You're a lot cooler than I would be if Ellie was my best friend," I say.

"Says the guy who's hooking up with a girl and his two brothers. It doesn't exactly make you conservative, man!"

I snort, realizing how odd this conversation is all around. "You have a point, Dornan."

He finishes his burger in two more bites and stuffs the rest of his fries into his mouth, washing it all down with some water. I try to eat too, but I have an odd feeling in my stomach that I'm not used to.

Anxiousness.

There's a lot on the line.

Even if Dad can fix his marriage, our hopes for a relationship with Ellie feel almost impossible.

As Dornan stands, nodding and saying, see you around, I weigh up what he said.

She'll be okay to keep things between the four of you.

Will she?

And would it even be fair to ask?

22

MICKY

In total, we spend two more nights at Molly's. With encouragement from us, Dad convinces Lara that he is genuinely regretful. She agrees to go on a two-week vacation to Jamaica to give them the time and space to sort things out.

Dad asks us to wait until they've left for the airport before we move back into our home, which we're happy to agree to. Even though we have done nothing wrong, we all feel awkward as hell about coming face-to-face with Lara. It sounds stupid, but I know I'd want to apologize to her on my dad's behalf.

We arrive in the late afternoon with our few possessions clutched in our hands. As Sebastian opens the front door and we step inside, I get the same feeling as when we've been away for a two-week vacation. Everything looks the same, but there is an awkward sense of unfamiliarity.

Ellie's car is in the driveway, confirming she's home, and even though we've had long discussions about what happens next, we are unsure how things will play out.

Music emanates from the kitchen, so we leave our bags

in the hallway, glancing at each other, seeking confirmation of our next step, before we make our way through.

When Ellie spots us, she stops grating cheese onto her pasta and stares without smiling. The unfamiliarity extends to our stepsister, too.

"Hey," I say, wanting to break the ice as quickly as possible, needing to see the same warmth and affection in her eyes as before.

"If you're looking for your dad, he left already," she says, dropping her gaze so that she can focus on the cheese grating again. It feels like she's using it as a distraction so that she doesn't have to look at us. My stomach twists into an uncomfortable knot.

"We know," I say. "He called to tell us the plans."

"A luxury vacation to bribe my mom," she says, still staring at her meal.

Colby, who's chosen to stand leaning against the wall near the door, clears his throat. "That isn't what it is, Ellie. It's a chance for them to spend time together."

"They could have spent time together here." Ellie waves the grater in a circle, spraying tiny fragments of cheese over the counter and onto the floor.

"With the four of us standing around watching?" Seb steps closer and smiles cautiously, expecting Ellie to be amused by the picture he just painted.

"Throwing money at an emotional problem is just masking the issues."

"Isn't it up to them to decide what to do about problems in their own marriage?" Colby asks.

"It's a good thing," I interrupt, already feeling the old tension between Ellie and my brother bubbling. None of us wants it to boil over, especially now. "They should take some time away. They haven't been on vacation for over a year."

"Men are all the same," Ellie says dryly. "They always let you down when you need them."

"That's a little harsh." I try to keep my tone soft to diffuse some of Ellie's tension, but it doesn't seem to work. "Dad made a mistake, and he's trying to make things right, but that doesn't mean you can tar half the world's population with the same brush."

"Can't I?" Turning to toss the grater into the sink, we get a full view of our stepsister's rigid posture. I don't know what I expected from our reunion, but it isn't this. At worst, I imagined her regretting what we did at Molly's motel. At best, I was hoping she'd sink into our arms and seek reassurance, which we'd be more than happy to give.

Taking her bowl of pasta, she starts towards the door, finished with the conversation.

Colby won't let her have the last word, though.

When he blocks her exit, there's a stare-off of epic proportions. I marvel at how she handles herself with such confidence, even though she's half the size of him. "We're not to blame for our father's mistake," Colby says slowly. "And just because he betrayed your mom doesn't mean that we will do the same to you."

"To me?" she cocks her head to one side. "You won't do anything to me because the dares are over now. We're finished."

"Finished?" Colby steps forward, looming over Ellie, but she doesn't flinch. "Oh, we're not finished, Princess. We're only just starting."

"What do you mean?" she asks, turning to find Seb and me in the room, eyes scanning our faces for answers.

"I mean, you don't get to just fuck us and leave us, Ellie. We're not allowing you to push us away like you usually do before we can get close."

"That isn't what I do," she says quickly, her lips tugging into a grim line.

"Of course it is." Colby reaches out to touch a strand of her hair, looking at it intensely. He folds in his bottom lip in the way that Hollywood heroes do in romance movies, as though he's remembering how she tastes. "Even Dornan admitted that's your MO."

"Dornan?"

"Just admit you liked it," Colby says as Seb moves closer.

"Just tell us what you want," Seb says.

I decide to get in on this conversation and take it to a less confrontational place. This is about more than sex and desire. This is about feelings. Maybe my brothers aren't comfortable acknowledging it, but I am. "Just tell us how you feel," I say softly, knowing full well that I'm asking Ellie the toughest question.

"I feel nothing," she says. "Other than pissed off that you're not listening to me." When she steps back, Seb crowds her from the behind, restricting how far she can move. We have her penned in, but I'm still unsure if the flush creeping over her cheeks is arousal or fury. With Ellie, those two emotions seem intrinsically linked.

"Oh, you feel something," Colby says.

"It's okay to admit it," Seb adds. "Because we do too."

"We do," I blurt. "We don't want to walk away from this, even though there are a million reasons right now that say we should. Doesn't that tell you something, Ellie? Can't you see how much we're willing to put aside for what we have between us?"

"You'd risk fucking up our parents' marriage for good because that's what will happen if they find out about this."

"So we keep it a secret," I say, raising my hand when Colby looks as though he's planning to interrupt. "We keep it a secret until they're in a better place, and then we take the heat - and there will be heat - because this is worth it."

She blinks, still clutching the pasta bowl close to her body like a shield. Her face, although flushed, is impassive, and I can't tell if I've gotten through to her. So I do what I vowed I wouldn't do.

"I dare you to have a relationship with us."

Colby and Seb stare at me as though I've broken a cardinal rule. I know this isn't the right thing to do. We're at a juncture where Ellie should be willing to take a step forward, but she's not ready, and I'm not willing to risk things falling apart.

"You can't dare me to do that," she says softly.

"Can't I?" I raise my eyebrows and move closer, looking down at the dark-eyed girl who stole my heart the moment I laid eyes on her. She has no idea how far I'd go to keep her in my arms and in my bed.

"Sex is one thing, but relationships need a whole lot more. Dares don't work when it comes to love."

"The dare won't make the love, Ellie. I know that. But maybe it'll give you enough time to see that we mean every word we say."

"You're daring me to fall in love with you?" she asks, looking between us all. Her wide eyes remind me of Bambi's, innocent but also fearful.

"I'm daring you to let yourself go and see what you feel," I say, taking the pasta bowl, easing it from her clenched fingers, and placing it on the countertop.

Her shoulders lower as we move closer, taking places around her like three points of a triangle, with Ellie at the center. I take her right hand, and Colby takes her left. I bring it to my lips, kissing it softly. "It's okay," I whisper, knowing she needs to hear it. "Everything's going to be okay."

When she collapses into my arms, I wrap her up against my chest and let her cry. It's like a dam has burst, and every emotion she's been bottling up comes rushing out. Colby's worried, and Seb is confused, but I nod, knowing this is part of Ellie's healing process. She has a lot to let go of, and we have show her that between the three of us, we will create a safe space for her. We can't let her down. Not ever. Because if we do, there will be no going back.

Not even a dare could fix it.

23

ELLIE

For two weeks, while our parents are away, we live like we don't have a single care in the world. We camp out in the living room, bringing two huge mattresses from upstairs and creating a comfortable platform for us all to sleep.

I say sleep, but we hardly get any shuteye at all. By day fourteen, we're all bleary-eyed and slightly dazed, our bodies sore and our minds exhausted.

I've never felt like this before about anyone. When I'm between Colby, Sebastian, and Micky, I can't get close enough. I scratch at their skin, desperate for more contact, more weight on me, more hands holding me down, more huge cocks between my bruised thighs. They kiss me so deeply it's as though they're searching for some kind of answer and never quite finding it.

But they don't give up.

They never give up.

Only when I succumb to exhaustion, do they leave me to sleep.

Micky's dare hangs over us every moment we're together. It pushes aside all thoughts of my mom and their dad and what's happening to the structure of our family. It hangs over me when I watch the triplets sleep and it's there in the recesses of my mind when I'm going through the motions of attending class and spending time with my friends because any time I'm away from my boys, I miss them.

I miss them so badly.

I let them do things to me I never thought I'd let anyone do. They explore my body with their tongues, leaving no part untouched. There's no embarrassment when I'm letting go with one of them, and I know the other two are watching. Instead of shame, I've come alive through this crazy relationship we're building on a stupid dare.

It shouldn't be possible to feel so much about three men. I've never been capable of these kinds of feelings with even one man before. But the Townsend triplets own me, physically and mentally. I'm the most content, the most whole, when each of them is inside me at the same time. I'm like the sun that they orbit around. We move perfectly, like one being.

I lay against Colby's front, my face pressed into his chest, and his cock buried deep in my pussy. "Don't move," he whispers. "Just relax. Seb's going to handle everything." His hand strokes over the back of my head, my neck, and lower over my back, soothing all the tension from me. Seb slicks cool lube over my taint, massaging slowly until his thumb has slid inside me. This is the first real intrusion there, and just one digit feels huge. Colby must sense me tensing again, but he carries on his slow stroking motion, whispering for me to relax, that they've got me, that they'll never hurt me.

It's the last part that wraps around my heart and squeezes. I know in this context that he means physically, but I wish I could believe that he means emotionally, too.

Seb pushes in another digit, twisting slowly inside me , and I grunt, the sensation strange and weirdly arousing. I shift on Colby's dick, but he anchors me tightly against him.

"It's going to feel so good," he says softly. "Trust me."

I wish I could let go of the one percent of doubt that I always have, clouding every relationship I ever build. I wish my dad hadn't shown me that even the people who are supposed to be the most reliable and trustworthy in my life can let me down.

As Seb works me until I'm slick and ready to take him, Micky moves closer, his cock hard and ready.

Anticipation thrills up my spine.

This isn't the first time I'm going to take them all inside me at once. Although at first, it seemed like an impossible idea, I've taken Micky and Seb inside my pussy at the same time and Colby in my mouth. It was the first time in my life that I've ever felt truly whole.

And now. This just feels like the next step.

Seb's heavy hand rests at the bottom of my spine. "Ready, Ellie?"

"Yes," I whisper. Colby's arms wrap around me so tightly that he squeezes the breath from my lungs, but I love it. Here with these men, I feel like nothing in the universe can touch me.

The press of Seb's cock against my taint is weird. I wish I could see what he's seeing. The impossible sight of something so big trying to penetrate something so tight.

But it isn't impossible. With the weight of his body, he eases inside me, inch by perfect inch, and I groan like an animal in heat. Colby's body is rigid, and I realize why. He can feel every movement through just a thin barrier inside me. How he's holding himself together, I don't know.

"Nearly there," Seb says. His voice is so gruff and out of control.

When I feel his thighs against mine, I know he's done it. He's deep inside me.

"Slowly," Colby tells his brother, the warning clear.

I raise onto my palms, turning to Micky and looking into his hungry green eyes. "Ready?" I ask him.

With a nod, he shifts, sliding the head of his cock between my lips.

When Seb moves, my mind spins. I make a guttural and primal sound, and Micky's hand flies to my hair, gripping to slow my movements. The sight of what his brothers are doing to me is blowing his mind.

It's blowing mine, too, tripping switches I didn't know existed.

Colby stays still, letting Seb do the work, and I can feel how difficult it is for him to maintain his control by the fierce grip of his fingertips on the flesh of my ass.

"Fuck," Micky says as I gaze into his eyes, all my inhibitions and reservations sliding away. I never imagined I could be this person. I never believed I could be enough to satisfy even one man, let alone three. But I can feel each of them desperately trying to hold off their impending orgasms.

None of them will come until I've fallen over the precipice into sexual oblivion.

I know it's coming. As Seb mashes my pelvis against Colby's, my clit swells, and my pussy tightens.

"That's it," Colby says, shifting his hips for the first time. He nudges upwards, once, twice, three times, and I gasp around Micky.

"Fuck."

I lose control of my body, my head hanging as wave after wave of warm pleasure spills through me.

At that moment, I lose control of my mind too.

We can do this, I think. We really can. We can be this

perfect union of three men and one woman and show the world a new kind of love.

I can be enough.

I am enough.

They show me every day just how much I mean to them.

All doubt leaves me in the wake of bliss.

Seb's the first to come, his cock a deep, throbbing pulse inside me. Colby is next, rutting into my pussy as he loses all control at the end. Micky is last, showering my back and shoulders with his cum.

They tell me I'm beautiful. They clean me up as though I'm precious and worthy of their care.

The lay around me; a pride of content lions with me at the center, and everything feels good and right and infinitely possible.

Until the day our parents return.

Colby collects them from the airport while the rest of us clear away all evidence of our sordid activity. I restore the space that we filled with our laughter and happiness to the formal place designed by my mom to impress Harry's friends.

I spend too much time in my room, hiding from what I feel is already slipping through my fingers. Although the triplets are happy to keep everything secret, I don't know if I can live that way. Lying to my mom every day. Skulking around the house, pretending to be siblings again.

Wanting them.

Needing them.

Having to make do with stolen snippets of time that will never feel long enough. Risking discovery and never being able to fully relax.

These last fourteen days have spoiled me.

When Colby's vehicle pulls into the driveway, I stand in my window, staring out at mom, who's laughing and smiling, tanned and vibrant, and then at my stepfather, who looks younger and maybe like he's shifted a few pounds. Colby makes conversation, and helps with the bags, and when mom puts her key into the front door, it feels like a punctuation mark of sorts.

An end to one era and the start of another.

"Ellie, we're home," she calls up the stairs. I should be overwhelmed with a rush of happiness at her singsong tone and her desire to see me as soon as she steps through the door. I should celebrate the healing of our family, but everything is tangled and complex. The tiny green shoots of our relationship are so tender and easily trampled.

I make my way slowly down the stairs, inhaling deeply and fixing a smile on my face. Mom's eyes are bright as she catches sight of me, and when I step off at the bottom, she tugs me into a tight, warm hug. "There she is," she says. "You've all grown up while we've been away."

"What do you mean?" I ask as she scans my face.

"I don't know. I just got a feeling from Colby, and now I'm getting a feeling from you. Maybe it's because you've all had to take care of yourselves this week. You've turned into adults while we've been on vacation."

My traitorous cheeks heat, recalling all the eighteen-plus activities that have taken place in this house. If the walls could talk, they'd be spilling erotic tales that would have made Hugh Hefner blush.

"You're so tan," I say, hoping to change the subject by moving the direction of the conversation onto her. My plan works as mom tells us all about the amazing place they stayed and all the delicious food they ate. It's as though they had a second honeymoon rather than a trip to reconcile after adultery.

Colby stands with his shoulder resting against the wall,

watching with as much discomfort as I'm feeling clear on his face. Seb babbles with questions, making mom laugh as usual. Micky's baked a cake which mom doesn't stop gushing about and we all drink coffee and sit around the long hardwood table in the kitchen, talking like nothing has changed.

But everything has.

My fingers tingle with the memory of touching my stepbrothers' skin. My tongue remembers their taste. Between my legs, I'm swollen and wet at the memory of how many times they've made me come.

I avoid looking at them because I'm like Pavlov's dog. Our eyes meet and my body primes for sex immediately.

When we've devoured half the cake, and mom has stacked the plates and cups into the dishwasher, I make my excuses and head up to my room.

My bed feels different; the mattress harder, and the comforter cooler than I remember. It's as though my room has shut down through the lack of an inhabitant. Or maybe I've just gotten used to being surrounded by so much strength and warmth that existing in my space is no longer comfortable or familiar.

Rather than waste time feeling lost without the Colby, Seb, and Micky, I get my head down and study, trying desperately to keep my thoughts engaged on work rather than the three men in this house who make me weak with desire. When it's time for dinner, I ask mom if I can eat it in my room, so I don't get behind, and in her excellent mood, nothing is too much trouble.

At eleven pm, there's a knock on my bedroom door, and when I tell whoever it is to come in, the door opens, and mom appears. "You're working hard, sweetie. I'm so proud of you."

They're words I've been desperate to hear for so long, but now they feel tainted with the creeping guilt of my lies.

"Thanks, Mom," I whisper, already imagining the change in her expression and attitude if she eventually discovers the truth.

"Are you going to sleep soon?"

"Another five minutes," I say.

Padding across my cream carpet, she rests a hand on my shoulder. On my shelf, there's a photo of us all on vacation two years ago that mom framed for me, as though the forced smiles we were all wearing could convince me we were a happy family. I look up at her and find her smiling strangely.

"Life is funny, isn't it?"

"I guess," I say, unsure where she intends to go with her statement.

"One minute, everything is fine. The next, you feel the world has been torn out from under your feet."

"I'm sorry about what happened," I say.

She squeezes my shoulder. "So is Harry. I didn't believe it at first, but I've never seen that man so humble. Everything feels different."

"Different good?"

She nods, squeezing my shoulder again. "I was worried about what kind of message I'd send if I accepted his apology and believed his regret. I don't want you to think his behavior is acceptable. But then I thought about the message of forgiveness and trying hard to make love work." She shrugs, and I understand why. Life isn't black and white, even though I try to make it that way. "Sometimes, we're hit with a curveball, and we have to decide if a relationship is worth fighting for. This one is, but that doesn't mean all of them will be."

I know she doesn't know about my feelings for her stepsons, but her words still feel strategically placed to make me feel bad.

How can anyone be sure which relationships are worth fighting for?

Is it a feeling? Does it come from having self-confidence? Whatever it is, I'm missing it.

"It's okay, Mom. I understand. Live your life for you." Do I even believe what I'm saying? It's certainly not how I've acted these past few weeks—hiding from myself and my feelings—hiding from our relationship and the implications it will have for others. Why is it so easy to give others advice that I would never give myself?

"I'm living it for you, too," she says. "This home, you, and the boys. You all deserve stability and parents who are around to support you."

The sinking feeling that's been weighing in my stomach from the morning plummets another ten feet. "We're almost grown, Mom."

"You are," she says softly. "You know, one of my biggest regrets was always that I hadn't given you a brother or sister to keep you company in life. Then I met Harry, and suddenly, there were three amazing big brothers to look out for you."

Amazing big brothers?

Amazing big brothers don't lick the places the Townsend triplets have licked. They don't slide inside you while holding your throat and tell you what a good girl you are. They don't spank your ass and make you gag on their cocks. They don't touch you like you're invincible and fragile and precious, all at the same time.

No, mom might have wanted to give me big brothers, but what she's given me is three huge live-in boyfriends. If she knew, she'd be horrified.

Disgusted.

Furious.

There's a thesaurus of words to describe my mom's potential disappointment.

"I'd better get some rest," I say, not wanting to risk hearing any more emotional platitudes.

Mom leaves after placing a kiss on the top of my head like she did when I was young, and I have to swallow four times to get rid of the lump in my throat.

Even though it's late, I shower, and when I've brushed my hair and covered my skin with cream, I slip between the cool sheets to sleep alone for the first time in a week.

I'm not alone for long.

24

ELLIE

Micky comes to me first, waking me with soft kisses on the back of my neck and his big warm hand resting against my belly. He makes a gentle shushing sound in my ear when I stir, tugging me back against the hard bar of his cock.

Giving into him is foolish.

The risk that I bowed to the first time we were together now feels magnified by a thousand. But I can't resist the slow stroke of his finger over my clit or the way he slides it inside me, testing how wet I am. He's so quick at rolling on a condom, and by the time he pushes into me from behind, I'm slick and open and ready. Biting my lip is the only way I can keep from crying out. It's so hot beneath the covers, but neither of us throws them off for fear of being naked and exposed. My mind goes to the possibility of being discovered by his father or my mother and the small chance I would be able to hide him beneath my comforter.

Stupid risks.

Amazing sex.

We rock together as though we've been dancing this

way for years. Everything between us is soft and fluid, urgent and beautiful.

I pull his hand to my face and take his thumb into my mouth, missing the multiple penetrations I've become used to so quickly. He realizes what I need immediately, sliding his other thumb between the cheeks of my ass and pushing against my taint with an alternating rhythm to his thrusts.

"Micky," I whisper softly against his thumb. "Seb, Colby." I'm used to all their names tumbling from my mouth before I come, and tonight is no different.

When I surrender to the orgasm, it's liquid and beautiful, slick, and black as oil, bright as the morning sun. Clenching around Micky, I want to draw him in so that our bodies never part.

A tear leaks from the corner of my eye, trickling over my temple and into my messy hair. I'm grateful that in the dark, Micky can't see how emotional I am.

He comes so quietly; I wouldn't have known, but for the swelling and pulsing of his cock. He's quick to pull out and clean up, kissing my neck and across the back of my shoulders.

I love you, dances in my mind but never makes it to my tongue because even just the fleeting thought makes me seize with fear.

Love isn't easy. It isn't kind. It doesn't care what mess it makes after. It's selfish and hurtful, filled with betrayal and loss. I don't want it to split my heart open like an overripe fruit.

"I'm going to go," Micky whispers, "just in case."

"Okay," I say softly. "Night."

One last lingering kiss before he leaves.

Three seconds of hesitation while he scans my face, looking for answers I'm not ready to provide, not sure enough to declare the truth for himself.

I love you.

It's in the tentative graze of his fingers over my cheek. It's in the softness of his green eyes which rest on me in the darkness.

He leaves and takes a piece of my heart with him.

Ten minutes pass, and I'm still awake when my door creaks again.

I don't turn to find out which of the brothers is calling on me next, but I know as soon as Colby grips my hip with his big, demanding hand that it's him.

"Did Micky warm you up?" he asks, letting his hand drift over my belly and breasts, seeking all the softness that I've come to realize he likes so much.

"Yes," I breathe, grateful that he's going to focus on the physical.

"Is your pussy wet?"

Oh god, the rumble of his voice and the warmth of his breath against my ear send a static rush of nerves up my neck and over my scalp.

"So wet." Just the way he likes it.

"That's good." Colby makes a low hum, like a cat purring with contentment, when he discovers it for himself. Thick fingers find out just how messy I am between my thighs. Clever fingers sheath his cock in record time. When he tries to turn me, I push my ass into him, hoping my veiled demand will be enough. I know I couldn't look at him without crying.

The first thrust of his huge cock burns despite how lubricated I am, but I've grown used to the feeling now. There's an element of violation that comes with fucking men who are this hung. An aspect that I know I won't ever be able to do without.

Colby rolls over me so that my body is almost face

down, and his big, muscular frame spreads out on top of me. It's hard to breathe this way, but it's fine. The more of his power I feel, the less I remember all the reasons we shouldn't be acting this way.

"You feel so good," he says, nipping the soft flesh between my neck and shoulder with his teeth and then using his tongue to soothe.

"You're so big," I say, gaining a growl in response.

With one hand, Colby grips my hair, tugging my face from the pillow. My scalp burns, and so do my cheeks, as he shoves his thumb into my mouth. I don't suck it as I did with Micky because that isn't what Colby wants. When I bite down, he shoves it deeper, pressing down the back of my tongue, and I know he remembers what it feels like when I swallow against the head of his cock. Maybe he's even remembering how it looks to watch his brothers pushing their cocks between my lips.

Once last week, they all stood in front of me, and I kneeled, moving between them, letting them use my mouth until I was a mess of their cum, and they were staring down at me, wide-eyed, as though they were struggling to reconcile the woman at their feet with the stepsister they'd practically grown up with.

Tonight, I come just from the stretch of Colby's cock and the thoughts that swell and travel like flames through my mind, biting down on his thumb and twitching against him, my body more out of control than it's ever been. And he follows, tightening his grip on my hair, seizing like lightning has struck him dead.

It's less about pleasure and more about exorcising our demons. I know Colby is as twisted up inside about this as me. I know the guilt about our lying to our parents is eating at him more than the others. It's because he doesn't want to be a disappointment. I see that part of him clearly because I'm exactly the same. Twisted up by expectations. Racked with self-reproach.

When we've both returned to our senses, Colby once again tries to roll me to my back, but I resist.

He pauses for a few moments as though there are questions on the tip of his tongue, but unlike his usually demanding self, he resists asking.

Does he suspect he won't like the answers? Probably.

Instead, he does what Micky did, kissing my neck, telling me I'm beautiful, reminding me that what we have is worth the risk, and trying to convince himself.

And I don't disagree.

But I don't agree either.

I love you, I think, but the words die in the warm cavern of my mouth, snuffed out by guilt and dread of what it will feel like to lose him.

Seb is the last to find his way to my room. I wonder if they drew straws or flipped a coin to decide the order. Have they worked out a schedule with times so that they don't cross paths, or is it their intention to come to me all at once sometimes? What would that look like, three huge men tiptoeing across the hall, sneaking into their stepsister's room?

It would look guilty. That's what it would look like.

Seb doesn't slide between my sheets in the way the others did. He walks around to the side of the bed I'm pretending to sleep on and kneels in front of me. His fingers graze my cheek, playing with my curls. His mouth whispers my name.

"Ellie, I know you're awake," he says.

I open my eyes slowly, finding him smiling at me in the dark.

"You know how I know?" he asks. "Because you breathe differently when you're really asleep."

I smile fleetingly. "Have you been perving over me

while I've been unconscious?"

"Definitely," he says. "You have no idea how sexy you look with your naked body splayed across my sheets and your mouth wide open." Chuckling, he grabs my hand when I try to swat his shoulder. The weight of feelings that have had me close to tears all night lift with his smile.

"I do not sleep with my mouth open," I whisper.

"Errr…you do," he grins, "but don't worry. I've got something meaty to put in that mouth."

"Gross." I screw up my nose, the image of his cock replaced with a thick red salami, and Seb laughs silently.

"That's not what you were saying the other day." He's got me there. "So, have my brothers worn out you, or do you still have some sexy-time energy left for me?"

"Definitely worn out," I say, but I lift the covers and scoot back across the sheets.

Seb kisses me deeply, and I surrender to everything he wants to do because it feels so right, even in all its wrongness. He spends time kissing across my clavicle, then lower, taking each nipple into his mouth and biting just perfectly to make me squirm. He sucks, kneading my breasts in a way that makes it seem like he seeks comfort in them as well as pleasure. Between my legs, my sensitized clit swells, ready for more.

My traitorous body that never reached a climax with anyone before Colby, Micky, and Seb, now stirs for their touch like an addict. Even when I should be spent, I'm not.

When Seb fucks me, he hooks his arm beneath my neck and holds me close to his chest. He whispers in my ear, telling me how good I make him feel. I grip his back, using my fingers to urge his thrusts, angling my hips to seek the perfect friction.

It feels like forever and no time at all, as though the clock in my room is spinning back and forth. My whole being is becoming confused by the pull and push of the universe and Sebastian.

I keep my eyes closed to the growing light in the room and the knowledge that it's nearly morning. I let Seb find his release inside me, and I shudder my own in his arms.

"You need to go," I tell him when I'm sure he has regained enough strength to walk. Seb makes a soft groaning sound, but he draws away, pressing a butterfly kiss to the end of my nose.

"One day, we won't have to do this," he whispers. "Just remember that, Ellie. There will come a time when we will be free to be with each other without worrying about what anyone else thinks."

I nod, but my heart doubts it all.

Because where my stepbrothers are hopeful, I'm a jaded realist.

I love you, bubbles inside me for Seb too. But what's the point of admitting it when I know my mom and their dad, and there will be no overcoming the fallout that would occur if we ever gave light to our secrets.

When Seb closes the door, I curl into my mattress, burying my face into the pillow. I try to find sleep, but there are too many thoughts buzzing around in my mind, too many reasons for slumber to remain a stranger.

After a while, I sit up to sip some water and feel a strange hollowness in my stomach. It's more than hunger. More than sadness. The water sits, cool and present beneath my ribs. Not quite right. My mouth fills with saliva, but I swallow it and lay back down, determined not to allow all of my anxieties about our situation to take control.

I sleep for an hour before my alarm rings, and when I sit up to switch it off, my stomach rolls, but this time, I have to run for the bathroom.

25

COLBY

The retching noise coming from the bathroom is loud enough to wake me. Rubbing my eyes, I open them wide enough to check the clock on my nightstand.

It's early, but not ridiculously so.

More retching.

I slide my legs from beneath the sheet and sit for a couple of seconds, trying to get my bearings. Then I follow the noise and find Ellie hunched over the toilet, her back heaving.

Shit.

I kneel next to her just as Micky's door opens.

"Ellie. Are you okay?" I ask.

"Stupid question, Colb," she says, retching and spitting again.

"Yeah. I guess it is," I admit, shifting to relieve the pain from my knees on the tiled floor.

"Shall I get her some water?" Micky asks from behind.

"Yeah and close the door."

Micky pulls the door toward him and disappears down

the hall, his quiet footsteps disappearing in the shadowed hallway.

"What the hell did you eat last night?" I stroke Ellie's damp her hair back from her clammy forehead.

"Same as you," she mumbles.

"And in the day?"

"Toast in the morning. I skipped lunch."

Frowning, I grab a washcloth from the vanity and stretch to wet it beneath the faucet.

When I press it to Ellie's forehead, she sighs.

"Must be a bug, then."

Ellie sits back, clutching the flannel to her forehead. Her eyes look up to the left, and her brow draws into a perplexed v.

"What is it?"

When her mouth drops open, and her hand lowers from her forehead, I lean forward, worrying she's going to be sick again. She shoves my shoulder, scrambling into a standing position and bending at the waist.

"What the hell, Ellie." I'm on my feet in a flash, worrying she's delirious and might be on the verge of fainting.

"I'm late, Colby," she hisses.

I glance at my watch, wondering what the fuck she's talking about. It's the ass crack of dawn. There's no way she needs to be in college at this ungodly hour.

"Not that kind of late. LATE." She points at her stomach, and that's when it hits me.

The night at Molly's Motel. The broken condom. The vomiting.

Fuck.

I feel like I need to hold on to something: the vanity, the toilet, the wall. Ellie.

My heart is in my throat, beating with a racing urgency that feels strange enough to make me woozy. But I can't be woozy right now. I have to consider Ellie and what she's feeling. It's my duty to give her what she needs.

"Get dressed," I say quickly, thinking rapidly about what we need to do next. "I'll meet you outside. We'll go to the store and buy a test."

Ellie nods, straightening and looking around the bathroom, her expression confused. I rest my hand on her arm. "Don't worry. Whatever the result is, I'm by your side through everything. Do you understand?"

She nods and blows out a long breath, her dark eyes closing. Whether she wants to shut me out or just hide from the reality of the situation we could be about to face, I don't know.

"Five minutes," I say, waiting for her to breathe and open her eyes before accompanying her to the door.

As she disappears into her room and shuts it quietly, Micky returns with the water. "Where is she?" he says, glancing around the empty bathroom.

"We need to go to the store," I say. "I'll talk to you and Seb when we get back. If dad or Lara asks anything, just say we popped out for last-minute supplies for a presentation."

"What kind of supplies?" he asks.

"I don't know. Make it up."

I brush past, planning what I need to do; find my black joggers, sneakers, and shirt; dress; sort out my messy hair; grab my keys, phone, and card; make it down the stairs without bumping into anyone.

Ellie's already by the door, waiting. We exit the house in silence, head over to my car without discussion, and make it halfway to the store before either of us says a word. My mind is a tangle of thoughts and feelings, panic, and excitement.

Is it stupid that I feel excited about the possibility of Ellie being pregnant with my child?

I glance over at her, finding her fingers clutching her purse so tightly her knuckles are white. She looks so adorable in her cream sweater and joggers set with her hair tied into a messy bun. I just want to pull her into my lap and kiss the fuck out of her.

"Are you still nauseous?" I ask eventually. "You can open the window if you need fresh air?"

"I'm okay," she says.

"I have water." Tugging open the glove box, I grab a bottle and hand it to Ellie. She takes it and sips it slowly.

"My mouth tastes horrible," she whispers.

"Drink a little. Not too much in case it makes you feel worse."

I tap my fingers on the steering wheel, the buzzing in my body needing an outlet. The closest store that's open this early is still another five minutes away.

Ellie lowers the bottle from her lips and stares out of the window blankly. Just a few hours ago, we were as intimate as two people can be, but now I feel like I'm a million miles away from her with a wall as tall as the sky between us. I wish I was better at understanding what she needs from me. I wish I had the empathy that Micky has or the ability to make her laugh like Seb. Sometimes, I feel a few steps outside the connection that the four of us have, a little less anchored by our relationship. But I can't let that affect how I deal with this situation. I know that what happens in the next few minutes could be remembered forever.

"There's a bathroom in this store. I think you should take the test there rather than at home."

"Okay." Ellie keeps her gaze fixed on the street and her grip tight on the water bottle.

I grit my teeth, imagining what it's going to be like to

go into the store and buy a pregnancy test. This isn't something I've ever even thought about doing, but I won't leave it to Ellie to make the transaction. I'm not sure she could do it without breaking down.

When we arrive at the store parking lot, I find a vacant space as close to the main entrance as I can. Jumping out of the car, I jog around to Ellie's side to open for her, but she's already halfway out when I get there. Her eyes seem a little bloodshot, but I haven't seen her cry.

My hand itches to reach out for her, to grasp her hand or hold her around her shoulders. I just want her close and for her to feel my steading presence. But she hugs her arms around herself like a shield, and I know she doesn't want to me to touch her. If nothing else, I've learned Ellie's body language well over the past few years.

"Come on," I say, locking the car.

We walk side by side, blinded by the low sun appearing behind the hulking store building. Ellie holds her hand up to shield her eyes, but I focus on the door.

There's a chance, a very big chance, that I'm going to walk through this door as one kind of man and out of it another kind entirely. I'm an overgrown kid now, still living under our parent's roof without responsibility for anything other than myself and getting decent enough grades to make something of my life.

If Ellie's pregnant, I'm going to walk out of here a man with people depending on me.

A woman and a child. My woman and child.

The automatic door whooshes open, and we pass through into the frigid, air-conditioned building. Ellie immediately shivers. "The pharmacy is over here," I say, pointing at the sign. We make our way past the vast displays of soda and chips that are on offer. The store is quiet, and large stacks of goods wait to be unloaded from steel cages.

The pregnancy tests are in the same aisle as the over-the-counter medicine and supplements; somehow, that doesn't seem right. It's not a treatment. It's not for sale to fix an illness.

Grabbing the smallest box, I check Ellie's expression.

She's still clutching her purse like it's stuffed with bullion.

We make our way to the nearest register, and Ellie hangs back while I take care of everything. After, I walk ahead, leading her to the restrooms where we'll learn the truth.

I wish I could go in with her. I want to stand outside the stall so that she can feel my presence, but I'm confident that other women using the facilities wouldn't welcome it.

Holding the door open, I try to come up with something reassuring to say, but I'm lost for words. This feels momentous. Ellie looks into my eyes as she passes, and I hope she sees reassurance rather than fear.

When the door shuts behind her, I press my back against the wall and close my eyes, but not for long. I glance at my watch, working out how long it'll be before I should expect her to come out. Waiting isn't something I'm good at. Patience is not my virtue.

I pace for the first minute, knowing she's probably unwrapped the package and maybe peed on the stick by now. The test we chose provides results in two minutes.

Two fucking minutes. Can't they produce a test that works faster?

After a minute, the door squeaks open behind me, and I whirl to find Ellie, eyes wide. "Are you okay? Did you do the test?"

She holds out the white plastic stick to me, her face strained. "I couldn't wait in there alone. I just couldn't. There's another minute to go."

We stare at each other for a second, like two people about to engage in a duel. Then, I decide I don't give a fuck about how defensive Ellie's body language is. I need her close to me. I need her to feel how much I love her.

Love is such a tiny word, but it holds the greatest significance.

I've denied the depth of my feelings for this girl for so long because they weren't reciprocated, and maybe they're still not, but I don't care anymore.

When I throw my arm around Ellie's slight frame, she's rigid for a second, but then collapses into my chest. I hold her close, whispering that everything's going to be fine because I believe it will be. She's the girl I love, and we may or may not be having a child. Our circumstances aren't the easiest, but people have gone through a lot worse.

Seconds pass, but it's like we're wading through water as time slows by the magnitude of the result we're waiting for.

"Is it ready?" she asks softly.

Looking at my watch, I calculate there are another thirty seconds. "Not long now," I murmur against her strawberry-scented hair.

A tired-looking man dressed in a security uniform passes us, staring at the odd picture we make. He disappears into the men's restroom, and then we're alone again. I should look now. I should be brave enough to find out, but I wait another ten seconds just to be sure. Then, with the girl I love curled in my arms, her face pressed to my heart, I finally raise the pregnancy test so I can see the result.

It's positive.

My heart skitters and then thuds, racing too fast and then pausing with the momentousness of the result.

"It's positive, isn't it?" Ellie says without raising her

head. "I can tell. You went really still."

"It's positive, honey," I say.

"What are we going to do?" she whispers softly.

"We're going to get in the car and go home, and then we're going to talk to Seb and Micky about what you want to do next. But I need you to know that whatever you decide, you're our girl. We'll always be next to you through thick and thin."

Her body trembles in my arms, and I worry that she's going to cry, but instead, she draws back, looking up and searching my face.

I don't know if she finds what she's looking for in my expression, but when she turns to head out of the door, she reaches for my hand instead of walking alone.

26

ELLIE

How can I have a baby when I'm at college? How will it even work?

My hands tremble as I pull the seatbelt across my body, but before I can even think about anything else, Colby takes my other hand in his.

"You're shaking," he says. "Just take a deep breath."

I inhale slowly, closing my eyes. When I swallow, my stomach feels hollow and a little sick.

"How?" I say, even though it's obvious what's gotten us into this situation. "It was only once."

"Once is all it takes." The comment could have sounded grim, but it doesn't. There's a lightness to Colby's voice that I don't understand.

"Why do you sound happy about it?" I say, twisting to watch him as he reverses the car out of the parking space.

"Just do me a favor and listen," he says, keeping his gaze fixed on the road. "I want you to close your eyes and imagine our parents are happy when they find out. Your friends are throwing a baby shower. We're picking out a crib and lots of tiny clothes. The three of us are there to support you and help with everything."

I try to create pictures in my head of my mom's smiling face. She's holding up a cute outfit with a bear on the front. Dornan is there with a baby bath, and Micky and Seb are working out how to assemble the white wooden crib. Colby has his arms wrapped around me and his hand resting on my swollen belly.

And instead of a sinking feeling of sickness in my stomach, I feel happy. Contented. Relieved.

"See," he says. When I open my eyes, he's smiling at me. "You feel it too. You're just dwelling on the worry about what people will think and how they'll react. You're stressing about facing the future alone, but you don't have to."

"Colby, you don't have to stay with me because of the baby," I say, even though deep down, it's the exact opposite of what I want.

His brow lowers, and his hands flex on the wheel. "Ellie. You are so fucking stubborn, you know that? Why won't you accept how we feel about you? Why do you always want to push us away? Don't you know we wanted a future with you before this morning? You've been acting like you can't wait to get rid of us now that our parents are home."

My heart skitters, and I place my hand over it, blinking against tears that threaten to spill. I don't know why I find it so hard to hear his claims about his feelings or why I can't ever accept them to be more than just words. My heart longs for the picture that Colby painted, a future where everything is happy and filled with love.

But the problem in the picture isn't everyone else.

It's me.

It doesn't matter how hard I try; I never feel as though I belong at the center of the happiness he's suggesting is within my grasp. I'm on the outside. The black sheep. The little girl who wasn't brave enough. The one whose father left and never looked back.

"I just need to go home," I say. "I need some time to myself. I don't even know what I'm thinking or how I'm feeling."

Colby clears his throat, and I know he's frustrated. I can feel the tenseness of his body sitting so near to mine. He's near, but still feels so far away.

"Just promise me you won't shut us out," he says, his voice gentler than I've ever heard it.

"I promise." The words pass uncomfortably from my lips because I don't know what it will take for me to mean them.

Back at the house, I disappear into my room and lock the door. I have classes to prepare for, but I can't face anyone. How do I listen to people rambling on about things that seemed important and vital yesterday but are now totally irrelevant to my life?

When it's time for the boys to leave, they knock on my door.

I take a deep breath to steel myself to open it. Facing them when I feel so lost and confused is hard. I trust Colby has shared our joyful news. How his brothers have reacted isn't something I can predict.

When I tug the door open, they're all there, faces a little grave, eyes worried.

"Are you feeling okay?" Colby asks, looking at the sloth pajamas I've thrown on.

"No," I say. "I'm not going in today. Can you tell my mom I'm ill and resting?"

"Of course," Micky says.

"We won't be back too late," Seb adds. "Just message us if you need anything. We can be back in less than twenty minutes."

"I'll be fine," I say, even as I want to rest my hand on my belly and tremble at the prospect of the life growing inside me.

"Okay. We'll talk later," Colby says, shifting uncomfortably. "We'll make a plan together."

Of course, that's what he'd want to do. Colby can't cope without everything being set out in an orderly way that he can manage. Life isn't like that, though. It's messy and filled with curve balls that smack you on the side of the head when you are least expecting them.

Hasn't he realized that? He plays enough football.

"Sure."

My hand is on the doorknob, ready to shut them out, but Micky puts his foot in front. The memory of Colby doing the same thing the day after our seven minutes in heaven almost knocks me off my feet. So many events connected like a chain have brought us to this place. "We will talk later, Ellie, because we're a team now, and that's how teams work."

A team? Team fucking disaster.

"Sure," I say again, and this time, they allow me to close the door.

Mom appears seconds later with an offer of chicken soup that makes me want to hurl all over her feet. I shouldn't be ungrateful but having anyone in my space right now is invasive.

After a few hours, Dornan calls me, and it's only when I see his name emblazoned across the phone screen, I remember we were supposed to meet. Shit. I hate letting friends down, but I can't face hearing his jolly voice right now, even if it's just for long enough for me to make excuses.

I go for most of the day, curled up in a ball on my bed, hiding under my favorite blue spotted fleece blanket, staring at the wall. Nausea comes and goes, but with a few sips of water, I manage to get through it without needing to use the bathroom. I don't notice time passing until shadows creep across my room, and I hear the rumble of Colby's car outside and their footsteps when they enter the house.

They're going to want to talk, but I don't know what to say. I don't know how I feel. I don't know what to do.

I'm a kid. A glorified child whose mom still washes her underwear. What the fuck do I know about raising another human being? I'm not even raising myself yet. And the three men who want to be my support are glorified kids, too. What the hell kind of parents could we make?

Well, Micky would be really caring. He'd know all the baby's distinct cries and be able to tell exactly what they need to be content. He'd be the best at getting them to sleep.

And Seb would be the fun dad. He'd make up silly rhymes and be the first to hear the baby's laugh. He'd be able to diffuse tantrums and turn everyone's frown upside down.

Colby would be outstanding at keeping track of milestones and knowing what activities our baby would need to thrive. He'd have their college fund set up before they're born and have them reciting their ABCs and 123s before any other kids the same age.

Really, now I think about it, they'd be awesome fathers in all the ways that count. They've already shown the men they are with all their voluntary work and the way they're so responsible within the family.

It's me I can't picture within any of that. It's me who has no substance.

They'd be great fathers, and I'd be a terrible mother.

Would they have to dare me through every decision just to keep me moving? I'm a shambles. A person with no backbone. Someone who needs a sharp object placed at the small of their back to do anything.

When there's a knock at the door, I tell them to come in, and they all lumber into my dark room, scanning for me until they see my pathetic curled shape on the bed.

"Ellie." Micky is the first to reach my side, his face drawn with worry as he kneels in front of me. His hand presses against my forehead, and he looks up at Colby and Seb, who stand behind him.

"She's not hot."

"I'm fine," I say. "Just tired and sick."

"That's totally normal," Micky whispers. "I've done some research today. This stage of pregnancy can be tough, but it rarely lasts more than a couple of months."

"Months?" I gasp. "Are you serious?"

"Dry crackers and cookies with ginger will make you feel better," he says. Of course, Micky would know that. Of course, he'd be the first to find out the things that would help.

"We need to tell our parents," Colby says out of nowhere.

"Not now," Seb says quickly. "Ellie needs time. There's no rush."

"There's a rush," Colby says. "There's no hiding what's coming."

"If it's coming," I snap.

Silence falls like a thick winter blanket over the room, spreading inside me like poison. It's my right to choose what I want to do. Of that, I'm certain. But I don't want to hurt these men who are trying their best to be what I need. I don't want to be cruel.

At the same time, I'm unsure how to express what I'm feeling, and I don't know what I want.

Well, I do. I want to go back to that night at Molly's, to

the moment before I left this house. I want to undo everything that's happened so I can go back to being the Ellie at Dornan's party who didn't have a care in the world.

But at the same time, that would mean never knowing how it felt to rest in their arms, to never know the warmth and strength of their presence in my life. It would mean never discovering the person I am with them.

Alive.

Fearless.

Carefree.

Our lives are like a rope of experiences, all woven and tangled together. We can't pull out just one to discard it without changing everything that comes after. Even though it's hard to accept, I get it too.

We walk forward.

That's all we can do.

And I have to find the strength to face what's happening to me and do what needs to be done. I have to, but finding the courage and strength is another matter.

Micky's hand rests on my shoulder. "Take your time, Ellie. Work out what it is you want to do. Work out what you need from us. Let's keep talking, okay?" Then he does something that makes all the bottled-up feelings spill over. He kisses me with all the sweetness that he has inside him, and suddenly, I'm crying. In seconds, the three of them are around me, holding me and kissing me wherever they can find space.

It's so risky when we could get caught at any moment, but in my time of distress, none of us has any care of the risks. This pregnancy has put a different perspective on everything that I thought was important. It's as though my lens has been shattered, and all I can see are the parts and pieces of my past concerns and hopes.

Colby's hand touches my belly, and I flinch, but he

doesn't pull away, and the warmth of his hand sends a flush through me.

We stay like that for minutes that feel like hours, and in the cradle of their arms, I feel more like myself again. But then mom calls us down for dinner and breaks our secret world of security and peace once more.

For three days, I stay in bed. On day two, Seb encourages me to shower. Micky brings me toast with butter and cool ginger tea to sip. Colby waits by the door like a worried parent. On day three, Micky's the one who takes my hand and leads me to the bathroom, and when I come back, I find my bed stripped and remade.

Mom floats around during the day. She makes the soup and insists I take a few sips, but it only makes me feel more nauseous. Her hands flutter as I stare grimly at her from my pillow.

I can't tell her why, though. I can't share what's going on because I don't want to shatter her fragile happiness.

On the evening of the fourth day, after avoiding phone calls from all my friends, an unfamiliar-sounding car pulls up outside the house, and the doorbell rings.

Voices sound in the hall, but not loud enough for me to make out who it is. Footsteps start up the stairs, and mom calls through the door, "Ellie, Dornan, Gabriella, and Celine are here. Shall I let them in?"

I scramble out of bed, catching sight of my wild hair and pale face in the mirror. At least my PJs and sheets are clean, but I still feel as though my room smells of sickness.

You're not ill, I remind myself.

"Err…, just give me a minute."

Grabbing a clip, I twist my hair and pin it on the back of my head. I quickly use a cleansing wipe to freshen up my face and throw open my window, letting the cool night air spill into the room.

I feel fine, which makes my past three days of isolation

seem very self-indulgent.

I open the door a crack and see four worried faces peering in. Dornan doesn't give me a chance to say come in. He approaches so quickly that I'm forced to whip the door open wide enough to let him pass. Celine and Gabriella troop in behind him.

"You're looking better," mom says, smiling but uncertain.

"Thanks." She leaves, but not without a backward glance to check all is right.

My room could certainly be tidier, but that isn't what my friends have come over to talk about.

When I perch on the mattress, Dornan glances at the still-open door and strides over to close it.

"What's going on, Ellie?" he demands.

"Nothing," I say, hating that I have to keep secrets from him.

"Don't lie to me," he says, sitting next to me. The mattress bows beneath his weight, and my thigh rests against him, reminding me of how solid his presence has always been in my life. "You would have answered the phone if that was all it was. I know you, don't forget. This isn't you. There's something bigger going on, and I want to know."

"You don't," I whisper, keeping my eyes focused on the floor by Celine's feet.

"Did you break up with the triplets? Is that what it is?" Gabriella asks, chewing her gum.

"No," I say.

"Then what?" Dornan presses. His hand finds mine and tugs it into his lap, squeezing tightly. "Tell me, so I know what to do to help you. That's what friendship is all about, Ellie. Sharing our troubles."

"I can't," I say.

"Of course you can," Celine says. "Maybe you just don't want to."

"What could it be that you don't want to share with me?" Dornan sounds so hurt that I want to cry. When I glance up at Celine, her eyes are narrowed. She looks over at my nightstand, finding a packet of crackers and a half-finished cup of ginger tea. Reaching out for the mug, she takes a long inhale.

"Ginger," she says knowingly, and my eyes widen with realization. Celine's older sister has just had a baby. She went through awful morning sickness, which Celine knows all about.

I see the moment that the cogs in Celine's sharp brain click into place. "You're pregnant," she says, confirming my fear.

Dornan's and Gabriella's heads snap to stare at me, and I bury my face in my hands.

"Fuck," Dornan says. "It's true?"

"Of course it is," Celine says. "I'm not an idiot."

"How?" Dornan asks, earning a scoff from Celine.

"She rode the big pipe a little too enthusiastically."

I want to laugh like I usually do when Celine employs her filthy humor, but none of this is funny.

"Ellie?" The look on Dornan's face seems a lot like disappointment, and for the millionth time today, I start to cry.

"Fuck." Rather than hugging me like I expect him to, he stands. I stare up at my friend, watery-eyed and devastated, as he raises his hands to his head and grips his hair. "Fuck. This is all my fault."

"Dornan…" I don't get the chance to finish my sentence before he storms to the door, yanks it open and disappears.

"Oh, this isn't good," Gabriella says, skipping after

him, closely followed by Celine. I leap up as soon as I realize what's going to happen, but I'm too late to stop anything. Before I reach the bedroom door, Dornan is yelling. It sounds like Colby is yelling back, and then Gabriella and Celine join in, and there are too many voices to hear anything other than the colossal mess that will have my mom and Harry storming up the stairs.

"SHUT UP," I yell as loud as I can. "ALL OF YOU…"

But it's too late. Mom appears behind Dornan with Harry next to her. And when enough people notice, the noise reduces until an uneasy silence settles over the group. Celine's eyes are wide, flitting between my mom and me.

"What is going on up here?" Harry's voice is stern, and his expression matches it exactly.

Dornan, who is still holding a handful of Colby's shirt, takes a step back.

"I think you need to leave," Harry says, stepping forward to get closer to his son. Colby puts his hand up, though, and the look on his face tells me everything. He doesn't want Dornan to get in trouble for being protective of me. He understands, but this isn't the time to talk, not with our parents here.

"It's okay," I say quickly, moving closer and resting my hand on Dornan's arm.

"It isn't okay," Dornan says, shaking Colby by the shirt. "I trusted you. I told you to look after her. How the fuck is getting her pregnant looking after her?"

"Pregnant," Harry says. "Who's pregnant? Colby, have you gotten someone into trouble?"

I want to laugh at the turn of phrase because what fucking decade are we living in?

"We don't need to talk about this now," I say. "Not with an audience."

Dornan's eyes are blazing, and I know he's too far gone

to hear what I'm trying to say. He's gone into full-blown protection mode. "Just explain to me how this has happened, Colby?" He turns, finding Seb and Micky walking slowly from their rooms towards the disturbance. "And you. And you…tell me how you've gotten Ellie into this situation."

"DORNAN," I shout, grabbing his arm, desperate for him to hear me.

"Ellie?" Mom says. "What situation?"

Dornan's face is flushed and tense, veins bulging at his temples. I've never seen him enraged to where he's lost all concept of what's happening around him. "SHE'S PREGNANT," he yells, shoving Colby again. "And one of these fuckers is responsible!"

I stare at Dornan, horror flooding through me in an ice-cold rush. My mouth drops open as I watch my mom stepping back, the news like a bullet to her heart. Colby's eyes are wide with the same alarm, knowing that this turn of events has robbed us of the opportunity to deal with this pregnancy and our relationship with any kind of privacy. Seb and Micky are frozen, with eyes trained on their father's face.

I don't know how many seconds pass before I react, but it feels like many.

Dornan didn't mean to do it. I know he loves me, but that love has just blown my universe apart.

❦❦❦❦

27

SEBASTIAN

For a second, I have no idea what to do. Dornan has just blurted out our secret in the most terrible way, and Ellie is standing frozen like he stabbed her in the heart. Dornan still has Colby's shirt in his fist, and I can see his other hand flexing as though he intends to throw a punch. There's no way he's hitting Colby with his monster sized fist.

I edge forward, intending to try to smooth the situation over when Ellie bolts. She flies past her mom on the stairs, traveling so quickly, my heart is in my mouth. The front door is yanked open and slammed before any of us can react to her exit. Micky steps in next to Colby, putting his hands up to diffuse Dornan's anger.

"What is going on?" Lara says. "Ellie's not pregnant. She has a stomach bug." Even as she says the words, I can see the truth dawning. "She's pregnant?" Her attention turns to the stairs and focuses down into the hallway below. "She's gone."

That gets Dornan's attention. He drops Colby's shirt and spins to look for Ellie. "Where did she go?"

The sound of an engine starting outside sets everyone

in motion. Colby shoulders past dad and stomps down the stairs like a whirlwind. I'm not far behind, and Dornan and Micky follow closely. Lara is still yelling for an explanation, and dad bellows we need to get back upstairs and explain ourselves, but no one is listening.

Colby flings open the front door as Ellie's car speeds out of the drive. She's going too fast.

For fuck's sake.

"We need to get her back," Micky says quickly. He grabs the car keys from the console, but I raise my hand. "We're not going to find her if we follow now. She's long gone." Turning, I focus my attention on Lara. "Check her room. We need to know if she has her phone on her?"

She blinks, still lost in the turmoil of what's just happened. Celine disappears up the stairs, jogging to Ellie's room.

"She's pregnant?" Lara says again, her eyes wide. "Who. Who's gotten Ellie pregnant?"

"COLBY. EXPLAIN. RIGHT NOW," Dad yells.

"Her phone's not here," Celine calls.

"Lara, can you track Ellie's phone? Can you tell us where she's going?"

Lara dashes into the kitchen with her long hair streaming behind her, filled with an urgency that I know she doesn't quite understand. Everything feels so frantic and crazy.

"EXPLAIN," Dad yells again.

"Harry, wait," Lara says. "Here." She hands me her unlocked phone, and I search to find the app that can track Ellie. The girl I love is reduced to a moving dot on a map.

"Have you found her?" Dornan asks.

"Yeah, but she's still moving."

"Let's take the phone. We can follow her." Micky is

already sprinting to his car, his bare feet out of place on the driveway.

"COLBY," dad yells, his eyeballs bugging out of his head.

"Not now, Dad. Let us find her first."

Lara puts her hand up to stop the conversation as we all pile out of the door and into Micky's waiting car. I haven't even gotten my door closed before he spins us to the end of the driveway. "Yell directions," he orders.

"RIGHT," I bellow, clutching Lara's phone like it's the key to the universe. I'm trying to find where Ellie is, and where she might go, and where we are, and where we have to go to follow her. It's confusing as shit.

"Now?" Micky yells.

"LEFT," I shout, turning the phone and squinting down at it in the dark.

"Give it here," Dornan says, snatching it out of my hands. He holds it close to his face, the blue light illuminating his flared nose and flushed cheeks.

"She's stopped...hang on..."

"Give it here," Colby says, snatching it from Dornan.

Fuck. There's going to be a flight over the phone now.

"Can you fuckers just tell me where to go?" Micky yells, frustrated.

"Molly's. She's stopped at Molly's Motel."

"Why the fuck has she gone there?" Dornan asks. When none of us says anything, he growls. "You took her to Molly's? You put a baby in her at Molly's?"

"We didn't mean to," Micky says. "It was an accident."

"I mean, the place is a dive."

"It's not that bad," I say. "And anyway, that's not the point right now. Let's just find Ellie and make sure she's okay."

"Maybe things might be different if you'd been thinking more like that when you were last at Molly's."

Colby turns from the front seat to stare at Ellie's best friend. "Listen, Dornan. I know you're worried about Ellie. And I know this situation is fucked up. But we're handling it. We want to be there for Ellie."

"Be there? What the hell does that mean?"

"It means that we love her, and we want to be there for her and the baby."

"Be there?" Dornan says. "Be there as what?"

"As whatever she wants us to be," Micky says.

"But what do you want?" Dornan flexes his hands in frustration, his biceps tensing.

"We want to be the men in her life," I say. "Whatever that might look like."

"And who's the father? I'm guessing you know or did you all 'have an accident'." He places the last part of his comment into air quotes.

"Colby," I say.

"Fuck." Dornan shakes his head, and past him, I can see the lights of Molly's sign illuminating the night sky.

Micky swings the car into the lot, and we all scan for Ellie's car. It's over in the corner furthest from reception, and all the lights are off.

"She better not have gotten out of that car," Colby says, glancing around at the grim neighborhood.

"She hasn't. She's there," I say. Micky pulls up a few spots down, and everyone's hands fly to the door handles. "Only one of us should go," I say. "She's going to get overwhelmed if we all spring on her."

"I'll go," Colby says.

"It should be me," I say.

"Now isn't the time for jokes, Seb," Micky says. "Ellie

233

needs a careful hand."

"I can be careful," I say. "Trust me."

I rarely put myself out there like this, and my brothers stare at me through the gap between the seats.

"It can't be me," Dornan says, hanging his head. "She's never going to speak to me again."

It isn't the time or place to console him about the way he behaved. I throw the door open before anyone can disagree and jog over to Ellie's car. She's slumped over in the front seat, her head resting against the steering wheel, her hair concealing her face. Her hands have braced either side, knuckles white as bone.

I try the door, but it's locked. She jumps when I tap on the window, and her head swivels to see who's there.

"Open up," I say.

"Leave me alone," she yells. "Can't I get even five minutes to myself? Do I get no privacy?"

"Please," I say. "Just give me five minutes."

Ellie closes her eyes and shakes her head, and even in the darkness, her face seems shadowed with exhaustion.

"Please, honey. I promise we'll give you all the space you need after these five minutes are done."

In my heart of hearts, I'm expecting her to remain stubborn because I'd be the same in her shoes. In just a few days, she's lost control of her body and of who knows her secrets. She must be so overwhelmed.

When the lock clicks, I don't waste a second. I'm in that front seat, slamming the door closed and locking the car from the inside. This is my five minutes, and I'm going to make sure no one else can get in this car and undermine it.

I take Ellie's hand, finding it cold and resistant. I bring it to my lips and kiss it gently. "You know all we want is for you to be okay. That means being okay with whatever you decide. I know Colby's told you we want you, not just because of some stupid dares or because it's convenient, but because you're a part of us."

Ellie tries to pull her hand out of mine, but I resist. She has to hear me, and I won't let her pull away again. Not this time.

"You heard Dornan, and mom, and your dad. They're all disgusted," she whispers.

"I heard Dornan mad as hell because he feels we didn't protect you, and he's right, in a way. He only said all that because he loves you. I saw your mom freaking out when you left because she loves you, and nothing matters more than you being safe. And I saw our dad mad as hell at us for being irresponsible. None of it has anything to do with you and the pregnancy."

"Of course it does. Nobody will want me to keep the baby. I'm too young and still studying. I'll become a burden. It's not fair."

"Not fair on who? The baby will be a gift, honey. And we can overcome every obstacle you can think of."

"You just feel guilty," Ellie says softly. "I know if this hadn't happened, you'd all eventually move on and find girlfriends. This was all just a dare. None of it was real."

"It was real for me," I say. "Real as anything I've ever known. Can't you see that, Ellie? Can't you feel it?" I place her hand on my heart, knowing it's racing. Doubting my ability to convince her of the truth is enough to make me panic.

Ellie's eyes widen, and I nod. "I've wanted you every day since you moved into our house. Every day I've found another reason to love you. My brothers too. And we're not letting you push us away because you doubt yourself and your worthiness. Dares can only take you so far, honey. After that, you have to be prepared to take a leap. I just need you to know that whatever you decide, me,

Micky, and Colby will be with you all the way. You're our forever girl, Ellie."

She blinks, tears welling in the corners of her eyes.

"Forever's a long time?"

"Here's hoping," I say, sliding closer. Now's my chance to pull her into my arms and really show her what it means to have us in her life, a reliable presence to make everything easier. "We'll protect you and the baby, Ellie. We'll make sure everything works out."

She gazes up at me with wide eyes as black as night. "Will you dare me, Seb?"

"No more dares," I say softly, stroking her cheek. "You don't need dares, sweetie. You're strong and kind and loyal and fierce. You've got the strength to face any situation and come out on top. I see it. Colby sees it. Micky sees it. The only person left to see it is you."

Taking a shuddery breath, she closes her eyes and relaxes against my chest.

I stroke Ellie's soft hair, finding it still damp with her tears, but she's not crying now. She's relaxed and pliant. It's hard for me to sit with her in silence. The urge to fill the space with a joke tickles the back of my throat, but I resist. This isn't a moment for humor. It's a moment to face up to the parts of ourselves that hold us back from becoming who we truly are.

Ellie's hand finds the hem of my shirt and slides beneath to rest against the warm skin of my abs. I hope she finds comfort in our skin-to-skin contact the way I do. Her face moves against my shirt as though she's smiling. "You know, when you're not telling jokes, you're pretty wise, Seb."

"Don't go too far, Ellie," I say. "Wise is Colby's domain."

"Maybe I need to dare you to do something," she whispers.

"And what would that be?"

She lifts her head from my chest, her pretty eyes searching my face and a smile playing on her lips. "I dare you to take the lead in talking to our parents about what's happened."

Drawing my head back, I frown. "Why me?"

"They won't expect it, and I think you'll do the best job."

"You do?"

"Sure." She rests her warm hand on my cheek. In my pocket, Lara's phone rings.

"As much as I'm enjoying this hug, should go back," I say. "Are you ready to face the music?"

"As ready as I'll ever be." Ellie places her hand over her belly, smiling as her eyebrows draw together in a quizzical v. "I'm pregnant, Seb," she whispers.

I rest my hand next to hers, overwhelmed by the significance of the moment. "You're having our baby," I tell her softly. When she frowns, I laugh, and it's a bubbling, happy sound. "We're identical triplets, honey. You get pregnant with one of us, you get pregnant with all of us."

"Shit, I never thought of it that way," she smiles. "How perfect is that?"

Perfect.

It absolutely is.

28

ELLIE

My heart beats triple-time for the entire journey home, even with Seb by my side.

Walking up to the front door in my nightwear and without shoes doesn't help my anxiety. The quietness of the men surrounding me adds to the tension.

As soon as Seb puts the key into the lock, the door is yanked open from the other side. Harry looms large, even though he's a few inches shorter than his sons.

Before he says a word, mom barrels past and grabs me, pulling me into the fiercest hug she's ever given me. "You scared me," she says. "You scared me so much. Don't ever do anything like that again."

I stare wide-eyed over her shoulder at Celine and Gabriella, who lurk in the hallway, watching everything. Celine has her hand over her mouth in a rare display of emotion.

"Dad, we're going to explain," Seb says calmly. "Can we go into the living room?"

Harry opens his mouth to say something, but mom puts up her hand. "Let them talk," she says softly.

We all troop into the rarely used formal space and sit on the nice sofas, looking completely out of place. Colby's eyes meet mine, and I can tell he's itching to take over, but after our conversation in the parking lot at Molly's, he understands what I want.

Seb, who's sitting next to me, takes my hand and holds it in his lap. Everyone in the room follows the action. "Before I say anything about what happened tonight," Seb says in a tone that I've never heard from him before, "I want you to understand that me, Micky, and Colby love Ellie. We've loved her for a long time but did nothing about it because of our family situation."

"LOVE?" Harry spits like it's a dirty word that tastes foul in his mouth.

Rather than rising to it, Seb holds up his hand calmly. "We held back out of respect for Ellie and for you both, but there came the point where we couldn't anymore."

"So you've been messing around together behind our backs?" Harry says. "All of you?" The look of disgust that twists his face is enough to enrage Colby. His jaw ticks, and his shoulders bunch, but Micky rests a calming hand on his back, and Seb continues, unaffected.

"Ellie's pregnant," he says softly. "It isn't something that any of us intended, but it's something we're all happy about. We're not innocent of what it's going to take for us to care for a child. Changes will need to be made, but all you need to know is that we're together in wanting this child and the future that it's going to bring with it."

"You can't be serious," Harry says. "This situation has to be dealt with."

Seb is quick to raise his hand, and he leans forward, narrowing his eyes. "Dad, I'm going to let that comment go one time. ONE TIME. But if you say it again, we're going to have a big problem. That's our child you're talking about. Don't forget that."

"Do you even know whose child it is?" he asks, the sneer still tugging his lips.

"We share DNA," Micky says. "We share love. We share Ellie. This baby will be all of ours."

Seb nods. "Exactly."

Mom puts her hand over her mouth, her eyes blinking rapidly. "You're having a baby?"

I nod, resting my hand over my belly. "I'm having a baby." She starts to cry, and I'm not sure if they're happy or sad tears. I suspect it's a mix of both. "Mom?"

Turning to Colby and Micky, her expression makes me fearful that she will explode on them. If I were in her shoes, I'd be gouging out eyes and skewering dicks.

"Are you going to look after my baby?" she asks softly. "And my grandbaby?"

"Yes, ma'am," all the triplets say at once.

"Well, I guess that's it." She brushes her hands over her slacks, once, twice, punctuating the end of the conversation. "I'll set up an appointment with an OB-GYN. I want to ensure you're doing everything you need to stay healthy and help that baby grow big and strong."

"Less of the big, Mom," I say. "If it's anything like its daddies, it's going to be huge."

"Well, you reap what you sow, baby," she says. A smile plays on her lips, and I'm so fucking confused that I laugh.

"What is it, Mom? Why aren't you yelling?"

Seb pretends to cover my mouth. "Ignore her. She doesn't know what she's saying…pregnancy brain."

Mom laughs and shakes her head. "You know I love you all, right? And maybe it's odd, but I'm so happy that my daughter has found men I respect to fall in love with."

The surprise on the triplets' faces is enough to make my heart ache. In fact, a little tear leaks from the corner of my eye at their pride and happiness. We all look at Harry, waiting to see what his response will be. He's staring at my mom like he's seeing her for the first time. I guess hearing her validation of his sons has taken away some of his anger at the situation.

It should.

"Dad?" Micky asks. The hopefulness in his voice forces another tear from my eye.

"Well, the ship has sailed," he says gruffly. "No point in me having anything to say on the matter."

"We'd like you to say that you're with us rather than against us," Seb says, squeezing my hand.

Harry shrugs his shoulders, glancing around the room. "I just want you to all make sure that you're not giving up important parts of your future. Between the four of you, you can work out how to still do the things that are necessary for your long-term happiness and security. I guess I can help you all with that."

Seb nods, and I swallow the lump in my throat. "We'd appreciate your help and advice."

From the corner of the room, Celine clears her throat. "Well, isn't this just awesome? One big, soon to be even bigger, happy family."

"Yeah, congratulations, Ellie," Gabriella says.

"Congratulations," Dornan adds, still unable to look at me. Even though his outburst sent me running tonight, I can't hold a grudge. His motives were decent, and that is all that matters. I stand from the couch, striding across to him, placing my hands on his face and forcing him to look me in the eye.

"It's okay," I say. "You're my best friend."

His ocean eyes blink once, twice, surprise raising his blond brows. He pulls me into a relieved bear hug, and I sink happily into his warm embrace.

"Hey, not too long," Colby growls, even as he smiles.

"That's our girl."

"Baby momma," Celine says with a wink.

"Can we not start using that phrase?" Mom says, shaking her head.

"Girl is fine," I smile, drawing away from Dornan and gazing around the room at all the people I love. The people who love me.

My heart feels fuller than it ever has. The space in my chest that I didn't realize was empty is warm and happy, and I blink quickly in surprise.

It started as a dare, but Seb, Colby, and Micky have shown me I have the strength and conviction to take my own steps forward to a bright future with them by my side. The baby growing inside me is just the beginning for us all.

EPILOGUE

COLBY

When Lara insisted on throwing us a huge graduation party, I thought she was crazy. Yes, it's an important day, but since Noah's arrival, nothing else holds the same weight. If I'm honest, I would rather dad and Lara spend the party money on things for the baby than alcohol for our friends, but this goes back to what dad said that night in the den. He wanted to make sure we don't miss out on the important things.

They have decorated the yard with congratulations banners and what seems like a million shiny gold balloons. Caterers have provided a buffet table that would have been perfect for a wedding, and a bar has been set up next to the kitchen where beer, wine, and spirits are available.

I look around, finding our friends chatting in groups, holding plates, and balancing plastic cups. Seb is at the center of the football team, telling them a hilarious story that has half of them bent at the waist with laughter. Micky is introducing Lara to some students from his course, and they're all cooing over my beautiful son as he lays sleeping in her arms.

I can't find Ellie, so I turn, heading back into the

house. Our girl isn't graduating with us today. She should be, but she took a year out to be with Noah. She's signed up to finish her studies next year. Dad insisted she go back as soon as possible. He realizes that any more time out would make it harder for her to pick up the student lifestyle again. Sure, she's going to miss Noah, but it's important that she doesn't compromise the life she had planned for herself before she got pregnant.

That's one of the major benefits of there being four of us in our relationship. There is always someone able to pick up the slack.

Ellie's not in the kitchen or in the lounge. The front door opens, and I find her in the driveway, greeting Celine and Gabriella. I swear, her friends are the craziest girls on campus. They arrived in fancy dress to a party with a smart dress code. Gabriella is dressed as an angel with huge silver feathery wings, and Celine has painted her face with moons and stars.

"There you are," I say when Ellie turns and sees me.

"Checking up on me, Big Boy," she laughs, shaking her perfectly curled black hair. In her shimmery black dress, she looks like one of those old Hollywood movie stars. Classy and sassy, strong and bold. Ellie is everything I ever wanted in a woman, and she's mine.

Well, ours technically.

But sharing with my brothers isn't like sharing would be with anyone else.

"Of course," I say. "It's my job."

"Why can't I find a big sexy man who wants to check up on me?" Gabriella moans.

"Maybe because you're dressed like a celestial being," I say.

Gabriella rests her hands on her hips and scowls at me. "Don't criticize the costume, Colby."

"I thought guys love sexy fancy dress?" Celine says,

twirling around in her silver tutu. "Eddie sure appreciated me in this one!"

"Maybe a maid's outfit or a raunchy devil," I say. Ellie raises a perfectly arched eyebrow.

"Oh really, Colby. You just admitted to being a total cliché!"

I put out my hands, palms first, and my cufflinks glint in the sunshine. "I said nothing about me liking those things."

Nodding knowingly, Ellie grabs my arm and steers me back into the house. "Of course you didn't," she laughs.

"But if you have one of those costumes lying around…"

She snorts and swats my bicep. "As if I'd have a sexy costume lying around. I've only just stopped breastfeeding. Red latex and lactation do not mix."

I lean closer, brushing her ear with my lips. "Talk about your breasts again, and I'm going to have you over my shoulder and up those stairs in a flash."

"Promises, promises," she says, but then she stops, reaching up to smooth the shoulders of my new black suit and straighten my tie. "You know, you and your brothers really look handsome tonight."

"Handsome? Do people even use that word anymore if they aren't talking about little boys dressed up in sailor suits for weddings?"

She laughs, sliding her hand around my middle, and presses a kiss to the side of my neck. "Well, I could say you look good enough to fuck, but that wouldn't be appropriate in such polite company," she whispers.

We both take in the party; the decorations Ellie's mom has been fussing over for weeks, and our classmates, dressed up like they're going to prom. It really is an event that we'll remember forever.

"After we're done celebrating," I say, hooking my arm around Ellie's shoulders and pulling her close. "We have a surprise for you."

"A surprise? I'm not sure I like those."

"You'll like this one." Kissing her temple, I breathe in the scent of my woman, feeling a bone-deep satisfaction. It's the kind of feeling you don't know you're missing until it settles inside you, and then you never want to be without it.

"Maybe you should just tell me now," she says, gazing up with wide, hopeful eyes.

"Maybe you need to take a class in patience," I say with a wolfish grin.

"It's not on the class list," she smiles.

We've been keeping Ellie in the dark about something for months, but we've finally pulled it off. The next few hours will be fun, knowing that she knows we have a secret. Our girl doesn't enjoy waiting for things, and she doesn't like not knowing.

It's going to drive her mad.

And me? Well, her nickname for me is CF, which doesn't stand for Colby Fantastic, unfortunately. It stands for control freak, and I guess it's fitting because I'm going to love every minute of her frustration!

MICKY

Ellie has begged me to tell her about the surprise at least ten times, and I've resisted. She's pressing me because she knows I'm a soft touch. I hate seeing her so frustrated, which I why I made Colby promise not to tell her before today. If he had his way, the sick fuck would have made her wait a week to find out.

"I can't tell you, baby. Colby would have my nuts."

"I like your nuts," she says, smoothing her hand down the front of my dress shirt until it reaches my belt. A little too close to my nuts. Things that shouldn't stir in polite company start to come to life, and I snatch her hand away.

"You'll find out in an hour. Just be patient, okay?"

"Do you know me?" she says, scowling prettily. "Patience is not a virtue I have in abundance."

"But you have plenty of other virtues in abundance," I smile.

"I'm not going to get anywhere with you, am I?" she says, hanging her shoulders. Fuck, this girl makes me want to tell her everything, but the surprise is too big and too important.

"Sorry, baby. I would if I could, but my brothers would tear me a new one."

"Not an image I want to dwell on," she snorts. I watch as her eyes scan the party, searching out Seb. He's the last one she hasn't tried to crack, but he's talking to our dad and Ellie's mom while bouncing Noah in his arms.

"Seb won't tell you either," I say. "It's too big of a surprise to spoil."

"Big?" she says, realizing I've given her something without intending to. "Big as in actual size or just big in significance."

"Just big," I smile, leaning down to press a kiss to the top of her head. She smells of coconuts and her own unique scent. When I kiss our son in the same place, he smells just like his momma.

Noah begins to fuss, and Ellie smiles up at me before dashing across the yard. Her hips sway in her clingy black dress, and I marvel at how her shape has changed since carrying Noah. Everything about our girl is gorgeous.

I follow, too, wanting to remind Seb of the importance of remaining tightlipped. I might be the softy around here, but Seb is the most loose-lipped of all of us.

"He's hungry," Lara says as Seb hands Noah to Ellie. He's so big now that she seems swamped by his size and weight.

"Poor baby. Everyone else has been eating, and he's famished."

"There are yogurts in the fridge," Lara says.

"He wants milk," Ellie says, kissing Noah's pudgy cheek.

"I'll help you to make it," I say.

As Ellie walks towards the house, her heels sinking into the grass, I nudge my brother.

"She's asking for details of the secret. You can't tell her, okay?"

He brings his hand to his forehead in a clipped salute. "Yes, Sir! Thank you, Sir!"

All he gets in return is an eye roll.

Ellie has strapped Noah into the highchair in the kitchen, and he's grumbling. "It's okay, son," I say, ruffling his dark curls. "Mommy will have your milk soon."

"Give him one of these," Ellie says, passing me a spongy biscuit that Noah loves. "But put this on first."

She hands me a muslin which I tuck around Noah's neck to keep his special party outfit biscuit and milk free. "There you go, No No, it's biscuit time." He snatches it from my hand and rams it into his mouth so quickly he gags. "Hey, go slow," I say.

"No," he replies, stuffing it back in again.

And there it is. Noah's favorite word and the origin of his nickname.

"This will be you next year," I say, watching Ellie shake Noah's sippy cup of milk.

"It will." When she smiles, I see genuine excitement at

the prospect of graduating, which fills me with relief. Dad was so definite about her completing her studies, and me, Colby and Seb were worried this was just another thing Ellie was allowing herself to get pushed into. I guess there is a difference between encouraging something and force, although dad still treads a very fine line.

Colby steps into the kitchen, laughing loudly with Dornan, and Noah scrunches his nose.

"Daddy noisy," he says, spitting biscuit crumbs over the tray table.

"Yeah, daddy is noisy," I laugh.

Dornan grabs Ellie's hand and spins her around. "I hope these douchebags have told you how gorgeous you look today."

"They have," she says.

"Less of the douchebag talk," Colby grumbles. "You might be Ellie's best friend, but that doesn't put you outside of an ass whooping."

"I'd like to see you try."

Colby and Dornan face up to each other. Two huge guys, almost the same height, puffing out their chests like arguing birds, fighting over a prospective mate. It's so funny that Noah starts giggling, and then we're all laughing.

And it's in moments like these that I know that this love between us all was meant to be.

SEBASTIAN

Don't ask me how I keep the secret because I have no idea. It's been burning my tongue for three months, and it is even worse now Ellie knows.

"Please, Seb," she says, and I want to run away because when Ellie begs, I only want to give her what she wants.

"Ellie-Belly, now is not the time."

"Oh, you didn't," she says, reaching out to pinch my pec.

Dornan told us his childhood nickname for Ellie when she was eight months pregnant. At the time, it was hilarious because she was just one giant belly. She hasn't forgiven him.

"I, for one, think that nickname is cute. Better than Smelly-Ellie anyway."

"Oh, hell no." Shifting Noah on her hip, she licks her teeth as though she's preparing for war. "You are not starting that stupid nickname. I swear I'll start sleeping in my room and locking the door."

That threat is enough to make me retreat.

"Are you guys ready?" Colby yells from the kitchen. "We're done cleaning up."

"Yeah, Noah's in his PJs," I call back.

Lara appears, reaching out for her grandson. "Come here, little man. It's time for beddy-byes."

Noah clings to his mom for a couple of seconds, then allows himself to be passed across. "Nana's going to read your favorite story."

"Belly button," he yells.

"Yes. The one about baby's belly button."

We all laugh as Colby, Micky, and dad gather by the front door.

"I'm proud of you, boys," Dad says out of the blue. I guess it isn't every day that a man watches his triplet sons' graduate.

"Thanks, Dad," Micky says, stepping forward to hug him. Dad claps him on the back with a flourish and does the same to Colby, too. Then he's searching for me.

I don't know why it's always been a little awkward between us. Maybe because I try not to take life too seriously, and dad is all about control and focus. He's always had lower expectations for me than my brothers, but thankfully that didn't lead to me having lower expectations about myself. "Well done, son," he says, hugging me tight and patting my shoulder.

"Not bad for the class clown," I say, catching Ellie's eyes and seeing them fill with tears.

"Funny and clever. That's got to be a winning combination," Dad says. "At least you'll be able to grease a few more wheels than I've ever been able to."

Is he seriously complimenting me right now?

Seeing my discomfort, Ellie steps forward. "Are you finally going to put me out of my misery now?"

"I guess so." Colby takes her hand, and I follow with Micky. I turn quickly, finding Dad and Lara smiling at each other. It's a far cry from where the family was all those months ago.

It's funny that the very thing we worried had the potential to tear the family apart turned out to be what brought us all together in the end.

ELLIE

I glance across at Colby, who's driving, trying to work out something, anything, from his stoic expression. This surprise really is just that. I have no clue where they're taking me. I bite the corner of my nail, and Colby reaches to take my hand. "No nibbling," he says softly. "This isn't something for you to stress about. It's something good."

"Can't you just tell me?" I moan.

"We're almost there."

When he comes to a stop, it's outside a house that looks as though it hasn't been lived in for years. The yard is overgrown, and the windows seem dark with dirt. There are no lights on, and a pot that used to contain flowers stands empty by the door except for three dry sticks protruding from the earth. I look around the car, waiting for someone to tell me what's going on.

Seb clears his throat. "We know our current living arrangements haven't been ideal," he says. "Our parents have been accommodating, but they tend to cramp our style."

I snigger, remembering last week when they banged on the wall because one of us was being too noisy. We all died a little inside that night.

"So, we've pooled all the money that mom saved for us before she died, and the life insurance payout, and dad has stepped in to lend us the rest, just until we can secure a mortgage," Micky says.

"It might not look like much right now," Colby adds, rubbing his top lip. "But we can take our time to renovate. We can put our stamp on it."

"Are you telling me you bought this house?" I say, completely stunned.

"YES!" they all say together. They've been so focused on keeping this a surprise that they forgot what they needed to tell me.

"Oh my god. I can't believe it." Clasping my hands over my mouth, I gaze up at the house I now know is ours. Our first home. "Do you have keys?"

Colby pulls a set from his pocket and dangles them on his index finger. "We sure do."

I snatch them and fling the car door open, not waiting for them to follow me as I dash across the driveway to the front door. I notice things I hadn't before: the original door with glass detail, a brass knocker, and the black and white tiled step.

My hands are trembling too much for me to open the door, so Colby reaches out to help.

The staircase leads up to a second floor that I can't wait to explore. Micky finds the light, and suddenly, the house is illuminated. The downstairs is mostly open plan with hardwood flooring and a kitchen that has seen better days. There's a lot to do to make it a home, but I can see why they chose this house. I can picture us here together, with our son and maybe more children in the future.

"Do you like it?" Micky asks, watching me from where he's leaning against the wall.

"I love it!" I gasp. "I can't believe you managed this. I can't believe you all kept it a secret."

"It wasn't easy," Seb admits. "But it was totally worth it."

"How many bedrooms?" I ask, resting my foot on the bottom step.

"Four," Colby says, and I detect a sense of pride.

We don't need that many now, providing at least one bedroom can fit a bed that's big enough for me and my three perfect men.

"Noah gets his own room," I say excitedly.

"We'll decorate that one first," Micky says.

"Can I pick the theme?" I ask hopefully, and they all laugh.

"You think we'd be any good at interior decorating?" Colby asks.

"The whole place is yours to design," Seb adds, grinning. "Although I'm pretty sure your mom is going to want to be involved too!"

Before I take any more steps, I look down at my three amazing men who've gone to such lengths to put a roof over our heads and a smile on my face, and I still don't know what I did to deserve them. I move toward them, grabbing Colby's hand and then Micky's and leading them closer to Seb. I stand on my tiptoes to kiss them all, one after another, and then I ask for a hug.

Hugging in a relationship like ours can be a complicated operation but I need all my men around me tonight, and that's what I get. I slide my arms around Sebastian's waist, and Colby wraps his arms around both of us, followed by Micky, who finishes our bundle. The laughter that bubbles up from somewhere around my heart feels so overwhelming that it becomes a sob.

"Hey, no crying," Micky says.

"They're happy tears," I blub.

As we pull apart and I swipe my face, there's only one thing left to say.

"I dare you to live happily ever after with me," I say.

"Now that's a dare I'd be happy to take," Colby says.

"It's a dare we're all happy to take," Seb says.

"Damn right," Micky adds.

So that's what we do.

ABOUT THE AUTHOR

International bestselling author Stephanie Brother writes high heat love stories with a hint of the forbidden. Since 2015, she's been bringing to life handsome, flawed heroes who know how to treat their women. If you enjoy stories involving multiple lovers, including twins, triplets, stepbrothers, and their friends, you're in the right place. When it comes to books and men, Stephanie truly believes it's the more, the merrier.

She spends most of her day typing, drinking coffee, and interacting with readers.

Her books have been translated into German, French, and Spanish, and she has hit the Amazon bestseller list in seven countries.

Printed in Great Britain
by Amazon